carolina girls
SUNSET BEACH

camille harwood

carolina girls

SUNSET BEACH

PALMETTO
PUBLISHING
Charleston, SC
www.PalmettoPublishing.com

Copyright © 2025 by Camille Harwood

All rights reserved

No portion of this book may be reproduced, stored in a retrieval system, or transmitted in any form by any means–electronic, mechanical, photocopy, recording, or other–except for brief quotations in printed reviews, without prior permission of the author.

Paperback ISBN: 979-8-8229-8670-1
eBook ISBN: 979-8-8229-8671-8

*To my core who believe in me,
and my two who make me believe.*

chapter one

MILLIE LOOKED AROUND her city, the place she had lived longer than any other. North Carolina always meant comfort to her, but she felt at home in Raleigh. It was a town feel, wrapped in city trimmings. The move to the City of Oaks was the only time she had chosen a move. Her Army brat upbringing sent her to multiple high schools and several schools before that, and although she loved her time in Savannah, she had never been able to commit to one spot before now.

So, she took it all in. The trees blowing in the wind stirred up scents from different restaurants downtown. There were people walking through the park who seemed to have nowhere to be today and others who were rushing for the sake of rushing, never looking up from their smartphones. She saw children holding their parent's hands, watching the bustle in innocent awe. One little boy made her smile when he waved a sticky hand at her. Millie loved children, and they had always loved her in return. She thought children were a great judge of character, so she waved back with a big smile.

She was an extremely shy child, but so many military bases had forced her to make new friends and learn how to get along with a smorgasbord of personalities. She was as comfortable at a fancy restaurant as she was at a hole-in-the-wall barbeque joint.

Her core group of friends was proof of it. They were polar opposites of each other, but each had a good mix of incredible kindness and deep-rooted sarcasm, so it all worked somehow. She was the glue that held the crazy bunch together. She was young enough to know there were a lot of changes ahead for her girls, but old enough to know they were the core group of friends she would grow old with.

Rory was already conquering the financial world and was the voice of reason in the group. She was dating someone new and walked around with that smile you get at the beginning of a relationship when everything they say is brilliantly wonderful. He seemed to adore her, though, so the girls agreed to wait one more month before they let their eye rolling loose whenever she announced the latest "sweetest thing" he did.

Audrey was on her way to becoming a doctor and the "grown-up" of the group. Delivering babies was her dream. She said it was like witnessing a miracle every day. She was recently divorced and still trying to put her life back in order. The waste of oxygen that left her with loaded credit cards and limited bank accounts was nowhere to be found, and they were all grateful the douche canoe was gone, no matter the costs… literally.

Then, there was Cate, a teacher who kept them entertained with the soap opera of kindergarten life. She was a great teacher, but they all knew she would be out of the classroom and running a school within ten years. Cate was focused on her career but was dating a hysterical man who was as focused on his career as he was on her. So, for them, it worked.

Millie took a deep breath and soaked in the beautiful day. She had chosen a waffle cone with coffee ice cream for lunch and was determined to enjoy every drop.

She wasn't exactly thin, but the grueling workouts and classes at the gym kept her figure in check, allowing her to eat like a college frat boy. A large pizza didn't stand a chance in her presence, and neither did this ice cream cone.

She was taking the last bite when she spotted him. Taylor Fitzpatrick was on his phone. He was probably making another killer deal but carried himself with a relaxed smile, as always. His suit was obviously tailor-made because it fit him beautifully, showcasing his broad shoulders and long legs. His olive skin was a complete contrast to her porcelain complexion, and he had a head full of jet-black hair that curled just past his collar. They had worked together for a few months now, and Millie thought she could quote every word he had ever said to her.

She grinned, thinking about their first real conversation. They were in his office talking about an upcoming book signing and laughing at the author's book cover when they were interrupted by a large man with a larger-than-life personality. "What's so funny?" he said, with a gleam in his eye. "And who the hell approved that cover? My grandson could have come up with that," he chuckled.

Millie, never one to shy away from matching wits, said, "I'm the author. My grandmother painted that before she passed away last year."

Larger-than-life's eyes grew large, his mouth gaped, and his cheeks blushed.

"Just kidding. Millie Sullivan, nice to meet you. Couldn't agree more about the cover."

The man threw his head back in laughter. "Hellfire, you scared me. Watch this one, Fitzpatrick," and winked at her as he walked away.

Millie turned back to Taylor at the sound of him clearing his throat to hide a laugh. "Do you know who that was?"

"No, but I like him. Who is he?" she asked, waiting to be let in on the joke.

Amused, he stepped towards her and crossed his arms. "That would be Greg Staton… the President of the company."

She felt her heart stop beating for a split second as the reality of what she had just said to the CEO sank in. She regrouped quickly, "Well, it's good that he thinks I'm funny then," she laughed. It had become a joke between them, and never failed to earn a big laugh when he told anyone in the office about it.

"What are you grinning at, Millie?" She blinked away the memory and had to shield her eyes from the sun to look up at him. Good Lord, he was gorgeous.

"Hey, Taylor. I was thinking about you, actually, and wondering if you knew your fly was open."

She laughed out loud at the jolt he made to check his zipper. "Very funny," he chuckled as he sat beside her on the bench. "Great day for an ice cream cone. What flavor was it?"

She looked at him with surprise. She didn't think he had noticed her. "Coffee with a cinnamon cone."

"I'll have to try that. Get the sea salt caramel next time. I swear it's the best ice cream I've ever had."

They sat quietly for a minute, his arm stretched behind her on the back of the bench and legs stretched out with his ankles crossed. She wondered if he was always this comfortable in his own skin and if she would ever be as relaxed with him this close to her.

She schooled her breathing and was about to continue the small talk when he slapped his knee. "Better get back to the grind. These books don't seem to want to sell themselves today." He stood up slowly, almost reluctantly, she thought. "Care to walk with me?"

Everything in her wanted to jump at the offer and walk anywhere he wanted to take her. But as he buttoned his suit jacket, his ring caught the light, sending a sparkling reminder of reality. He was married to an incredibly kind and beautiful woman who Millie had met at the company picnic.

His wife, Carrie, recognized that Millie was sitting at a table alone and, without hesitation, saved Millie from herself. She could still get shy in big groups, and Carrie saved the day by walking her around and introducing her to anyone and everyone she could. Millie left that picnic grateful but crushed after learning whose wife she was.

"I think I'll enjoy the quiet for a few more minutes. The team has been gridlocked all morning over the launch details for next month, and I could use a little more air before the back and forth begins again." That was a lie, of course. The details had been set in stone weeks ago, but she was determined to stop thinking about this charming man, so walks in the park were not on the agenda.

"I'll see you in there then. Good luck with the gridlock." He grinned at her in that special way he could, that made you feel like you were the only other soul on the planet he wanted to talk with at that moment, and walked away.

She was smitten, was all. Just a little crush. *Who wouldn't be attracted to him?* she thought. He seemed to be perfect in every way. He was kind, hysterically funny, and easygoing, but obviously had a passion for his work and was incredibly smart. Above all, though, she loved the kind of leader he was. He encouraged everyone around him to be better, do better, and see the great in the ordinary.

She put her head in her hands in frustration and thought how spot-on Alanis Morrissette had it. Meeting the man of her dreams and then meeting his beautiful wife seemed like a cruel irony. She could sit there feeling sorry for herself or she could move on and hope her heart followed suit. Millie was as stubborn as they came when she wanted to be, so she would keep filling her days, leaving no time to think of anything but work. She got up determined to pull it together. One more ice cream should help.

She took her last bite as she walked into the building that still took her breath away. The outside of the building was all glass, and on a sunny day, it came alive with sparkle and shine. On a cloudy day, you could see the reflection of the weather, which made you wonder where the clouds stopped and the glass began. No matter the day, the building itself had an energy about it that made it special from all the rest.

The main lobby was always bustling with various professionals connected to the publishing world or, for some, those hoping to be part of it. Its grandeur was never lost on Millie. She respected its opulence and what that signified. This was a place where dreams came true. The writers that walked the halls of this building were world-renowned Pulitzer winners, senators, humanitarians, and even a Nobel Prize winner. *And they all started somewhere*, she thought.

It was still surreal for her that she belonged here, but from the moment she walked through those doors for her interview almost a year ago, she knew this was exactly where she should be. It took some convincing, but grit and wit won her the job, according to Samantha Rothchild, Vice President of Sales.

Samantha was hard, harsh, ballsy, and brilliant, with just enough couth and charisma to make her phenomenal in sales. She was in no way easy to work for, but Millie knew she was learning, and that was all that mattered. She didn't need easy. She only needed a foot in the door to educate herself on the ins and outs of the publishing business.

Millie had always been determined, or, as her mother called it, bullheaded. She was smart, but she had to work hard to achieve the high grades she received in school. She had common sense but never saw that as an extraordinary attribute because most people had at least some sense. Whether they chose to use it was another story.

She saw the world in black and white – you make a mistake, you take ownership; you see that someone needs help, you do what you can; you see something you want, you go for it until it's yours. Her drive didn't always leave room for outside opinions, which is why it surprised Millie that she and Samantha got along so well. They had butted heads several times in the last few months, but at the end of the day, she appreciated the mutual respect they had for one another.

As the elevator doors opened, she zeroed in on her schedule for the rest of the day. There were still a few minor details to confirm for the launch next month. A new author was scheduled to arrive in an hour to go over sales projections for the year. Samantha's speech for the Women in Business dinner needed a few more tweaks, and she needed to meet with IT to update some things on the website.

She sat at her desk, took a deep breath, and got to work. Her passion for what she was doing made any menial chore important to her. She didn't mind dealing with the details because she found the more detailed she became, the more important her assignments became. Her plan was simple – learn all she could, work as hard as possible, and never forget where she began. She knew her work ethic would take her where she wanted to go, which was all the way to the top.

The afternoon flew by, and before she knew it, it was quitting time. Millie got up to rinse her coffee cup, an absolute necessity in her life, when she saw Taylor walking towards her.

"Come with me. I need you."

Her legs actually went limp, and she had to grab the counter to keep upright. She was acutely aware that sentence would haunt her dreams tonight.

Since her entire vocabulary had apparently left her mind, she just stood there staring and feeling foolish. "OK," was all she could muster as he took hold of her arm, and she rushed to keep up with him down the hall.

He stopped her outside the small conference room. "Samantha is still with the newbie writer. I need someone to help close this deal, and you're it. Do you have the numbers for last quarter's company sales? Anything you've got that would prove to him that we are where he needs to invest?"

She had worked on the spreadsheet earlier and knew enough to get by but was afraid to quote any real figures.

"Let me see if I can rush Samantha for you. She'll be able to help better than I…"

"No time for that," he interrupted. "He's on the edge. I can feel it. You can do this."

Her heart was going to burst out of her chest… he believed in her. With newfound confidence, she felt his hand on her back, guiding her into the room. Was it possible for a person to actually set your skin on fire with an innocent touch? She pulled her mind from the gutter long enough to look around the room and see four men staring at her. The oldest stood as Taylor escorted her to a chair at the table.

"Gentlemen, this is Millie Sullivan, the latest addition to the team and our rising star. Millie, this is Chester Montgomery and his partners." As Taylor introduced everyone, she shook hands with each man and decided to make this moment count. It was risky, so she decided to break the ice.

"It's very nice to meet you all. I had no idea we were auditioning models today." The resounding laughter gave her one more boost of confidence and a seat at the grown-up's table with who she would soon learn was the President and Founder of Vikings Banking and Loan. As one of the largest banks in the U.S., she found herself seated next to one of the wealthiest and most influential men in the country, a leader in its economic growth. God, she loved her job.

"Young lady," Mr. Montgomery began in a deep Southern drawl, "we are pleased to have you join our discussion. Mr. Fitzpatrick obviously knew when to bring in the big guns."

She knew he was patronizing her, but it only fueled the fire in her belly to prove herself. "Our Mr. Fitzpatrick doesn't need additional ammunition, sir. His holster is quite full already. What he does need is last quarter's figures, and

I'd be happy to go over those if you like. This company has performed extremely well over the last year. In comparison to our competitors... well, there is no comparison. In the last quarter, however, we have seen a rise in distribution, client and customer satisfaction, endorsements, and sales like no other, which has awarded us the possibility of working more closely with companies such as yours... or others perhaps."

She cocked her eyebrow for effect and then went on, hoping to God that what came out of her mouth sounded articulate or at least coherent. The more she spoke, the quieter the room got. At one point, she turned to Taylor to beg him to jump in with only a look, but he just stared. They all just stared. She could feel beads of sweat forming, but she couldn't seem to stop talking. Why hadn't she gotten Samantha? She should have stood up to Taylor instead of going all gaga. Stupid!

When she finally finished, the room was silent. She saw the men look at each other and then back at her. She just lost the deal for Taylor and the company. She knew it. Taylor would be furious and would have to explain why the deal tanked. How mad could Samantha really be? The idea of cleaning out her desk and doing the office walk of shame clouded her mind as her hands began to shake.

Mr. Montgomery cleared his throat. "Mr. Fitzpatrick, I must say, I am disappointed." She saw Taylor's nerves show for the first time as his jaw locked slightly, and her heart sank for him. "Over the last few weeks, we have had several meetings and wasted everyone's time." All breath left her lungs. Crap! "In the future, I would recommend bringing the big gun in sooner. My partners and I will review the contract one more time, but I'd say you could expect a signed copy next week."

The men stood as Mr. Montgomery rose from his chair, everyone buttoning their jackets and shaking hands with Taylor. Mr. Montgomery walked around the table and offered his hand to Millie. She accepted it gratefully. She still hadn't taken a deep breath. "I certainly am glad to meet you, Miss Sullivan. Well done, young lady."

She shook hands with the men as they left the room and wished them a great weekend. Her legs were still wobbling, so she walked to the window to balance herself in the empty room. Had that just happened? She went through the play-by-play in her head, hoping the numbers she spouted out had been correct. She made herself stop for a second and appreciate the moment. A smile grew, and she couldn't help the happy dance that came along with it.

That is how Taylor found her, doing an unreserved version of The Carlton and smiling like a lottery winner. Immersed in her excitement, he watched until the imaginary beat took over, and he joined her with a clap and a moonwalk. Millie jumped at the clap, feeling absolutely ridiculous, but when Taylor kept dancing, she jumped right back into the groove.

Grateful that she would include him in her happiness, he grabbed her and spun her around like a slap-happy ballerina. When the spinning stopped, they were still holding hands, breathing hard, with their eyes locked on each other.

The seconds seemed like minutes, and the sparks between them lit up the room. He broke eye contact to look at her mouth, and she knew that he would kiss her if she leaned in. Her chest was tight with desire, but she knew she wanted more than he could offer. She stepped back, never losing eye contact but freeing her hands from his. An understanding shared between them, the moment was broken.

They made themselves busy cleaning papers off the table and pushing chairs back into position. The heat lingered, but frustration had replaced desire.

"Thank you," was all he said, but his eyes spoke volumes.

"Anytime," she replied, not exactly sure what he was thanking her for. She didn't want to break the connection but knew it was time to go.

She walked to her desk to collect her things and was grateful she already had plans with her girls that night. She was going to need a full night of friend therapy after today.

chapter two

HER PHONE WAS blowing up with plans and changes of plans. The girls had decided to get all dolled up and go out tonight, a rarity for the four of them. She looked out the window and hoped for the best. The heavens had opened up about an hour ago, and it was pouring buckets, making everyone late, especially Millie.

In a group message, she texted,

Crazy late but coming!

She tossed the phone on the bed so she could change her clothes. Her phone beeped, and she saw Rory's reply.

*There's a revelation.
Almost there. I'll get a
table. Had to work late,
coming straight from the
office so no one is to
get TOO gorgeous.*

She smiled at that because Rory was a Farrah Fawcett meets Julia Roberts combination. She was beautiful, and if she hadn't been so nice, Millie would have loved to hate her for it.

She caught her reflection in the mirror and stopped cold. Is this what she looked like all day, or was it just in the last few hours that she started to look like a character from a Hitchcock movie? Gravity had taken hold of her eyeliner and mascara, making huge dark circles around her eyes. A streetwalker would have been proud of this look. Her fine brown hair, usually stick-straight, had grown with the humidity, making her the poster child for why you should keep your fingers out of electrical sockets.

She thought back to the conference room and hoped this Halloween makeover had happened on the way home after the happy dance. She sat on the edge of the bathtub and sighed. There were so many days in the office that she wished for a moment with Taylor or caught herself watching him. She would hear him laugh and imagine it was her telling the joke. After the dance, though, she wanted more than just a moment with him, which scared her to her core.

She was a good person with a good heart. Pining away for someone else's husband just wasn't something she ever thought she would face. She bowed her head and said a prayer for guidance, ending it as she always did, *"Thank You for everything You have given me and everything You haven't."* She always felt better after prayer, like some of the weight of her problems had been lifted, but today was different. She felt guilty, not for the wanting but for not feeling guilty for the wanting. "You're rambling again," she said to herself out loud.

Millie stood up and looked in the mirror again. She needed to talk this out with the girls, and the only way to do that was to tame the beast sitting on her head, wipe the scary clown makeup from her face, and open the app to order a ride to the restaurant. She decided washing her face and starting fresh would save time, and a ponytail was the only way to conquer the frizz. She was out the door in 15 minutes, only to find that the rain had stopped, but the humidity had increased. Lord help the hair band holding on for dear life around her ponytail. She pulled it tighter, just in case.

The driver seemed less than thrilled to have a rider in the car that day, so other than asking where to go, he was silent. She felt like she was in an elevator, where there is that unspoken rule (pun intended) that you can't speak above a whisper. Usually, Millie liked the silence, but today, it gave her more time to think. She had a bad habit of over-analyzing things anyway, and the quiet only kept the conference room in her mind like a play she could rewind over and over again.

When the car pulled up to their favorite restaurant, she paid the man and stepped out into the damp night air. As she was getting out, she saw a shiny penny face up. She smiled, a little good luck never hurt anyone. As she bent down to pick it up, a car driving way too fast in the parking lot swerved past her, hitting a small wading pool of a puddle, splashing her from head to toe. She stood there shocked for a minute, dripping wet, while the car gunned out of sight.

"Are you freaking kidding me?!" she yelled. Why did things like this always happen to her? And where had the damn penny gone that she was picking up in the first place?

"Perfect," she muttered and turned to walk into the restaurant.

Her friends waved as she passed the hostess, but their smiles dropped when they saw her soaking clothes. Millie headed straight to the bathroom, where the girls met her and peppered her with questions.

Millie took them through the story, from the quiet drive there, to the stupid lucky penny and finally to her ride on Splash Mountain. She cussed and fussed about the weather wreaking havoc with her life and hair, all while the girls used paper towels to pat her dry.

She was boiling, not something she managed often. She was so mad with life in general. This was just the cherry on top. "I should just go," she barked. "I'm not going to do anyone any favors by being here. I'm a mess."

"You know, things like this only happen to you, Millie," Cate grinned. "There's a whole restaurant full of people who got here without wetting their pants."

That did the trick. They erupted in the kind of breathless laughter that only happens once in a blue moon and makes your stomach and cheeks ache in the best way.

Cate gave her a big hug, wetting the front of her shirt. "See, now we're both a mess." After a group hug and a few more paper towels, she decided to toast the night instead of ending it.

Sitting at the table, drinks in hand, Rory raised her glass. "To our first wet and wild-themed girls' night. May there be many more adventures tonight."

"To adventures," the girls said in unison. They were still giggling through their order to the waitress, who brought Millie a free drink after hearing her story, when lightning crashed outside and scared everyone in the restaurant.

"Good glory! We may need more paper towels. That scared the bejesus out of me." Cate's southern accent always made Millie smile. It was a mix of country and old south, which gave her a sweet drawl and funny adages.

"Alright, Sullivan. There's a looker at your two o'clock. He's either waiting for a date or hoping that drink will solve his problems. I say you walk up there and take his mind off either."

Millie rolled her eyes, "I am not walking up to anyone looking like this. And this is a girl's night. Stop trying to pawn me off." She knew her friend meant well, but since Cate and Rory were so happy in their relationships, it had become their mission to find someone for Millie. They knew Audrey wasn't ready for that after the divorce, so Millie got their full attention. Lucky her.

"I don't like the look of that one anyway," Rory chimed in. "Too skinny. You need someone who knows how to cook. Skinny men don't cook or don't do it well anyway."

As they continued to search for Mr. Right Now, Millie noticed how quiet Audrey was. She was smiling, but her eyes were sad, and the circles were there again, which meant she wasn't sleeping.

"You two need to shut up. I'm off the market tonight. Audrey, how's the world of wombs these days? Any good stories you want to share before the food gets here?"

Audrey chuckled and played with her napkin. "No stories to tell, although we did have a woman who nearly delivered in the lobby the other day. She walked in, saying she needed to push. I guess we didn't react fast enough for her, so she lifted her dress and showed us the baby's head."

Audrey lit up from the inside out when she spoke about her work. You could see her passion for it, and lately, it was the only thing that could put the sparkle back in her eyes. So even though no one at the table wanted the picture of a stretching vagina in their head, they asked questions and listened to every bloody detail, each understanding that it made her happy.

As the food was placed on the table, Audrey got quiet again. "Aud, is there something going on? Is that baby going to be alright?" Rory asked.

Rory was sensitive to Audrey's attachment to her patients, having lost her mother when she was little. Rory knew that losing patients wasn't only hard on the families.

"Oh yeah, the baby is fine." Audrey sighed. "My Mom called today. She said someone called the house asking for me. She wouldn't say his name, but it was David. He thought I was still living with them and didn't know my new cell number. He's back in Charleston." Rory and Cate reached for Audrey's hands, trying to give all the support they could. None of them knew what to say to make her hurt any better, so they just listened whenever she wanted to talk about her horse's ass of an ex-husband.

"There is no way your Mom gave that ass wipe your number, and I doubt he wants your dad to know where to find him, so how do you know he's in Charleston?" Cate was ready to spit nails, but to her credit, she kept her voice light and caring.

It took Audrey a second before she whispered, "I called him." In that one tiny sentence, they knew he had managed to do more damage. Everyone at the table would have loved five minutes alone with him and a heavy bat, but right now, Audrey was more important.

"He's living with her in *our* apartment. He wanted to know when I would get the rest of my stuff because she wants to redecorate. They think a contemporary leather couch would look good along the window wall." She wasn't talking to anyone in particular now, just reliving the conversation and the hatred and hurt that she held for this man who had promised to love and cherish her all the days of her life.

"I asked him what he thought I left behind, and he said there were a few pieces of furniture, some clothes, and odds and ends. The best part was the dog. She is allergic to dogs, so he's got to live with me or be put down." Her eyes came alive with the hatred now. "Can you believe he said that? Like those are the only two options! I've wanted that dog from the minute this whole thing blew up, but it's only when that whore has the sniffles that I can pick him up or let him die."

She was shaking now, but any tears that may have formed a few minutes ago had been replaced with rage. They nicknamed her "Street Fighter" because of her temper, but they had only seen it twice between them. Ironically, neither time had been directed at David, so frankly, they were glad to see it aimed his way.

"I still can't believe this happened. We were OK."

In unison, all three girls said, "Ummmmm."

"Well, maybe not, but one late-night hook-up at the office, and he needs time to think about where he wants his life to go and what a crushing disappointment I am as a wife. Who does that? He's made the whole thing my fault! After all he did…" she shook her head to escape the memories. "What kind of person goes after a man without any thought about the marriage she's destroying? And what kind of son of a bitch tells his wife to be happy for him that he's found a soul mate in someone else?"

They were all shaking now, all in tears, and all touching her in some way to give support. Their friend was hurting like none of them had ever hurt before. Millie looked down at the wet dot on the tablecloth. Her tears weren't just for her friend. They were for her attraction to Taylor. Audrey's words had been like a knife to her heart, and without knowing it, her friend had shamed her with the lashing of her life. She took every word Audrey had said to heart, and the judgment she felt was horrendous. She knew none of it was meant for her, but it didn't change the effect.

She tucked her hurt away and decided in that second that no matter the chemistry, she would distance herself from the temptation of Taylor. Audrey had given her some balance back.

THANKFULLY, THE NEXT FEW weeks were slammed at work. Millie liked to work and really enjoyed what she did, but even she was feeling the strain. With six big events behind her, she had one last launch before she could relax. The book launch for the newbie author was tonight, and it seemed like everyone was racing around the office, taking care of the little details that come up when you're planning an event.

She popped into Samantha's office to give her the rundown of essential information and stopped short at the door. She had nothing but respect for Samantha. She was tough but kind to her and always gave credit where credit was due. Millie knew that wasn't always the case with top leaders in a company. So the sight of her boss standing behind the desk, making out with Jake from accounting, nearly had her jaw hitting the floor.

She cleared her throat and watched the show continue. Unbelievable. She cleared her throat louder and watched as the pair jumped apart in surprise, like they had been caught after curfew by their parents. Millie grinned and raised an eyebrow. With her hands on her hips, she tried to break the tension.

"The neighbors called. They were watching the show but asked if you would move a little to the left. The plant is blocking their view."

Millie laughed out loud as both of their heads jerked around to see the building next door. "Kidding! But it was a hell of a show."

"You are awful!" Samantha said as she pulled herself together. "Jake, I believe you know Millie, our resident comedian."

"Yes," he said with a big smile, "I know Millie. Always good to see you. Well… I should be going. Lots of facts and figures to plow through before tonight." He gave Samantha a wink, and with their eyes locked, he took her hand very sweetly and kissed it. She blushed like a schoolgirl, and Millie sighed louder than she intended.

Where do men learn those moves that make women swoon? It's like they pull them aside in college before graduation and introduce them to the art of seduction. Most men, in her limited experience, failed the course. But the ones who studied could keep your mind in the clouds and the gutter simultaneously.

"Have a good day, ladies." Jake closed the office door with one more wink. Millie smiled at Samantha and waited. There would either be a confession, or it would be back to work as if the whole scene had never happened. Fortunately for her, Samantha smiled in return and covered her still-rosy cheeks.

"It's new," she said, "but it's been coming for a long time. We were both in relationships, and our timing was off."

"I'm familiar with that myself," Millie rolled her eyes.

Samantha smiled in commiseration, "We both worked late one night a few weeks ago. He got on the elevator on my way down, and we started talking. We kept talking in the lobby at first, then at the coffee shop around the corner. We talked for hours that night."

Samantha was smiling to herself now, that dreamy smile that Rory still had. It was sweet and annoying at the same time.

Millie started talking about the launch details, but her focus was on that blissful smile. That smile reminded her of how lonely she was for the first time in weeks. They had been working so hard, it had taken lonely's place. She wondered when she would have that happy smile again.

She had dated a few people here and there, but there was always something wrong with them. Too tall. Not tall enough. Too serious. Too goofy. Too handsy. Too driven. Not driven enough. Too concerned about what his mother thought.

That one had been a doozy. He actually asked her to stand so he could take a picture of her to send to his mother for approval. She got her dessert to go that night and wished him and his mother well.

Her favorite story, so far, was a man Cate had gone out with a couple of times. On the second date, he "forgot" to feed his dog and asked if she would mind coming to his house for a quick second. As they walked in the front door, he told her to make herself comfortable while he fed Lucy, the puppy. From the back of the house, he asked her to get him a water bottle from the fridge. When she brought the water back to the living room, there he stood – completely naked, with one foot propped on the table like Captain Morgan, showing off every little bit God had given him. According to Cate, God had only given him a little bit.

Millie had only seen a profile picture of him, fully clothed, but would forever use his face as an example of why neutering shouldn't only apply to dogs. Who has the time or patience to deal with men who appear normal at first glance but are that level of special?

"Millie? Honey, are you OK?" Millie blinked at Samantha's worried expression and snapped out of the past. "Oh, I'm fine. I'm sorry," she blushed. "I was lost in the details of tonight. You were saying?"

Samantha walked around the desk to the girl who reminded her so much of herself at that age. With her hands on her shoulders, she said, "Tonight will be perfect. I've been watching you, Millie. No one has worked as hard as you have for this book, not even the author. Tonight will be perfect."

Suddenly aware of her nerves, Millie took a deep breath. "As perfect as it can be, given we're launching on a llama farm." They both burst into laughter at the craziness of the venue. The author had insisted on the location from the beginning and had unknowingly been the butt of countless jokes.

As Millie pulled into the parking area, she saw the joke was on them. The lights had been strung, creating a ceiling of sorts, and were starting to glow as the sun hung tired in the sky. The sconces hung from the trees, lining the walkway, and when the candles were lit, they would transform it into a golden path to another world. The arbor had been placed at the entry of the beautiful white tent and was now covered in magnolias.

Millie had been monitoring every detail of this event almost from the get-go. She knew where every arrangement should sit, what music would be played and when, the name of every hors d'oeuvres, and how many would be passed around. She had arranged the schedule ten different ways but finally settled on the rhythm of the night when she found out the author's entire family was flying in from all over the country.

This night would be magical for the author, and she was proud to have constructed it for him. He seemed like such a great guy. It would be a stellar event with a small-town, family feel. She walked through the enormous tent, looking for all the details she had spent hours planning. She had the staff move the chocolate fountain to another corner, made sure there was a signed copy of the book at every place setting, tested the microphone, and spoke to the band about the schedule and playlist.

Everything was perfect.

She walked to the back of the tent to tie back the plastic doors for a view of the lake. When she opened the left flap, she walked right into Taylor and Carrie in the middle of an argument. She tried to step backward and disappear without interrupting, but they both turned to stare at her. "I'm so sorry, I didn't realize… I'm sorry." She pulled the flap closed again and heard angry whispering.

She stood there for a second in disbelief. She would never assume that any relationship was perfect, but they truly seemed like the perfect couple. What on Earth did they have to fight about? She had this image of them at home, laughing at each other's jokes, looking lovingly into each other's eyes, probably in front of a crackling fire, wanting to hear every little idea that popped into the other's head. She shook her head at the stupidity of that image. Life wasn't perfect. Even they must have *some* troubles.

Samantha walked through the front door with the guest of honor and gave Millie her focus back. She greeted them both with excitement and confidence, promising a night he would never forget, hoping with all her heart that nothing would get in the way of that.

As the tent began filling up with guests from all walks of life, Millie watched every detail like a hawk. She stepped in when any particulars needed attention, but for the most part, she watched while the night progressed perfectly. The author asked that his brother introduce the book, and although her team had encouraged him to let a professional do it, the presentation was an exceptional mix of humor, brotherly competition, compliments, and family pride.

The author gave a very gracious speech that was as unique as the man himself. The audience laughed at all the right moments, and there were even a few tears when he choked up at the end. He was getting rave reviews from the members of the press who attended, who were all encouraging it as "a great read" on social media. The night was perfect.

After the hors d'oeuvres were gone, the cake shaped like an open book had been eaten, the drinks had been drunk, and the author had left in a limo on cloud nine, Millie surveyed the room. By the looks of the mess, it was a great party, and she was extremely thankful she wasn't in charge of clean up.

She smiled wide and decided she deserved a glass of the expensive champagne she had yet to taste, sitting by the view she had yet to enjoy. She took a bubbling glass and walked through the back door to enjoy her moment. That's where she saw Taylor sitting at a table by himself with his elbows on his knees, staring out at the lake.

She found herself looking for him to check in throughout the night. Carrie left not long after their argument, and Millie figured that wasn't a good sign. Every time she spotted him, he was smiling and schmoozing with the guests or press, but his eyes had lost their sparkle.

She wondered how many people saw the sadness. He wore a black suit and tie for the event, which was far more formal than some of the author's family, but each person he spoke to received a compliment. He made each woman he spoke to feel like the prettiest girl at the ball and each man the most powerful guy to know. He had a good heart.

And good Lord, he was gorgeous.

chapter three

Taylor knew Millie was keeping an eye on him throughout the party. He wanted to be annoyed that she walked in on that scene with Carrie. He was usually in his element with the press and even enjoyed talking with them, but tonight, he wanted to scream at them for asking the same questions over and over again.

He was just off and couldn't shake it. He and Carrie had had arguments before, but not like this. Lately, they seemed to do nothing but argue, and he was tired—mind, body, and soul.

He knew the infertility treatments were a strain on her physically. He ached for her, for everything she was putting her body through for their dream. He would have given anything to take the pain of not getting pregnant from her and all that came with it.

The constant doctor appointments, the injections, the hope that was fading, the desperation that was replacing it. It was all just too much. The effects of the medications put her on a hormone roller coaster that he could never seem to keep up with.

None of that was her fault, and he made sure to tell her that, but over the last year, he had felt like he couldn't say anything right. The more she pulled away, the harder he tried to fill their days with anything other than doctors or babies.

He booked a cruise; she told him she couldn't take off that much time at work. He reserved a bed and breakfast in the mountains for the weekend; she said she and her sister had plans. He came home early to make dinners that were eaten in silence. He felt like a chunk of every paycheck was spent on bouquets of her favorite flowers.

They used to be best friends, but now he wasn't even sure if she loved him anymore. *Stop it*, he thought. He knew she loved him, but he wondered if she was *in* love with him, and that made all the difference in the world. He didn't know how to show her anymore. He was miserable and disappointed in himself for allowing it to get this bad.

So when the press had gone, and the limo had taken the author home, Taylor sat down at a table outside with a double whiskey neat and let the poison torch the pain away. He was a social drinker but never let himself get out of control. Tonight, however, he had had enough. He needed one night away from the reality that he couldn't seem to repair. He took a long sip, closed his eyes, and waited for the burn of relief.

That's how Millie found him. From the tent, she thought he was enjoying the scenery, but when she got to the table, she saw the pain even through his closed eyes. She sat next to him and took a deep breath. It was the first time she had sat down since arriving at the party. The launch had been an incredible success. She was on top of the world, and she was completely exhausted.

She called Rory earlier to share the details of her night with someone who would be just as excited as she was, but her voicemail picked up, which probably meant she was already asleep. Rory loved to sleep, and it was nearly impossible to wake her up once she was out.

All of the adrenaline had left her now, though, and she was grateful for the silence. She leaned her head back on the chair, closed her eyes, and let out a deep breath. She wouldn't bother Taylor with the conversation if he didn't want it but she needed to be near someone who could share in her success. Even if the sharing was silent.

"You did good, Millie." He was watching her now, thankful she hadn't come over asking questions. He tapped his glass to her champagne flute. "You deserve that drink. It was a hell of a launch."

Taylor downed the rest of his drink and hissed at the burn. He wanted another, and Millie was going to join him. "I'll be right back."

She leaned her head back on the chair again, ditched her shoes, and propped her feet on another chair to get comfortable. It wasn't exactly professional, but she had earned a minute of peace. She finished her champagne and wished she had another but was too tired to get up. She stretched in the satisfaction of a successful evening, a soft moan escaping when she felt the stretch in her aching calves.

Taylor stopped dead in his tracks. He knew from the second he met Millie that they clicked. She was one of those rare knockouts who had no idea how beautiful she was, but it was her sense of humor and smarts that had really impressed him.

He liked her, genuinely liked her, but watching her lean back in complete comfort with herself had him wishing.

Seeing her dress tighten over her chest with the stretch and hearing her moan like that had him wanting.

Taylor shook the idea from his head. *Don't go there*, he thought. He sat beside her with a bottle of whiskey for him and a bottle of champagne for her.

"Let me buy you a drink to celebrate. You made his dream come true tonight, Millie."

His smile sent shock waves down her spine, and his sincerity touched her heart. "No, I just planned the party. He did the hard work. Thank you. I was just wishing for a glass."

She watched Taylor pop the cork and laughed when the foam spilled all over the front of his pants. "Shit!" He jumped up, and without thinking, Millie grabbed a napkin to help clean up the champagne.

Taylor stilled immediately as she wiped at the spot. He smiled at the innocence of the scene, but even a saint had limits. He didn't want to embarrass her, but he also needed her to stop before he embarrassed himself. "You missed a spot."

She looked up and saw his ear-to-ear smile when it hit her like a ton of bricks. She was wiping this magnificent man with such concentration that she hadn't noticed she was rubbing up his thigh. "Oh my God! I'm sorry!" She backed away, mortified and in such a hurry that she tripped on the leg of her chair and nearly did a nose dive over the table.

Taylor grabbed her just before she hit the ground and held her tight. Millie closed her eyes to catch her breath and regain even a scrap of dignity before making eye contact with him. She took a deep breath to calm down, but that breath was filled with the incredible scent of cologne and man. It made her knees weak and sent a lightning bolt within her that she had never felt before.

She couldn't help herself. She took one more deep breath before looking up. Millie looked at his mouth and wondered what it would be like to kiss those lips. There was another world right there; she knew it. When she looked into his eyes, though, she saw the sadness again. It brought her out of the moment and had her backing up.

"I am like a walking *I Love Lucy* rerun. Good catch." She handed him the napkin, "Why don't you work on that spot while I pour the drinks. I warn you, there's a fifty-fifty shot that you'll need another napkin if you sit with me long enough."

Taylor finished wiping and sat down. "I'll chance it."

Millie poured the drinks and sat back in her chair. She banged her knee during her little fall, and it was throbbing. A big sip of champagne had her relaxing again. She put her feet back in the other chair to stretch it out.

"Can I ask you a question, Taylor?" She had been curious about their meeting in the conference room for weeks but had never asked him about it. She saw his tension rise. The poor guy looked like he was bracing himself for the "what were you fighting about" question, but she wouldn't probe, only listen.

"When you pulled me in the conference room a few weeks ago…"

"With Vikings?" he asked, relieved.

"Yes," she grinned. "Why did you do it?"

Now he looked at her puzzled. "What do you mean? Why wouldn't I?"

"I can think of ten solid reasons without trying. Was there literally no one else available?"

Taylor stared into his drink for a second and scoffed. It was Millie's turn to be puzzled. "What?"

Still staring at his drink, he chuckled. "I thought I had you figured out, is all. You surprise me."

"In the meeting room, you mean?"

He studied her, really looked at her—the kind of look that makes your thoughts and feelings visible to the naked eye but only to those who take the time to really understand you. It unnerved her to see him look at her that way like he was reading all of her secrets.

"No, not in the meeting. Right now. I pulled you into the conference room because I knew you had been working on the latest figures earlier that day. I just prayed to God that you remembered a few of them. But what you did, Millie, was far beyond anything I thought a fairly new employee would be able to do. You not only saved my ass, you made me look good doing it. This drink is far overdue, now that I think about it."

Taylor held out his glass to toast her but pulled back before she could tap her flute to his. "Cheers to you, Millie, and the bar that you raised for the rest of us when you joined the team. May you always be there to save my ass and launch our books."

He tapped her flute and knocked back the double shot. Millie took her sip, but her mind was racing. She turned to him, "If the meeting isn't what surprised you, what did?"

"Honestly, your confidence. Or rather, the lack of. I had you pegged wrong. At work, you seem to have it all figured out. It's kind of relieving to know you don't."

"That's funny. I feel the same about you." They stared at each other with understanding. There was no need to talk about the details or his argument earlier.

"How did you get your start in the publishing world?" She needed to get to know him better. She was sitting next to this man she had fantasized about for months and wanted more.

He poured them another drink and told her all about his dream of writing the perfect timeless novel that would inspire acceptance and encourage understanding between generations. He rolled his eyes at himself.

"What's stopping you?"

His sigh was heavy with reasons. "Life."

"If you could push pause on life, what would the main character's name be?" She was afraid to ask why he wasn't writing, but she wanted to encourage his passion for writing itself.

"His name would be Isaac. It was my grandpa's name. He was a medic in the Army who became a barber after he came home from the war. He died before I was born, so I don't know much about him, but I've kind of made a life for him in my head."

"I love that. And does Isaac have a partner in crime?"

Taylor laughed, and Millie looked at him in awe.

Good Lord, he was gorgeous.

"Yes, I guess that's a good way to put it. He and Amelia want to be together, but their backgrounds are so different, and their families disapprove. Think *West Side Story* meets *Romeo and Juliet*, but with more focus on the history aspect, and neither of them dies for their choices in the end."

Millie was quiet but smirked into her drink as she sipped.

"What? No good?"

"Oh no, it sounds like the classic American novel is in your hands. I hope to read it one day." She smiled again.

"What?"

"The names. I just really like the names. So Amelia and Isaac, are they star-crossed lovers who defeat the odds and live happily ever after?"

"After some trials and tribulations, that's the idea." Taylor swirled his drink and looked into it like a crystal ball. "Do you think it exists?"

"What?"

"Happily ever after." He looked at her now, hopeful and miserable.

"Oh, I'm not the right person to ask, Taylor. No one has offered me a happily ever after." She looked out at the lake. "I hope it exists. Otherwise, what's the point?"

She grinned and filled their glasses again. She already felt the bubbles in her head and knew Taylor must be feeling the whiskey. There was no way they were driving home, so they may as well have one more.

"I think people miss their happily ever after because it's not what they expected."

He took the drink she offered. "Thanks. How do you mean?"

"Well, people have these expectations of who or what it will be or look like. Happily ever after can be with someone, but it can also be about publishing the next great American novel. People don't need other people to be happy. It's just a bonus when you get to share it with someone, but even then, that person has to respect what makes you tick, and if you're unsure of what that is, you can't expect them to know."

"Makes sense." His face was expressionless as he stared into the night. She felt like she had unintentionally hit too close to home. She had a hard time filtering on any given day. Add alcohol, and she was a walking advertisement for foot-in-mouth syndrome.

"I didn't mean to upset you, Taylor. I was talking about me." She put her drink down. She was officially tapped.

He rubbed his face with his hands and sighed again. "I used to know. I used to know exactly what I wanted, exactly where my life was headed. It was a good plan…"

The defeat in his voice made her heart ache for him, but the loss of his dream made her reach out and touch him. His arm tensed under her hand, but she ignored it and squeezed. "No plan is foolproof. You've hit a bump in the road. Now's the time to fight for it."

"That's all we've been doing!" he exploded out of his chair. "I'm tired of fighting!"

She had never seen him lose his cool before. He grew larger in that moment and became intimidating in a way she didn't think possible. The anger seared through his eyes, leaving her paralyzed, not from fear but from shock. How did he hide all of this every day? He was charming and happy to everyone but had so much bottled inside.

"I envy you and those fights," she whispered.

It made him stop pacing long enough to take a breath. "Do not sit there and give me some bullshit line about the grass being greener. You have no idea what it's like to feel like you are married to a stranger. To want nothing more than to have her in your arms telling you she loves you, but at the very same time being ready to run as fast as you can from this epidemic of frustration and spite that your most important relationship has dissolved into."

He sat down beside her again, and she saw him wobble from the drinks for the first time.

"Have you ever fantasized about what it would be like, for just a moment, to be someone else? What that life would offer, and who that life would introduce you to?"

She rolled her eyes in commiseration, "All the time. But I always come back to this one. It fits me, even when it sucks."

He laughed out loud and looked at her with a genuine smile. "Thank you for listening to my rambling. I'm sorry I'm ruining your night. You should be walking on air, not witnessing a crazy person's breakdown." He shifted to face her, bumping their knees together. "Thank you."

The sincerity in his eyes kept her still. The fire she felt growing had her frozen. She saw the want in his eyes and wanted to reach for him again.

"Taylor." Her voice was low and sultry. Her eyes were on his mouth again. She licked her lips and bit her lower one out of habit.

His eyes were on her mouth now, and he felt a fire burning inside him that had been gone for too long. "Millie."

"Amelia. My name is Amelia. Millie is a nickname."

His eyes darted to hers in surprise. They were breathing harder, both imagining what it would be like, wishing and wanting. She was offering him something he wasn't free to take, and if she wasn't careful, she knew things would go too far. "I'm going to call for a car. It's time to go home."

Taylor let out a deep breath and sank back in his chair. Another moment with him was broken, but the desire was unbearable. Millie reached for her purse and used her phone to get a car.

He rubbed his hands on his face again, but this time, it made him more unsettled. "We better wait up front. We'll never hear the car out here." He stood and offered his hand. She took it without hesitation, but when she stood, he weaved his fingers with hers and held it as they walked through the empty tent.

They stood in silence until the car pulled up. They climbed into the car, still holding hands and still silent except for the address she gave the driver. His thumb rubbed her hand absently as they rode towards her house. It seemed ridiculous to be overcome by this level of desire simply by the brush of a finger. She had never been affected by another living soul the way this man could affect her without even trying. She knew holding her hand was an innocent need after their talk tonight.

She turned to look at his profile and found him looking at their joined hands. At that moment, he looked like a lost child, hoping for reassurance and kindness. He looked up and smiled at her with those sad eyes.

When they arrived at her apartment, he asked the driver to wait while he walked her to her door. As the car door closed, Millie stood beside it, completely conflicted, playing with her keys.

"Everything OK?" He held out his hand to walk her home, but she couldn't move. She was terrified of what would happen if he got anywhere near her front door. She hated this feeling but had to admit to herself that, for the first time in her life, she didn't trust herself. It broke her heart. This man brought something out in her that no one else ever had, and she could never truly know the freedom of it.

She looked at him and knew that no matter how many years passed or who she met in the future, tonight would be imprinted on her heart forever. She stepped forward and brushed his cheek softly with her hand. He held that hand to his heart with understanding. She leaned forward to kiss his cheek and stayed close to breathe him in one last time.

"Goodnight, Taylor," she whispered, walking away as fast as she could without looking back. It took all of her strength to say goodbye, and she knew her willpower wouldn't hold if she turned to see him.

Taylor watched her walk away. She was so full of light and life, everything he missed most in Carrie. He stood there hoping and fearing that she would turn around and give him any sign of the pull he felt. So many emotions were warring inside of him. He had to believe she felt them, too.

She disappeared around the corner, and his hope faded while his mind hazed. He blamed the alcohol but knew in his heart that if Millie had given him the signal, he would have taken advantage of the night.

What is wrong with you? he thought. Suddenly mad as hell, he got in the car and slammed the door. This was not the man he was. Wanting a woman who wasn't his wife so badly that chasing her into her apartment sounded rational. He was better than this, and he respected Millie more than that.

He had never been a ladies' man, despite what people said about him. He liked being with women, their smells and soft skin, but he appreciated the strength behind their softness more than anything. They were deceiving in that way, which is why he thought so many men didn't understand them. They didn't admire the significance of the whole package. He did.

He was appalled with himself for the way he felt tonight, but he was confused by his sense of guilt. It wasn't towards his wife, who he loved, but for this woman who had enchanted him.

Over the last year, he had caught himself watching her at work, blaming it on the close quarters. He caught himself thinking about her at home and called himself a workaholic. Tonight, he was honest with himself. His thoughts about her had nothing to do with work.

With a deep sigh and confused to his core, he gave the driver his address and left the first true temptation he had ever faced.

From the walkway, hidden in the shadows of a crepe myrtle, Millie watched Taylor get into the car. The feelings that had been churning within her broke free, and a lonely tear rolled down her cheek as the car drove away.

chapter four

MILLIE WOKE UP to her phone ringing and the headache she knew she deserved. She texted Samantha the truth after she got home last night about having a bit too much to drink and that she would be late. She was such a lightweight. She rolled out of bed as slowly as possible to prevent her head from actually shattering.

She found her phone in the kitchen and thought about putting it in the disposal, but that would surely send her headache into the kill-me-now level. Without looking to see who was on the other end of the line, she answered, "What."

"Where are you?" Rory yelled into the phone and made Millie's ears ring. *Kill me now*, she thought.

"Millie! I'm at your office. Where are you?"

"I'm at home, recovering from a lobotomy currently with no pain meds in my system. Hold, please."

She put the phone down and laid her head on the counter beside it. "Shoot me." A deep breath gave her just enough energy to get some medicine from the cabinet and chug some sweet tea from the pitcher.

One thing she always had was Southern sweet tea in the fridge, just like Nannie used to make. God, she missed that woman. She closed the fridge to see her grandmother's picture on the door—the smile that lit up her face, the laugh that lit up a room, and the heart that lit up a community.

Nannie had been her soulmate, her role model, and friend. It hit her like a freight train that her guardian angel knew what happened last night. Somewhere in the middle of the night, the passion she felt turned to shame, and now, looking in the face of virtue, she felt it wash over her again. She needed to talk to someone about all of this, and Rory was it.

Millie picked up the phone. "Thanks for waiting. I'm glad you called Rory. I really need to talk."

"I guess so! Everyone here is singing your praises. It must have been some party, Mil. Did you really take the day off for a hangover, though? How old are you? And what kind of wimp are you? This wouldn't have phased you in college."

You can say that again.

"I'm not taking a day off, just coming in late. Wait, why are you downtown this early in the morning? Your office is in Cary. It will take you an hour to get there now."

"Yeah, I know, I know, but I needed to show you something. How fast can you be here?"

Millie looked in the mirror for the first time that morning and gasped. She looked like the bride of Frankenstein, and a zombie from The Walking Dead had born a love child. You know that look you get when you don't wash your makeup off the night before, and somewhere in the middle of the night, it runs all over your face and crusts in place? Millie had worn a little more makeup than usual for the launch, and now every bit of it was either smeared across her eyelids or holding on for dear life under her eyes.

"It's going to be a while. Just tell me over the phone."

"I can't goofball, or I wouldn't have come all the way down here. Get ready as fast as you can. I'll have coffee and breakfast ready when you get here. Hurry!"

Millie fell backward on the bed when the line went dead. Being awake was too much for her right now. How could she be expected to function today in the real world? And what was the real world going to present? She was a big believer in karma, and as she sat up groaning, she knew that hers was shot.

An hour later, she was pulling into the parking deck. She had pulled herself together in record time with the help of one more Advil and a Pepcid. In the course of that hour, she had stubbed the same toe twice, pinched her eyelid with the eyelash curler, and broken a nail opening the car door. Karma was after her—big time.

She pulled into her usual spot, turned the car off, and laid her head back. Taylor was up there. Would it be awkward? Would he ignore her? Should she ignore him? Would the whole office know about the almost-kiss in the parking lot?

Deep breath, she thought. *Time to hike the big girl panties up and face the music.*

Millie took the longest elevator ride of her life to the 24th floor. She stepped into the lobby and got a generic wave with a genuine smile from the receptionist. She expected to see Rory waiting, but since she wasn't there, Millie walked to her desk.

She had just turned the corner when she spotted Rory laughing with Taylor over muffins and coffee.

Good Lord, he was gorgeous.

"That better be mine." She put her coat on the back of her chair and was handed a large coffee.

She took a long chug of the steaming caffeine goodness. Rory could usually guess what she would order from nearly any restaurant in Raleigh, but she could always be trusted to get her coffee right.

She moaned a little as the caffeine worked its magic. She opened her eyes to see Taylor grinning at her. "You weren't kidding."

"Nope," Rory laughed. "My Millie needs an hour and a cup of coffee before the woman we know and love comes out to play."

They both laughed at her, but she didn't care. In fact, the laughter soothed her. The awful awkwardness she feared was nowhere to be found.

"Well, I'll let you ladies start your day. I'm headed to Birdie's for a moan-worthy coffee."

That brought Millie to attention. She choked on her sip and had Rory banging on her back while Taylor muffled a laugh and walked away.

"You OK?"

"Yep, went down the wrong pipe."

"You have an admirer in that one," Rory smiled, nodding in Taylor's direction.

"Yeah. Wait, what? What did he say?" Millie felt a shot of adrenaline course through her. This power he had over her was devastatingly irresistible.

"He told me all about last night."

Millie's heart stopped.

"Well, don't worry, he said it was perfect. That he wouldn't have changed a thing."

She plopped down in her chair. "He said that?"

"It's a great thing, Millie. Why are you upset?"

"Not upset, just exhausted. I need to talk to you about something, Rory. I, well, I don't know what is going on with me. I've lost my mind, I think."

"You do this all the time, you know." Rory cut her off.

"Do not!" Millie's eyebrow shot up. "Wait, do what exactly?"

"Yes, you do. You underestimate yourself. You are amazing at what you do. The party went perfectly. I'm sure the author was thrilled, and your boss will be too once the sales start spiking."

"Oh, yeah. The party. But…"

"Let me tell you why I came all the way downtown this freaking early in the morning to bug you."

So this was not the minute she would confess her sins and get the sage advice. She put on a happy face for her friend. "Alright, your turn. Shoot."

Rory's smile got so wide so quickly that she looked like a cartoon character. Her eyes lit up, her posture straightened, and her hand flew in front of Millie's face.

"I'M GETTING MARRIED!"

It was the last thing Millie thought she would say. This was nowhere on her radar. She and Will had only been going out for a handful of months. She was still getting to know him. She was still getting used to sharing her best friend. She wasn't ready to lose Rory to a new best friend.

"When did it happen? You were working late yesterday. You couldn't come to the launch last night because you had to work late."

Rory ignored the sting of Millie's reaction. *It was sudden*, she thought. *Give her a second to catch up.*

"I did work late. When I got home, there were flowers all over my apartment and tiramisu on the table with a card. As I was reading the card, Will snuck into the living room. I'm standing there bawling over what he wrote. I turned around to get a tissue, and there he was on one knee with the ring."

Rory looked at her hand in awe. She was radiating a level of happiness that Millie had never known, and she felt selfish for the jealousy that streaked through her.

Millie stood in tears, "What am I going to do without you?" was all she could get out before hugging her fiercely. They stood like that for a few minutes, softly crying until laughter through tears gave way to slap-happy giggles.

"Let me get a good look at this thing. Rory, it's huge! Did you pick it out?"

"Nope, he did this all on his own. Can you believe it? He took his grandmother's stone to CMI, and they helped him design it just for me."

She had to give Will credit. It fit Rory perfectly. It was delicate but strong, detailed but simple, and the biggest diamond she had ever seen outside of a jewelry store. This was real. She was getting married.

"It's incredible, doll, just perfect. How are we old enough for all this? I still don't feel like a grown-up most days, and here you are getting married."

She gave Rory one more hug, but this time, it was a genuine congratulations. She was happy, and that's all she ever wanted for her friend.

"While I have you trapped and crying already, I have a question for you, Mil. Will you be my maid of honor?"

All Millie could do was nod her head. There were no words to tell her how much she loved her, and she wouldn't be able to understand them through the blubbering anyway.

"Good, because we're getting married in three months, and I really need your help."

Millie laughed through the tears, "You know people are going to think you're pregnant."

"Is that you're way of asking?"

"Nah, you're too happy. If you were having a baby, there would be less blinking and more panic in your eyes." She finally let go of Rory and took a step back. She could see their whole friendship in that minute, from a chance meeting freshman year, all the college misadventures, the bad hair dye jobs, the synced cycles, the hatred and love for all the boys that breezed in and out of their lives, the countless conversations over cheesecake and, of course, the inside jokes that were only funny to them.

Millie never doubted they would be each other's maid of honor when the time came, but hearing her ask made it come to life.

"I'll help you plan, but please don't ask me questions like 'Which is better, taupe or tan?' And I'm calling in the troops if Bridezilla comes out."

They both laughed because Rory epitomized easygoing and low maintenance.

"Deal. I promise. You're going to look so beautiful in the pink taffeta dress I picked out. It has a big bow on the butt that will finally make you look like you have one."

"See, you think you're funny, but I already have exceptional ideas for my speech at the reception. You better be nice to me."

The two of them spent the next five minutes cackling over the awful choices of brides of the 80s. When Samantha came down the hall and saw the fun, she joined in with a few new trends they had never even heard of, which turned the hysterics into pure excitement.

About half an hour later, Millie walked into Samantha's office, still grinning.

"Thank you for that. Rory just left on top of the world and her head spinning with ideas."

"It was my pleasure. I didn't even know you had a sister."

Millie smiled. They heard that all the time. They looked enough alike to make people wonder, but watching them finish each other's sentences always had them asking.

"She's my sister from another mother. We met in college and have been inseparable ever since."

Samantha laughed, "I have a friend like that. I'll have to tell her the 'sister from another mother' line." She sat down behind her desk. "So let's talk about last night. You must be exhausted. I'm glad you came in late. You earned it. It was a wonderful launch, Millie. The author was incredibly happy with all the details. He had nothing but extraordinary things to say about you. He's already called this morning to say thank you again. I have to say, the location was amazing. Who knew a llama farm could be so spectacular? Let's keep it on the list of event space options. I wrote out some notes last night and emailed you, just things to remember in the future and details from the launch that we need to make standard at all of our launches. Have you had a chance to open your email yet?"

Millie was embarrassed to shake her head. She had come in late, eaten a leisurely breakfast, and was laughing with a friend at her desk instead of actually working.

"That's OK. I'd like to discuss an email you received this morning. It's from HR about last night."

Millie's heart sank. Would they fire her for an *almost* kiss in the parking lot? She cataloged all the people she had seen and who had seen her with Taylor after the event. Would they have gone to HR? She was about to let loose with the details when Samantha's phone rang.

"Hold on one second. This is Samantha."

Millie sat in her chair, legs crossed, foot shaking, and mind racing. She would beg if it came down to it. She loved this job and wouldn't let it go without a fight.

"Ok, Millie is with me now. I'll have her head on down to get the details, and we'll meet later today to put the pitch together. Good work. We'll be ready."

She smiled as she hung up and rolled her eyes. "Well, good news or bad news first?"

Millie braced herself and prepared to plea. "Bad."

"The break we were about to enjoy is over. That was Taylor. He is working on a new pitch and will need a lot of info. The prep will be awful, but the payout could be huge, his words. So, let's cut this short and start pulling resources. If you'll go down there and see where he's at and how we can help without reinventing the wheel, I'll start on this end. Let's meet up later before we talk to him to make the plan. Tell him we'll meet him at four."

Distracted by the workload, Millie's work ethic kicked in, and she got up excited by the new project. It wasn't until she was approaching Taylor's office that her nerves kicked in.

"Let the awkwardness commence," she whispered to herself—deep breath.

She knocked on the door and put on her best everything-is-fine smile. Taylor looked up with the same smile, and she laughed out loud. "Good, it's not just me."

"What's not you?"

"Nothing. So what's up, buttercup? Samantha says you've thrown the office into another tornado."

He smiled again, but this time, it was a grateful one.

Good Lord, he was gorgeous.

"I seem to be good at that lately. It's a great opportunity if we can manage it. I need to say something first, though. I want to apologize for last night. I've never done anything like that before."

He hadn't stopped twisting his pen since she walked in, which reassured her that he was as uneasy as she was.

"Listen, Taylor, you are a good man. I know it to be true. Last night wasn't something that needs to be an issue, especially at work. It was an exceptional night with an exceptional amount of alcohol. And bottom line, nothing happened."

Taylor waited for the 'but' or a "tell" that would show him that under her calm façade, he had inadvertently broken her trust. The hours of replaying the whole thing in his head last night had brought him to the same conclusion every time - he had crossed the line and was ready to pay the piper today.

As he watched her, she only radiated the calm that had made him open up to her in the first place. Her eyes were kind, with no hint of the torture he had felt all night. He was relieved not to have hurt her but felt a pang of frustration that the night hadn't affected her as it had him.

"You are one of a kind, Millie. I am sorry though, and…"

"No need for apologies, Taylor. Really."

Cut off and surprised by the sting, he tried to regroup. This conversation hadn't gone at all how he thought it would. He couldn't tell if he was more relieved or frustrated, which frustrated him more.

"Ok, well, the deal kind of came out of nowhere, so I've done very little prep, unfortunately. I'll put together the proposal outline and break down what I need from you. Why don't you pull the updated numbers for total sales by quarter, with year-to-date as well last year's breakdown."

Millie was taking notes furiously and adding things she thought he might need. She stopped for a second to listen to the long list of requests Taylor was giving her and started writing again. Out of habit, she put the tip of her pen to her lips. It was an automatic response when she was deep in thought.

Taylor was rambling off different ideas for the proposal but stopped cold when he looked up from his stacks and lists. Her lips were full and even bare, they were a soft rose red. Her eyes were grayish blue today, but he dreamed about their soft green color all night. He wondered how it was possible that she had no idea how sexy she was. He could tell she had no clue, which only made her that much more alluring.

She caught him staring, and their gazes held. The air sizzled between them, and for a brief second, she had the urge to knock everything off the desk and pull him on her. She grinned at the idea and how bold she had become in her fantasies of him. If he only knew some of the scenes she had come up with during staff meetings, he would be shocked.

"Your eyes are gray today."

Millie blinked away the fantasy. "What?"

"They were green last night, with a dark blue ring around them. Now they're gray."

The fact that he knew her eye color sent a thrill up her spine. It was a silly little thing, but it meant he had been paying attention. Their eyes were locked, and her head was swimming. The whole room went hazy, but his face was crystal clear. She looked at his mouth and saw endless possibilities waiting, but they were someone else's possibilities.

Pull yourself together, for God's sake.

"They change with my moods. I think I have what I need here. I'm going to get started."

"You're telling me you have mood-ring eyes? How many colors are in there?"

Millie collected her papers and answered him absently. "They are usually gray. Different shades come out at different times. When I cry, they are a really intense bright blue."

"What mood makes them green?" he interrupted.

She stopped organizing the papers and let out a deep sigh. "I don't know," Millie lied, picking up her folder. She needed to get out of there. The wanting was only getting stronger. She needed to break the connection so she could think clearly again.

She grabbed her pen off his desk and knocked a stack of files off the side, sending papers hang-gliding to the floor.

"Dammit! I'm so sorry!" Millie slammed everything back down on his desk to pick the papers up. She was on her hands and knees before she realized he was kneeling in front of her without a second thought about the mess.

Taylor put his hand on hers and made her stop fussing. "Please don't worry about it, Millie."

She looked at his hand on hers and back up at him.

Good Lord, he was gorgeous.

"You don't seem to care that half the Holland, Inc. file is mixed up on your floor."

"What mood makes them green?" His eyes were intense, and they were set on hers.

"Taylor, focus. This is a hot mess. Hand me those pages over there, and I'll get them organized again."

"They weren't in any order on my desk. You just shuffled them a bit. What mood makes them green?"

He still had her hand in his and rubbed it with his thumb like he had in the car. She felt the fire in her belly stirring and a new feeling of comfort she had missed last night in the heat of the moment.

Millie looked up at his big brown eyes, "Taylor, I need to get started on this project. You need to give me my hand back."

Taylor shifted closer to her in the scattered papers. He couldn't explain why, but he needed to be closer to her, to know her better. "What mood makes them green?" he whispered.

She was lost in his eyes, his scent, his presence. She felt all sense leave her, and the wanting take over. "They turn green when I..."

"Knock, knock."

Millie jumped out of her skin and snatched her hand away to collect more papers. Taylor didn't blink, but she saw the disappointment in his face at the interruption.

Hank Mendenhall walked in with gusto and an arrogance that somehow wasn't off-putting but more comical coming from him. His features were odd when you looked closely, but put together, they made for a very handsome man. It was his eyes that made him attractive though, they were cocky but kind.

"Whoa, what happened in here? Millie, why are you cleaning up this mess by yourself? Thank goodness a gentleman is here to help you." Hank knelt next to her and shot his best friend a look that meant they were going to talk about this little scene at the first opportunity.

Millie was mortified. "I'll just let you two handle this then. I've got some leg work to prep." She stood up quickly and grabbed her things. "I'll get you something by the end of the day. You have a meeting with Samantha at four." She turned and was out the door before either of them could respond.

Taylor was left to explain why he was holding someone's hand who wasn't his wife.

chapter five

MILLIE SANK IN her chair and threw the stack of papers on her desk. She had never been so embarrassed in her life. Not only was she a klutz, but she seemed to be incapable of using any part of her brain when she was in Taylor's presence. He had this power over her common sense. It shut off when he was near. No one had ever had this effect on her, and as much as she had grown to love the rush he gave her, she knew she couldn't keep this up.

She turned her computer on and sorted through the mess of papers while it booted up. She was going to screw her head back on straight and get to work. Work was the only thing that could save her at this point. She dove into the financials and started pulling the details together that would make up the proposal. Hours flew by before her need for coffee reappeared, along with her headache.

She stretched in her chair and took stock of her progress. She had made great headway, but it wasn't enough. From everything Taylor had said about the deal, they needed a wow factor, and right now, it just wasn't there.

Coffee. She needed to clear her head and get a fresh perspective. She minimized the screen she had been working on to find her email. She rolled her eyes at the number of new emails when the message from HR caught her eye. She had been so preoccupied with Taylor and his project, she had forgotten all about Samantha's warning about the HR email.

She took a deep breath to relieve some of the instant dread that filled her chest. Whatever was on the other side of that email, she would fight for her job and make them listen to her side of the story. She just had to figure out how much of the story they knew.

Millie opened the email to find it short and sweet.

Subject: *HR* meeting request

Good morning Millie,
I understand you are coming in late this morning. When you catch your breath, I'd like to speak to you. Just see me whenever you are free today.
Thanks!

Brenda Crawford
Director of Human Resources
Grant Publishing, Inc.

So there it was. Her future at the company she loved rested in the hands of a woman she had only spoken to in passing. The fact that it was the Director of HR worried her. She read the email over and over again, hoping to decode some subtext that would give her insight into the meeting. There was nothing to do but face the fire and hope for the best.

Her headache was back with a vengeance, so she grabbed one more Advil on her way to the kitchen for the coffee. The blessed smell of caffeine gave her hope that the drummer inside her head would rest his sticks. She popped the little pill and took a long sip of coffee. She probably should have waited for the medicine to kick in, but she wanted this meeting over and done.

She got on the elevator with her coffee in hand and pressed the button for the 18th floor. She always felt sorry for the people who worked on the lower floors. Their view was good, but the view from the 24th was amazing. She looked into her coffee and sighed. She dreamed of working on the 28th floor eventually. What a view they must have.

The doors opened, and she walked out slowly. As the doors shut behind her, a revelation hit. Why wasn't Taylor in this meeting? If it was such a big deal for employees to be… whatever they were… then he should be here to face the music with her. With every step she took toward the director's office, she grew madder and bolder. This was completely hypocritical, and she was going to let this woman know it. She was in human resources, for God's sake. Surely, she should know that it takes two to tango.

By the time Millie found the director's office, she had built a case around inequality and glass ceilings that would make Gloria Steinem proud. She knocked on the door a little too hard to let her know she was there and meant business. They said their hellos as she sat on the other side of the desk but instantly regretted bringing the coffee because she caught herself shaking a bit.

She hated that she did this. Whenever she got the least bit nervous, her hands would shake and go ice cold. If the nervousness got bad enough, the shaking would spread to her whole body. It didn't happen often, but always at the most inconvenient times.

'Lock it up!' kept running through her head. She closed her eyes and took a deep breath when Brenda closed the door. That was good. She didn't want everyone to hear her begging anyway.

Brenda sat down at her desk, seeming so official. The shaking in her hands kicked up a notch. "Do you mind if I put this here?" she asked as she put the mug on Brenda's desk. If it took sitting on her hands to get herself under control, she was going to do it quickly before it got any worse.

"Thank you for coming in today. I know you have a lot of follow-up to do after last night. I heard great things, though. The author was apparently thrilled with everything."

Brenda was smiling, but Millie was too nervous for the small talk. "He did the hard work. I just helped celebrate it."

"I think you're being modest, but well done anyway. Well, I imagine you are wondering why I brought you down here."

Millie shifted in her seat and felt the shakes kick up another notch. She would wait a minute before the pleading began but had no control over the damn shakes.

"We are creating a new position outside of sales, although you would still be working with them closely."

Millie sat there blinking. Maybe they weren't going to fire her, just demote her and force her to quit? There went her severance package. Tricky.

She got a flashback from last night and the stolen moment in time. Was it worth losing the job she loved at a company where she already felt at home?

Hell no. Time to fight for it. She opened her mouth to begin her pleas when she heard Brenda say, "It's a great opportunity, and it's yours if you want it."

"I'm sorry?"

"I said, the job is yours if you want it. Here is a list of responsibilities we have come up with so far. Since the position is being created, you would have the opportunity to make it your own and edit this as you go. What do you think?"

Millie sat there speed-reading through the duties and was awe-struck. While she had been preparing for battle in her head, Brenda had been offering her a dream job: Director of Events at Grant Publishing.

"Are you serious? You're offering me a promotion?" Millie was still scanning the page, trying her best to read it.

"I'm surprised that you're surprised." Brenda laughed, "This company likes to reward hard workers, and we always prefer to promote within."

"But I've only been here for a short time, just under a year."

"And in that short time, for nearly a year now, you have caught the attention of several VPs. You have proven yourself in ways I'm not sure you were even aware of." Brenda laughed again, "You know, it's not often that I have to convince a staff member to accept a better job with more responsibility and pay."

That snapped Millie out of the dumb-founded trance she had fallen into. "A raise?"

"Absolutely. You'll see the pay structure on the second sheet, including bonus options, all laid out. It really is competitive with the market now and a significant increase from your current salary. There is also an employee stock program you are eligible for that is excellent if you're interested."

Millie blinked for the first time in too long. "Stock options?" she whispered.

"If you accept, that is." Brenda looked at Millie above her reading glasses and smiled. "You can do this, Millie. It's a tremendous offer."

It was Millie's turn to laugh out loud. Brenda mistook her silence for a confidence issue when, in reality, it was pure relief.

"I'm sorry, I'm not often speechless. Yes, I accept. Thank you." She could hear herself talking over the details with Brenda, but nothing was registering. It was a dream. Any minute, she would wake up with half her sandwich stuck to her face because she had fallen asleep at her desk. But it wasn't a dream, it was real. Holy crap!

She shook Brenda's hand and walked to the elevator, still dazed. Had they talked about a start date? Was she doing both jobs for now? Had anyone spoken to Samantha? Was she supposed to give Samantha her two-week notice?

Ugh! Why didn't you pay attention?!

The elevator doors opened, startling her back into reality. She just accepted a job without confirming any of the actual details. All she knew was that she was moving into a new chapter, and she was going to make the best of her significant raise. She headed straight for Samantha's office but realized almost immediately that she had forgotten her coffee cup downstairs. She did an about-face and nearly slammed into Taylor.

"We can't keep running into each other like this." He smiled and pushed the down button. "Heading down?"

Millie gave a half smile but was still distracted by her conversation with Brenda. Taylor saw that her heart wasn't in the smile and immediately felt that guilt again. He was positive he should steer clear of her, but he just wasn't sure he had the willpower to do it.

"No, I left my mug downstairs, but I think I'll get it later though. You?"

"Yep, I'm meeting Hank for a drink. You're welcome to join?" As soon as the words came out of his mouth, he feared both a yes and no from her. He knew he wanted more time with her, but more time meant wanting more of everything else. And if he was going to be honest, if he was going to spend time with her, he wanted her alone.

"Sorry, I can't. I need to talk to Samantha about the job."

"Hmmm, you're not leaving us already, are you?" He pushed the down button again, relieved that he wouldn't spend another night out falling for this woman but frustrated that he would spend the weekend wishing he had been able to spend time with her.

He looked at her then. She was unusually pale and definitely distracted.

"I still can't believe it. I don't even know how it happened. I just need to talk to Samantha. Have a good weekend."

"Whoa! I was kidding, turkey! You can't take another job!"

"I know. It's crazy. I wasn't even looking for it." She was rubbing her forehead like she did when she was worried. She needed to slow down and wrap her head around all of this.

"Millie. Seriously. You can't leave." He was holding her by the shoulders now and knew people were watching. The elevator doors opened. "Get in. We need to talk."

"But, I…"

"Get in!"

He had her by the arm, but it was his eyes that held her still. There was worry and fear behind them.

The minute the doors closed, she braced herself for the yelling she thought would come. Taylor stared at her in a daze. "I'm so sorry" was all he could say. He still had her arm but held a gentle grip. He needed to hold on to her, even for just a minute more.

She stepped closer without thinking. "What is happening up there? Talk to me."

"You are! You're what's going on up here. I'm an idiot. There's no reason to leave a job you clearly love. We can figure something out, Millie. Please don't take it. Don't go."

"Taylor, I've already accepted the new position. It's a great opportunity." Or at least that's what she remembered Brenda saying. "I'm sure…"

"No! This is ridiculous!" He slammed the elevator's stop button. "We haven't even… I mean, I wanted to, but we haven't! Even though the moment was there, it would have been the perfect moment. Maybe I should have so you would be as tormented as I am. You're so cool, not a *cool* cool either. Why am I the only one yelling! Why aren't you yelling back?"

Millie laughed out loud. "Because you are the only one who knows what you're talking about." He wanted to be offended. He wanted to resent that she wasn't as confused as he was, but she had this sweet southern calm about her that brought a smirk before he could control it.

"You could at least get a little crazy to make me feel better."

"Tell me why you think this job is such a bad idea. You don't think I can do it?"

She had taken his little tantrum in a completely different way than he meant it. His face dropped immediately, "Oh no, Millie. I think you can do anything. You've got such a great head on your shoulders. Even though I want you here, whoever snatched you is lucky to have you. I just don't want you to leave because of me."

It was Millie's turn to feel like the fool. Until that moment, she truly hadn't believed that last night had affected Taylor in the same way it had her.

Sure, she had felt the spark. Sure, she wanted to think that he felt it, too. In her heart of hearts, though, she didn't really believe it.

"You want me?"

It was said so innocently that he wanted to pull her to him and wrap his arms around her. He was more confused than ever.

"How can you not feel that?" He stepped closer but made a point not to touch her. He would show her how much he wanted her if he didn't get control of himself.

She looked down, shy and unsure. She whispered, "You couldn't want me. Not really. It was just the whiskey."

"What?"

"I thought it was just me imagining things and the whiskey." She was trying to convince herself more than him. She couldn't hope like this. It would destroy her in the end.

"I've made a mess of things, Millie, but you must feel what's happening here. At the very least, you have to feel the electricity every time we're in a room together?"

He took a deep breath and another step forward. "You have to know how incredible I think you are. I've wanted to know you since the first day you walked into the office.

You were wearing this sleeveless white sweater. You took my breath away."

She looked up in shock. "You liked this shirt?" She put her hands on her stomach and was suddenly very aware of the shape it gave her.

Again, the innocence overwhelmed him. She had no idea how beautiful she was.

"I like this shirt. But I love you in it."

She blushed and stepped back in disbelief. She shook her head to clear it, but her mind was spinning. A rush of desire took her breath away. "Taylor."

She was irresistible. "Millie, of course I want you." He stepped forward and put his mouth to hers gently. His arms were around her, holding her close, and were the only thing keeping her from melting.

Her moan was enough to send his brain swirling. This was the kind of kiss that time stood still for.

Her hands slid up his back between his shirt and jacket, and she felt every muscle under them tense. He wanted her. There was chemistry here, not just lust but a real connection to another soul.

As their hands explored and their tongues danced, she felt his need and wished they were anywhere else. She put months of feelings into the kiss, and tenderness quickly turned to desperation.

The elevator alarm rang, shocking them apart, both gasping for air and needing the handrail to steady themselves. It was almost like an alarm clock had gone off, waking them from the kind of dream that makes your fantasies come to life. Only it wasn't a dream. An actual fantasy was coming to life, and neither of them knew what to do about it.

"Taylor, I…"

"Please don't," he said as he hit the lobby button and turned off the alarm. "We need to talk about this, but please let me get my head on straight first."

He turned to look at her. Her face was flushed, and her lips were swollen. He had done that, but she had done so much more to him. He laughed at what he must look like.

"What's funny? Taylor, my head is on a roller coaster right now. I'm glad you're having a good time, but I want off the ride."

The doors opened as if in queue, and she walked away from him with as much conviction as she could muster. She made it through the doors and was nearly in the parking lot before it occurred to her that she hadn't meant to leave the building and didn't have her keys.

"What is wrong with me!" She turned to go back upstairs and saw Taylor sitting on a bench by the door.

"I thought I'd wait here for you."

His smirk was usually incredibly sexy to her, but at this moment, she wanted to kick him in the teeth.

"And there is nothing wrong with you. That's the problem. Will you sit?" He held his hand up to his forehead to shield his eyes from the sun and look at her. "Please?"

She loved and hated his pull on her. Even when she was mad, she wanted to be near him.

"Why would you laugh? Forget that, actually. Why would you kiss me? Taylor, I feel like I'm going out of my mind here. You aren't available for me to have."

His eyebrow cocked up, and the smirk was back. "*Have*, huh? Where is your mind, Miss Millie?"

She laughed before she could catch it. "Shut up." She said and plopped down next to him.

"I'm so sorry for all of this, Millie. I really am."

It stung so badly that her eyes filled with tears before he even finished. "Oh, I see," she took a deep breath. "It's fine. I need to get back up there, so I'll just…"

"Now you shut up." He said, still smirking, needing her to listen. "I'm not sorry for the kiss. You pack a mean punch, by the way. I still haven't … recovered. I couldn't chase you. I needed to sit down. I just hoped like hell you didn't have your keys on you."

She was blushing again. She was irresistible again. And she still had no idea how sexy she was.

Focus, he told himself. He looked at her lips, how full they were and how they had taken him completely by surprise.

"I laughed because that alarm scared the shit out of me. I felt like the principal had caught us under the bleachers. And because your lips were swollen, your face was flushed, and your hair was all over the place. If I did that to you, I must have looked like I had walked through a tornado."

He ran his hand through his hair out of habit, unconcerned with the tornado. Millie, on the other hand, started fixing hers.

"Please stop. You're beautiful. I didn't say that to make you self-conscious. I just wanted you to know why I laughed. Nervous habit." He looked down at her mouth, "I have a lot of those with you."

Now, it was her turn to laugh. "Right. You're the most confident person I know. Even when you're not up to it."

"What do you mean?"

"At the launch party, you were distracted. You were hurting, and you had absolutely no interest in talking to anyone, but you did it. Not only did it, but you made everyone feel like they were the only person at the party you wanted to talk to."

She kept going, even though the shy was pushing her to stop. "And other times, when there is a deadline no one could meet. You walk in and utilize everyone's strengths to make it happen, to bring out their best. You're great at that."

"Thank you." He could feel her looking at him, but he kept his eyes on the ground. "Congratulations on the new job, Millie. Whatever it is, I know you'll be amazing at it."

He took a deep breath and whispered again, like he had on the elevator. "I'm so sorry for making such a mess of this. I won't sit here and make excuses. You know too much about me and my life to make them."

He turned to her then so she could see his sincerity.

"But I need you to believe me, Millie. I don't want to hurt you, and I never meant to lead you on. The connection between us is something I've never known." He looked away, "That sounds terrible, considering. God, I'm becoming the cliché I've always hated."

He ran his hand through his hair again, like the answers were hidden in the roots, but his eyes were lost.

"Taylor, listen to me. This wasn't your fault. I was a willing participant. You have become this fantasy for me that I never dreamed possible. You've made me feel things I've never felt before, and you've never touched me until today. I'm not naïve. I know you love Carrie. You're in a rough patch, and I'm not willing to be the complication that ruins your marriage. I wish life were different, but it's just not."

She watched him for some sign of agreement, but he didn't respond at all. She leaned down to see his face and saw a single tear fall down his cheek. Millie reached over and wiped the tear gently.

"And I'm sorry too. I should have been stronger."

He looked up at her, lost and hopeless. "What am I going to do? I don't know what to do anymore. I love her so much. She's a wonderful person. I can't remember not having her in my life."

He squeezed his eyes shut like the words were slicing through him. "But I'm not *in* love with her. I haven't been for a long time. I wanted to be. I tried to be. I tried to do the things people do when they are crazy about each other, but in the end, it just showed me what I already knew."

He jumped off the bench to pace. "With everything going on in our world, how can I break her heart like this? How can I leave when she's doing so much to make my dreams come true? I've wanted to be a father since my dad taught me to ride a bike. I wanted to teach my son with the same patience he had. Now, I am questioning the very relationship that could make that happen. So, do I give up on the whole thing or make it work for the sake of the children we may or may not have? Tell me. What do I do!"

Millie fought tears. She ached for him and the whole situation. He needed a friend right now, not a temptation. No matter how strong their feelings were for each other, he belonged with Carrie. All the flirting she was doing was only hurting him more, and now, knowing the whole story, it felt like a punch to her gut.

In her most soothing voice, she let him free. "Taylor, I can't answer that for you. I can't fix this for you either. It'll only make things worse for you. You need to talk to her. Let her know how lonely you are, how much you're hurting. Have you ever thought that she may be hurting in the same way?"

"Are you kidding me? You're going to sit there and tell me I'm making her life miserable because I can't stop thinking about another woman, even though that woman is you! Unbelievable!"

"Stop it, Taylor. You want to yell and scream? Fine. But don't twist my words around to make me the villain here. I want to help you. I really do. I care about you. But I can't sit here and decide which path your life is going to take, and you know it."

"Just once, I would like someone to back *me* up! Just once, I would like someone to make *me* feel like the special one! I can't win!"

"Oh, stop it! Do you want me to feel sorry for you because you have two women who want to love you? Do you want me to beg you to be with me, to choose me and the potential we have? I don't want to *tell* someone to love me, Taylor. I want them to do it on their own. I don't want someone who is going to resent me for telling them to leave their family all because he was tired of trying!"

"I wouldn't leave Carrie over some cheap thrill in the elevator. Get serious!"

As soon as the words came out, he wished for a rock big enough to crawl under and hide. He kept a tight leash on his temper for exactly this reason.

"Millie, please forgive me. That came out completely wrong."

He reached for her hand, but the damage had been done.

"Thank goodness you can see it for what it was. Glad to help work that out for you." She rose slowly, staring at him with daggers in her eyes. "If you'll excuse me, I need to go upstairs and tell Samantha the good news. I won't be a problem for you anymore, Taylor. Good luck."

There was no point in chasing after her. He had seen the sword strike her heart and make the cut that he couldn't take back.

"Damn it!"

As he walked to the car, he pulled out his phone to call Hank. He needed to yell, as she had put it, and Hank was the lucky son of a bitch who was going to listen to it.

"I'm heading to the Pub. You're buying."

Upstairs, Samantha was leaving a note for Millie at her desk. "Well, hey there, Miss Director of Events! Congratulations! I'm so thrilled for you!"

Millie was in a spine-popping bear hug before she could wipe the tears from her face.

"I'm going to miss working with you like this, but I'm just so happy for you! They came to me a few weeks ago and asked what I thought, but wow! They moved quickly!"

She let go and finally saw the tears. "Well, honey, there's no need for all that. We'll still work together on special projects. And there's always the oh-so-exciting department head meetings that you'll be forced to sit through now."

Millie was grateful for her dismissal of the tears. She did her best to regroup and focus her energy on the incredible opportunity instead of the incredible heartbreak. Her heart hurt. It actually hurt. Every beat hit the bruise his words left behind. Every beat was another second she was removed from any ties to him. Every beat was a new level of misery she had never known.

It was time to confess all of this to the girls and hope they understood her side of the "cheap thrill" she had with the very gorgeous, and very married, Taylor Fitzpatrick.

chapter six

TRUE TO FORM, Millie was the last to arrive at Audrey's apartment. Audrey had just put down her deposit the month before so the girls walked around the boxes with enthusiasm and a lot of imagination. They knew what this meant for Audrey. Freedom had come at a steep price for their friend, but this move was a huge step in the right direction.

"It's huge, Audrey! How are you going to fill this place up?"

Millie took the five-cent tour while the others popped a bottle of champagne.

"One piece at a time, I guess. The new bed will be delivered tomorrow. There are a few things from Mom and Dad's coming. I have a few new kitchen things that I bought, and of course, the Monet. I think I'm going to put it on this wall."

After graduation, Audrey had gone to Paris and walked through the Louvre. While there, she bought a print of *Water Lilies* and had it shipped home. It was her prize possession. For her, it symbolized peace. She had no idea then how desperately she would crave it or how precious peace would become.

"How are you with all of this?"

"I'm good. Exhausted, but good. I know it needs work, but it already feels like home. All the boxes are here now, so it's just a matter of finding time to unpack them." Audrey turned to her friend. "What about you? You good?"

Millie grinned but saw the worry on Audrey's face. She was the most sensitive in the group and was always the first to see the trouble any of the girls were hiding. Millie didn't want to go through the whole thing twice, but she really didn't want to go through the whole story with Audrey first. She knew Audrey would be disappointed in her and wanted to make sure she had the girls around to support them both.

"I'm good. Exhausted, but good. A lot happened at work today. I could use a glass of something potent before the debriefing."

Audrey laughed and joined arms with Millie. "That bad, huh? Well, I have a Solo cup with your name on it."

They joined Rory and Cate in the kitchen just in time to hear Cate scream bloody murder. Audrey ran over to her, "What in the world is wrong? OH MY GOSH RORY!!"

Millie felt like such a terrible friend. In all the drama of the day, she had completely forgotten about the tears of joy this day had started with. She stood there smiling at Rory spill every detail of the most romantic night of her life, teary-eyed and beaming, and knew there was nothing in the world she would do to take that away from her.

She put on a happy face and jumped into the excitement around her. Her story could wait. Tonight was Rory's time to shine.

After the details were given, tears were shed, and drinks were toasted, the real news broke.

"We talked earlier, and we agreed on a fall wedding. What are you guys doing Labor Day weekend?"

"Whoa, that's fast, girl." Audrey was already opening her calendar to clear weekends.

"The real question is if the baby's christening will be part of the wedding ceremony. Might as well get a two-for-one deal while you're at the church." Cate laughed at Rory's expression. "I'm with Audrey, what's the rush?"

"There's no rush, but there's also no reason to wait. I want to be with him, and I really want to be married to him. I just know this is right. And I want *right* to start right now. I would elope if I could, but that wouldn't exactly fly with the fam. So, we'll do the dress, the dinner, the whole shebang in the fall. Everyone wins."

The girls looked at each other in disbelief. "We have a hell of a lot of work to do, ladies." Millie put her head on Rory's shoulder and took a minute to appreciate the moment. "Go big or go home, right?"

Rory kissed the top of Millie's head and nodded. "I need you guys up there with me. Will you be in the wedding?"

"Oh, glory." Cate rolled her eyes, "You're not going to make us wear some awful dress with a big bow on the butt, are you?"

"She's already found it. It's pink taffeta!" Millie laughed.

"Twisted minds think alike." Rory laughed as she filled their cups up with the champagne. "To you, together we are the perfect person. May we each find the men who are brave enough to take us on."

The girls tapped their Solo cups, "To the brave."

"Should you drink that? It's not good for the baby." Cate joked. She was on the verge of tears and needed to lighten the mood.

"A sip won't hurt the twins." Rory put her drink down. "I take that back. That joke isn't funny, can you imagine?"

A belly laugh erupted that brought a different kind of tears. "Too late, mama, you've done it now!"

The girls laughed and planned until the yawning took over, and the quiet set in. "Ladies, I appreciate the focus group discussion, but I'm going to have to call it a night. I still need my beauty sleep until the license is signed."

Everyone rolled their eyes in unison. "Rory, why don't you shut up. You're beautiful. I actually don't know why I'm still friends with you." Millie held out her hand to make Rory help her up. "You'll be a much better wingman now that you have a rock on your hand. They'll have to look at me now."

"I've always been a good wingman, thank you. The problem is that you're too picky. What was wrong with the last one? He was great."

"His name was Stuart, and the problem was his black socks with sandals in the summertime. As we do not live in Florida and he is not 95 years old, I had to jump ship."

"Well, that is unfortunate," Rory smiled. "But it's nothing compared to some of the winners you've met. You should let him try again."

Cate jumped in, "What about the one that brought his mother on the date with him? What was his name?"

"That would be Ben. Nice guy, pity he couldn't wipe his own mouth or pay for the bill. Thank God we met there."

"And who was the one who only ordered food he could eat with his hands?" Audrey asked, breathlessly laughing.

"Ugh, Michael. I'll never forget the way he looked at his mashed potatoes, like they were some kind of puzzle he couldn't figure out."

The girls had clearly gotten their second wind and were laughing hysterically, but Millie was too tired to go through her roster of disastrous dates.

"I'm so glad we could take this stroll down memory lane, y'all, but I'm out of here. Audrey, the apartment is fantastic. Let me know if you need help with anything. I'll bring the big guns to help you move the light stuff." Millie gave her a big hug. "I'm proud of you, love. This is your fresh start."

The girls joined in for a big group hug and swayed back and forth a bit. They were all so proud of Audrey and wanted her to feel it at every opportunity.

"Lock this door behind us," Cate, ever the practical one, ordered. "Love ya, mean it."

Millie got out her phone as they walked to the elevator.

"Where's your car, Mil?" Rory was digging in her Mary Poppins bag for her keys.

"I left it at home. I didn't know how much celebrating was going down tonight." That app was proving to be very handy. She had used it two nights in a row now, both because of champagne.

"Just let me take you home, fruitcake. I drive right by your exit." Cate was holding the elevator door open for them. "That rock isn't going to put us over the weight limit, is it? Step in slowly."

Sarcasm was Cate's way of loving. The more sarcastic she was with you, the more comfortable she was with you.

"I'm too tired to take the stairs, so we'll just have to risk it." Rory looked at her hand. "He did good, didn't he." It wasn't a question. She was dazzled by her ring and by the man who gave it to her. They had never seen her so happy before.

"He got it perfect, doll. He did great." Millie saw the ring flash like fire in the elevator lights and wondered what it must feel like to know someone loved you that much. She watched Rory turn the ring around and around on her finger and wondered how it felt to be the one someone chose above all others.

She put on a smile, but her heart began to ache again. She was blessed with hours of distraction, but it was late, and all of the dread of the day was seeping its way back into focus. She still hadn't told them about her promotion. How sad was it that such big news had been diminished by the person who had put her on cloud nine and the seventh ring of hell, all in one afternoon.

When the doors opened, the girls hugged and took one last look at the ring. "Lunch on Sunday, 11:30 a.m. Don't be late… Mil. Night girls!" Rory turned on her car and watched as her friends got in Cate's car before she drove away, singing loudly to Jack Johnson.

"Where to, Ms. Daisy?" Cate buckled her seatbelt and let Millie get settled before she started with the questions.

"You've got something on your mind. You wanna share it now, or do I have to beat it out of you?"

"I'm fine, just tired. It was a long day." Millie turned the heated seat on and stretched.

"I swear, you turn that thing on in the heat of summer."

"It feels good on my back. I like it."

"Comes with the ride, my friend. Now dish." Cate backed out of the parking spot and turned out of the apartment complex. "You've got a heated couch and my full attention. Let the therapy begin."

"You don't have time for the kind of therapy I need." Millie reclined the seat a little and wiggled into the warmth.

"Try me."

"I'm tired, Cate, that's all. And definitely too tired for therapy."

"But there is something bothering you. Did the launch not go well? Rory said the office was still talking about what a great job you did. Don't let some little detail ruin the bigger picture."

"No, the launch was amazing. It's what got me the promotion."

She hit the brakes harder than she meant to at a red light. "You got a promotion today? Why didn't you say anything? God, you've only been there for five minutes, and now you're running the place! Tell me!"

Millie smiled at her, "Not the whole place, but a section of it. I'm the new Director of Events, as of… well, I don't know when I start actually. It's a new position, so I'm going to be making a lot of it up as I go along, but I'll have support staff, a pay raise, and stock options."

The whole idea of the job was still surreal to her, but telling Cate made her sit up a little taller.

"Shut the front door! Millie! That's amazing! You should have told us so we could toast you, too! Is that what you're worried about? Because honey, if anyone could do that job, it's you. It was made for you. Literally!"

The green glow of the street light lit up Cate's face and took her attention. She was genuinely excited for Millie, like any proud sister would be. Her women loved her, and she knew it. And they would always love her. She knew that, too. If today proved anything to her, it was that she needed to get her head on straight and get her focus back. And the quickest way to do that was with the slap of reality Cate would give her when she told her about Taylor.

"It's going to be great once I get going. I didn't want to steal Rory's ring thunder and Audrey's apartment lightning. There was enough great news today. Mine can keep. And it still hasn't sunk in yet, honestly, but I'm overwhelmed and excited. Samantha and I went over a lot of ideas this afternoon so I can spend the weekend overanalyzing and obsessing over everything that is going to happen on Monday."

Here goes nothing, she thought.

"It was what happened after that meeting that I need your Walmart counseling degree."

"I got it at Target, thank you very much. I got my doctorate at Walmart. I really should frame those for occasions like this."

"One day, I'm going to snag you a red shirt and blue vest so you can feel official during our sessions and charge more."

"You pay now. I'm just sneaky about it." Cate giggled, "So what's up?"

They got to Millie's apartment complex and sat in the parking lot for forty-five minutes while she went over every detail of the afternoon, the launch, after the launch, and the flirty work days that led up to it all. Cate only interrupted for clarification. The quieter she was, the more details Millie gave.

By the end of the story, Millie was beyond exhausted and more frustrated than ever. Hearing herself tell her friend that she had kissed someone else's husband was about as low as she had ever felt.

"Please say something. I know I just threw a lot at you, and you're disappointed in me, but I need some guidance here. Clearly, I need to go to church and have some holy water thrown in my face. What is wrong with me?"

"I don't think some holy water would hurt, but I can just say a little prayer while I hose you off in the yard here. Let's not wake the minister up tonight."

Millie laughed nervously and put her head on Cate's lap. "What is wrong with me?"

Cate took a deep breath. She was still searching for the right words to comfort her friend. "Do you love him?"

"What? No, of course not. He's not available for me to love. That's the point."

"Do you love him?"

"How can I love someone that I know I can't have? I'm not an idiot. I know this doesn't end well for me. And you heard what he said. It was just a cheap thrill for him."

"Millie, do you love him?"

The tears burned her eyes, but she refused to let them fall. She closed her eyes and felt shame and relief wash over her as she nodded her head. "I really think I could."

She never allowed herself to admit it before, but she had known for some time that he was special and everything she wanted wrapped up in one person. It was an awful and wonderful feeling then, and finally acknowledging it to Cate only heightened that.

"Does he love you?"

As much as she struggled to admit her own feelings, she was painfully aware of his. She shook her head, eyes still closed, but now had no control over the falling tears. "He can't, even if he wanted to, but he made it pretty clear what he thinks of me today."

Cate looked down at her friend with compassion. Now wasn't the time to say she wanted to kill the man who had shaken her friend's world like this. Now wasn't the time to give her hope that he may feel the same way. Now definitely wasn't the time to say someday she would find someone who deserved her.

So what the hell time was it? Cate thought. She and Millie were practical people, but heartbreak was never practical. Real heartbreak, no matter the cause, threw logic out the window and made even the strongest person weak.

Millie turned her head into Cate's lap and wept. How could she love someone she knew so little about? How could she love someone she knew didn't love her? How could she love someone who was married to someone else? When had she gone off the deep end and just completely lost her mind?

The whole world seemed to close in at that moment. She couldn't hold back the sobs. She cried for the love wasted, the love lost, and for the love of God to forgive her for getting into this mess in the first place.

To Cate's credit, she just let her cry while rubbing her back. At one point, she whispered, "Everything will be just fine," but Millie wasn't ready to believe her quite yet.

When the well had run dry and the tears stopped, she laid twisted in the seat. She felt stupid and small. What was so great about love? She was raw and wrecked with a dash of deflated and a gallon of guilt. She was starring in her own Lifetime movie, and she wouldn't even get the guy in the end.

"This sucks," surprised at how sharp and bitter she sounded. This wasn't her. She had never been this hung up on a guy before. She was the one who did the leaving before it got serious, and this was precisely why. Who in their right mind would sign up for this willingly or more than once?

She had heard fairy tales throughout her entire childhood, filled with love conquering all, the perfect man making the world right again, and everyone living happily ever after. The cartoons left out the part where Mr. Right couldn't be the hero because he was the main love interest in someone else's story.

She was more unsure of herself and her future than she had ever been, and that made her mad. "I've never been this frustrated before. It's not supposed to be this hard."

Cate laughed. "Life is hard, friend."

"You know what I mean. Why am I so upset about a relationship that clearly isn't an actual relationship and has no potential of being anything other than a disaster?"

"Because, as you finally admitted a few minutes ago, you love the disaster." Cate jumped a bit when Millie shot up in her seat with a wild look in her eyes.

"I swear to God, he better be twisted in as many knots as I am, wherever he is."

"I don't think you need to worry about him or his knots. If he's half the catch you say he is, he'll be beating himself up for the fling comment for a long time."

Downtown, a completely different scene was hearing a very similar conversation.

Hank watched his friend pace back and forth, talking in circles. He had gotten the full story sitting at the bar, but after about the sixth drink, Taylor's volume had gotten a little high. Hank took him to his condo to continue their conversation without an audience.

Now, here he sat, the pool lights casting an eerie glow over his friend, who was as close to falling apart as he had ever seen. They had been friends for over twenty years. They were more like brothers than their actual brothers. They could read each other's minds with a single look. So how had he missed that his friend was hurting this badly?

He watched as Taylor continued to pace, making no sense but talking through the whole situation in his own way. He wanted to help but had absolutely no idea how. "Why don't we take a long weekend and go somewhere? We haven't been on a trip in too long."

"She detests me. I know she does. She looked at me like I was the devil, like it was all in my master plan. Like I don't want the same things she wants. I know I can make it right if I just try. She deserves that. How can I make it right with her?"

"We can get some of the guys together. Deep sea fishing. Grill our food like men. Drink. Play cards. Lie to each other about how big our…"

"But how do I convince her I'm not the bad guy here? I mean, sure, I've screwed up. But I'm one of the good ones. Until all of this, I'll be honest, I thought I was one of the great ones. Now look at me, I'm a damn cliché. She'll never look at me the same way again."

"Didn't you say you wanted to go snorkeling? Why don't we set that up, too? We can make Jimmy teach us, practice here, and then go somewhere tropical this winter. How's Fiji?"

Taylor stopped in his tracks. "What did you say?"

"I doubt you've heard the last hour of what I've said, but I think we should take a long weekend."

"No, after that, you said Jimmy. I wonder if he still needs someone." A whole new obsession crossed his face, but this one worried Hank more than the women troubles.

"Jimmy always needs someone. This week it's Rebekah, she's the most beautiful thing he's ever seen. The trouble is, she's smarter than he is, and he's not sure it will work. The real trouble is that most of them are, but I haven't told him that yet."

Taylor rolled his eyes. "He asked me to come work out there a few months ago. I wonder if he found someone."

Hank stood now, "Taylor. You're not moving to the beach to sell snorkeling equipment. Come on. You have the job of your dreams. You bought a house. And, lest we forget, a wife and family that live in Raleigh."

"We don't have a family! And at this point, I'm not sure I want one."

"I meant me, you jackass. I'm your family! What will moving to the beach solve for you? Nothing. It's just running away from it all. You're better than that. I've listened to you ramble all night long about Carrie hating you and how you want to fix it. How will you fix anything two hundred miles away?"

"Dammit! I wasn't talking about Carrie tonight! I was talking about Millie!"

Hank leaned against the balcony railing and took a deep breath for patience, hoping he wouldn't sound like a scolding parent. "You have been talking in circles for nearly four hours. You're telling me that in all that time, I have listened to the whole story, or at least your take of it, and you're just now telling me you want it to work out with *Millie*? What the hell, T! Did you not think that was vital information to share at the beginning of the story? What about your wife?

What role does Carrie have in all of this? You've had a hard few months. I'll grant you that. What you two have been going through is awful, and I'm sorry for it, but are you just going to run off with someone else? Your job is to be her rock right now. I hate that the awful is lasting this long, but suck it up! Life is hard."

"Don't give me that bullshit! You know it hasn't been working with Carrie for a lot longer than the last few months. You see the way she is with me more than anyone. You should know how she has pulled away from me! Well, multiply that by ten when it's just the two of us at home. We don't speak unless it's about bills or something that needs to be fixed at the house. We stay in opposite corners of that house. Hell, I sleep in the room she decorated for this baby that we can't conceive! I'm telling you, at this point, I'm not sure we need to bring a baby into the world. We're a mess, a hot damn mess, and neither one of us cares enough to work on it. I've done all I know to do. We've talked to everyone I know to talk to. It's not working!"

Hank truly hadn't known how bad it had gotten. Taylor was right, though. He had noticed the way Carrie had pulled away over the last few years, but with everything going on, he thought it was exhaustion. "I'm sorry, Taylor. Really."

Taylor sat at one of the tables and put his head in his hands. "Tell me what to do. Just tell me what the right choice is. I stay with Carrie? We're both miserable, but God willing, we make this perfect little creature of our own to love and spoil forever in a house that is only happy because he or she came into it. Or I take a chance with this amazing woman who looks at me with hope and respect, someone who has already taken my heart, but…"

"I can't tell you what to do here, T, and you know it."

Taylor scoffed, "You sound like Millie."

"Wait, did you tell her all of that too? Did you tell her to decide?"

"No! Well, kind of. I don't know. Yes."

"Oh, Taylor, no." Hank shook his head, "You told her to choose for you and then called her a fling? I think her decision may have been made, brother."

"How did I screw this up so royally? Five years ago, I didn't have the perfect life, but I had a plan. That plan had potential. Now... now I don't know what I have."

"You still have it all, Taylor. You're just going to have to decide what you want and fight to get it. Let's start with this weekend. We'll drive east and get your head on straight. You'll come back and know what you have to do, but I'm going to throw this out there while you're calm enough to hear me. You and Carrie have been together for a long time, and you have loved her even longer. She deserves to know where your head is, especially considering everything she has been putting herself through to have a family. I'm not telling you where to follow your heart, but I'm telling you to step carefully when you start walking in whatever direction. Once you make that choice, there's no going back."

"I know," Taylor sighed. "Thanks, Hank."

Hank smacked his friend's shoulder out of solidarity. "You keep things interesting, that's for sure."

chapter seven

THE NEXT MORNING, Millie rolled over in bed and thanked God it was Saturday and she didn't have to get up. She was exhausted. She had cried to Cate in the car and again after walking into her apartment. Her home was usually a place of peace and comfort to her, but last night, it felt lonely and isolating.

Being a good friend, Cate called Rory after she had gotten out of the car and gave her the rundown of what had been happening. When Rory called Millie afterward, she was grateful she didn't have to retell the story. Rory sat on the phone for nearly two hours listening, consoling, and being the voice of reason Millie always depended on.

She put her hands over her eyes. They were sore and swollen from all the crying. She made a mental note not to look in a mirror for a few hours. No sense in making herself feel worse.

She stared at the ceiling and couldn't stop herself from wondering how Taylor's night had been. Was he sorry, really sorry, for the way he had spoken to her? Was she just a fling, and in the heat of the moment, the truth had slipped out? Did she make up the connection they had? Was she going straight to hell for wanting someone else's husband?

She wanted to think of herself as strong but knew her weakness for him would win. If Taylor walked in the front door right now and wanted to be with her, she knew she wouldn't hesitate to jump into his arms. That made prayers for forgiveness and guidance difficult.

"My life is a masterpiece and a mess," she muttered to herself.

How was she going to go to work on Monday and face this? She was grateful for the new job. It would more than keep her days busy, but there was no way she wouldn't run into Taylor. How could she act like it was a typical business day when she still held all this inside? Would he want to talk about all of this on Monday? Should she bring it up first to get some closure? Maybe she should start looking for another job. Hell, maybe she should start looking for another city.

"Enough!" Millie sat up in bed more frustrated than ever, but it was with herself this time. She was stronger than this! Since when did someone else hold all the power in her life? She picked up her phone with a new attitude. She started a group text to the girls.

I'm going to the beach,
will be back tomorrow.
I'm fine, promise. I just
need a break. Hoping
to see things clearly in
the saltwater.

She jumped out of bed with a mission. The beach was her favorite place on Earth and the one spot that never failed to bring her peace. A day on the sand, in the warm sun, listening to the waves with a margarita and a Nora Roberts book was all she needed to set herself right again.

She started throwing clothes and toiletries in her favorite overnight bag, just enough to make her comfortable on the beach and in the bed. She went to the kitchen to hunt for snacks and drinks to take so she could avoid having to go to restaurants for food.

When her bag was packed, she threw on a bathing suit and cover-up, brushed her teeth, and looked in the mirror. "Well, that's unfortunate." She had forgotten about her puffy eyes. Her face was still blotchy from the fire hydrant that seemed to blast from her eyes all night.

"Can only get better from here," she said to her reflection. And with that, she grabbed her bag, keys, and an apple for breakfast.

"Oh, don't want to scare the natives." She snatched her favorite sunglasses to cover the puff and locked the door behind her.

When she got to the car, there was a piece of paper stuck under the windshield wiper.

I just love you.
Call me if you need anything.
I'm only a car ride away.
Rory

That brought new, grateful tears. She always felt loved by all of the girls, but Rory just understood her. She didn't push, she didn't jump in to fix it, she just supported. She laughed out loud when she saw the bottom of the note.

PS – don't bother coming home without saltwater taffy.

She folded the note up and put it in her bag. "Fruitcake," she said with a smile. She had a new sense of freedom when she pulled out of the parking lot. With the windows down and the radio up, she sang at the top of her lungs for the next two hours.

The closer she got to the ocean, the more excitement she felt. It never failed. The ocean and all its breezes and scents lifted her spirits and brought out the optimist in her. She parked near the gazebo and got out of the car to take it in. The deep breath and the night's misery came and went. She was thankful for the respite, even if it was a temporary peace.

She walked up the ramp and smiled as the wind whipped little hairs free from her ponytail. She leaned on the railing to soak in an open view of the sparkling water. It looked like thousands of tiny diamonds were floating as far as the eye could see.

She felt peace wash over her, warming her from the inside out. She smiled at the water like she was reuniting with an old friend.

She lifted her sunglasses to her head to get the full effect. She hadn't realized how much she needed this, but was so thankful she had come. She lifted her face to the sun and felt completely at home.

Maybe she would leave Raleigh for a fresh start. Buy a little house on the water that would bring her this feeling every day. Millie laughed out loud. "Next paycheck", she mumbled to the sun. She hadn't even gotten that raise yet but was already living in a million-dollar house by the ocean – because, let's be honest, if you're wishing, wish big.

She stood there smiling at the sun, completely relaxed and loving her decision to come. She took a picture of the ocean and sent it to the girls.

That is how he found her. Taylor had split from Hank and Jimmy to take a walk and clear his head. Without even meaning to, he walked towards the pier where he had fished as a boy and had had countless conversations with his dad about life at the gazebo. He looked to it for answers and calm, and here it was, presenting this beautiful conflict on a golden platter.

Taylor watched Millie smile at the sky and felt her wonder at the ocean, wounded from the calm she held. What made her smile like that? He knew in that second that he wanted to be the reason someday. How could she be so happy when he was miserable and fighting an inner war of his own making?

He wanted to run up to her and wrap his arms around her until she had forgiven him for all of the hurt he had caused. He felt like he could tell her anything, and she would accept him just as he was. She helped him clear his head somehow with the questions she asked and the way she thought about things.

He ran his hands through his hair and acknowledged that he had failed her in that way. He hadn't allowed her to talk to him about… whatever was going on in her life. He rolled his eyes, willing to bet he was what she would need to talk about these days.

She looked so calm now, so peaceful. Something in him sank. He could only cause her pain right now. He had nothing to offer but empty promises and chaos until he got his life in order.

Good Lord, she was gorgeous.

He looked at her one more time, soaking in her raw beauty. She took his breath away at the office, but this was a whole new level of wanting. He loved her. He was sure of it, and one day soon, he would be the man she deserved and offer her a life to match.

Millie took one more deep breath and decided to check into a hotel after she hit the sand for a while. She turned around and stopped cold in her tracks. In the distance, she would swear she saw Taylor walking on the beach. She was so frustrated. Even strangers were starting to look like him to her now. She rubbed her eyes and put her sunglasses back on. "Like you're going to run into him here."

She walked to her car to get her things but turned back one more time. Why did she have to run into Taylor's doppelganger this weekend? She rolled her eyes. "Lock it up, Mil. You're losing it."

All cozy on the beach, she opened the book she brought and dove into the world of Nora Roberts. Where was a McKade brother when you needed one? She read for almost an hour before she thought to turn over. She had such a fair complexion that she really had to be mindful of the sun.

She rolled to her stomach, still immersed in the book. She caught the shadow of something in the corner of her eye, but by then, it was too late to react. A Frisbee came hurling at her and knocked her on the side of her head, just under her eyebrow. She grabbed her eye, trying to figure out what had hit her through the stars whirling around in her vision.

"Oh my God! Are you alright? I'm so sorry!" A man reached down to help her to her feet, but she wasn't quite ready to stand. He knelt and put his hand on her head.

"Oh shit, you're bleeding." He took his shirt off and twisted it into a ball. "Keep this on your head. I'll be right back."

Millie was in a daze, and the pounding behind her eye was getting worse. She reached for her bottle of water and saw the blood on her hand. "Oh, for God's sake." She firmed her grip on the shirt to stop the bleeding and did her best to open the water with one hand. Blood didn't bother her, but she had been in the sun for a while without much to drink.

"How you doin'? Let me see what we have here."

Where in the hell had the lifeguard come from? she thought.

"My name is Kevin. What's your name?"

"Millie."

"Do you know what day it is, Minnie?"

"My name is Millie. How old are you?"

"Sorry, Millie, I'm seventeen."

Millie rolled her eyes. "Is there no one of at least voting age at Baywatch HQ? No offense, Kevin, but I'll take some gauze and be on my way."

"Ma'am, I don't think you should stand just yet. The gash is still bleeding. And I don't have any gauze. I'm not a lifeguard, I'm visiting my grandma." He gave her a bashful smile. "At least wait for your boyfriend to get back. He's pulling the car up now."

"Who's pulling what car around? I don't have a boyfriend. I'm here for a freaking relaxing weekend!" Millie looked at the crowd that had formed around her and at poor Kevin's face. She had been too focused on the Frisbee hit to notice how green he was.

"I'm sorry, Kevin. Thanks for helping. Does blood make you queasy?"

Kevin looked at her pained, "Yes, ma'am."

"Do you feel like you're going to…" Right on cue, Kevin's lunch came up all over the beach beside him.

Millie closed her eyes and shook her head. "Wonderful." The crowd began to fan Kevin while she looked around for this "boyfriend" and his car. Nothing. Even her imaginary boyfriends couldn't be relied on.

She wanted to scream. Kevin sat up sheepishly while his grandmother handed him her water. "I think we better get him inside to cool off," Millie tried her best to be patient. "Is your house close?"

"You're not going anywhere with that cut gushing like that. I'll take you to the emergency room."

Millie looked up and couldn't believe her eyes. The author from the llama farm launch party was looking down at her with big puppy-dog eyes.

"It's the least I can do. After everything you've done for me, I just repaid you with an emergency room trip that's probably going to include stitches."

"*You* threw that Frisbee! What are the odds?"

She started to stand up and wobbled as he caught her. "You're very light on your feet, but I don't think now is the right time for a dance," he said.

Millie laughed out loud and winced at the new throbbing it produced. "Don't make me laugh until after the stitches are done and the meds have kicked in."

"I feel terrible, Millie. I'm so sorry. Can you stand, or do you need my arm?"

Millie wanted to be able to stand on her own two feet, but she was still a little light-headed.

"That hesitation says it all. Just hold on." He scooped her up and turned to Kevin. "I'll be back for you in a second. Just let me get her into the car."

"You don't have to carry me, mister. I'll walk." The crowd laughed and started helping the would-be-hero up.

"Glad to hear it. I'm acting tough now, but I'm not sure I'd make it to the car carrying you." He started to walk but turned back to Kevin. "Bring all her things, will you?" The crowd helped pack her small bag and waved them off, sending well wishes.

"So, just a 'freaking relaxing weekend on the beach', huh?"

Millie winced again, but this time it was from the quote, not the pain. "You heard that, did you?"

"Oh honey, the whole beach heard that. Besides the Frisbee of the past and the needle in the future, how's it going?"

"The present isn't too bad. I don't often get carried to my car. It's pretty nice, actually." She grinned at him. "Thank you for saving the day, Drew."

"You're most welcome. Thanks for helping launch my dream, Millie."

"You're most welcome."

Drew was not a big fan of hospitals, but knowing what was coming made it worse. They let him come to the room with Millie, but he was rethinking that brilliant decision as the nurse practitioner was laying out the tools they would use to sew her up.

Millie was talking to the staff like they were at a restaurant for lunch – no worries, no apprehension, just talking it up while holding the gauze in place. Where had his shirt gone, he wondered. It was one of his favorite t-shirts, but it would be covered in blood, and he wasn't sure he needed a reminder of what he had done to this poor girl.

As the nurse draped the blue cloth over Millie's face, he saw her first sign of nerves. Her hands were shaking just slightly. How had he not noticed? He reached over and held her hand in his. "I know you're fine, but she's about to start the buzz saw, and I don't want you to jump."

"Ha. Ha. Funny. When this is over, I will borrow that saw and show you just how funny you are."

"Quiet children," the nurse practitioner laughed. "Millie, I need you to be really still. I'm about to start. Can you feel this?" She poked Millie with the needle, once gently and again hard enough to send her a foot in the air without the numbing medicine.

"Nope, I'm good to go. Lace me up, doc." The woman made quick work of the cut, but Millie caught herself holding her breath several times.

"Breathe, Millie. It's almost over," Drew whispered. He lifted her hand and put it in his, rubbing her knuckles. She doubted he did it intentionally, but it was both calming and distracting, and she was grateful.

After the last stitch was in and the cloth was removed, Millie looked at Drew. "How bad is it? Bride of Frankenstein bad or clumsy in the kitchen bad?"

Drew laughed, "After the word 'Frisbee' fades away from your forehead in a few days, you could go with saving a puppy from a burning building and be the hero. But I'd say a little scar can't change beautiful."

"You two are too funny." The nurse practitioner gave him an all-knowing smile. "What he's not saying is that your wound is very swollen. It will get worse before it gets better. You'll need ibuprofen soon for the pain. No swimming in the pool or ocean for at least forty-eight hours. You need to keep those sutures dry. You can shower tomorrow, just keep the area as dry as possible. Just do it carefully. I'll want to see you back here next week to remove the stitches, but sooner if the area is red, more uncomfortable, or if you notice any drainage."

"Well, that's a problem. I live in Raleigh, and as much as I would love to be here for that long, I have a new job and have to go back."

"That's fine. You can go to your doctor at home then. But the same rules apply."

"Yes, ma'am." Millie gave a loose salute and managed to tap her new scar dead center.

"Careful now, don't mess with my work of art. Jenny will be in soon with your paperwork." She looked at Drew, "Remember that ibuprofen."

"Will do. I mean, I won't. I mean… thanks so much." Drew stood up to shake her hand.

"Be safe out there." She patted Millie's knee and walked out of the room, closing the door behind her.

"Well, I must say… this is not at all how I thought this day would go. I'm not usually the one telling stories about my adventurous weekend around the water cooler."

Drew looked down, wringing his hands. "Millie, I'm just so sorry. Whatever this costs, you have to promise to send me the bill. And whatever you need, you have to promise to let me know."

"Drew, please stop. It was an accident. Besides, how many people can say they had an award-winning author who was recently featured in Raleigh Magazine cut their head wide open and carry them to the hospital?"

"You saw that?" She smiled at the red that crept up his cheeks. "Can I tell you a secret? I got a call last week that someone is thinking about making a movie from the book. *My* book. It's crazy! That's why I came down for the weekend, to celebrate."

She hopped down from the exam table and hugged him like an old friend. "Drew! That's amazing! Oh my God! A movie!" She pulled away quickly. "I'm so sorry, that wasn't professional at all, was it?"

Drew laughed, "I think we left the professional part of our relationship in the pool of blood on the beach, Millie. Thanks for the enthusiasm. I'm pretty stoked about it, but the guys I'm with haven't offered a hug yet. You're the first."

"Where is your family? I know they must be over the moon."

"They don't know yet. It all happened so fast, and we are still in the early stages of the conversations. I don't want to tell everyone until it's all signed."

"But you told me?"

"Yes, I did." He smiled at her. "I think I can trust you."

She smiled at him in return. He wasn't just being nice. She could tell that he meant it, and after the way he held her hand through the procedure, she felt she could trust him right back.

The nurse came in with the paperwork she needed to check out. Drew gave the receptionist his credit card information to keep on file and insisted they charge him any balance. As they walked out, she pulled at his arm.

"You really didn't have to do that. It was an accident."

"An accident that I caused. Have I said sorry in the last few minutes?"

She lifted up on her tiptoes and kissed him on the cheek. "Thank you for today, Drew. You didn't have to stay, but I'm grateful you did."

"It was my pleasure. I wanted to make sure you made it out of there in one piece. Thanks for being so great about this whole thing."

"It's funny to me, actually."

"You have a twisted sense of humor, woman."

She laughed as they started walking towards the car. "Murphy's Law rules my life. If it can happen, it will happen to me. I choose to laugh." Millie shrugged, "It keeps things interesting, though."

"That's for sure. So where are you staying? Should I take you to your car or your hotel?"

It dawned on Millie in that second that the simple choice of hitting the beach before checking in had changed her weekend completely. "I'm actually not staying anywhere yet. This was a spur-of-the-moment trip. I was just going to find a hotel once I got here."

"Perfect. I have a house on the beach, just up from where you were attacked. You can stay there."

"Oh no, Drew. Thank you, but I'm fine getting a room somewhere."

"There are five bedrooms, Millie. You'll have plenty of space. You won't have to see me unless you want to, and there's a big breakfast in it for you in the morning."

"That sounds wonderful, Drew, but what about the friends you're with? I'm sure they don't want some random girl in the house for a guy's weekend."

"The guys live here. They have their own places to crash. I texted them an hour ago, telling them that I'd be playing nurse tonight."

That made her grin. "That's quite a visual."

"I won't wear the outfit, but I'm great at fetching. Please let me do this, Millie. I'll be worried about you all night anyway. You might as well be close so I don't have to keep calling you. I promise to stay in my half of the house and not to sing while I'm making breakfast. I make killer dry toast, by the way, but the singing may make you queasy."

Millie had to admit it was a good offer, and her head was already starting to hurt again. Maybe it would be smart to have someone close, just in case.

"Can we eat tonight, or do we have to wait for toast tomorrow?"

Drew smiled victoriously as he helped her into his car. "Let's get you home and settled and have something delivered. I've got some Advil with your name on it. I bet the meds are wearing off. Your eyes don't hide much, do they?"

Millie leaned back in the seat, "I've never been good at hiding my thoughts. I'm a work in progress."

"I think it's a good thing. Honesty is crucial to me."

That one statement sent her thoughts straight to Taylor. She knew he was a good man. She knew it to be true. She thought about the cheap fling comment, though, and her heartbeat hit the bruise he left.

She was so blinded by her desire for Taylor that she hadn't seen past his sweet talk. He wasn't interested in her, not all of her anyway. She closed her eyes and sighed. This Frisbee may have actually knocked some sense into her.

Drew's house wasn't too far from the urgent care, but by the time they got inside, her head was pounding. "Can I get that Advil, please?"

"I'll get it right now. You just sit and make yourself at home."

Before she had even gotten comfortable on the couch, he was back with the pills and some sweet tea. "I remember you drank a gallon of this at the launch."

She swallowed the pills and closed her eyes. "I had to go to the bathroom fifteen times that night, but everyone was toasting, so I needed a glass in hand. Thank you."

"Are you hungry? I can order some food now."

"Do you mind if I just sit for a second? I'm hurting. I'll be fine once the pills kick in."

"No problem, just relax. Put your feet up and cover up with this if you want."

He handed her a blanket made of old t-shirts. She sank into the couch and was asleep before she could ask him about it.

Millie rolled over and felt the ocean breeze on her face. She loved the beach so much. She opened her eyes slowly and took a second to get her surroundings into focus. She must have slept for hours because the sun was starting to set. She sat up slowly to measure the pain, but other than an ache, she was fine.

She loved watching the sunset over the water and wanted a closer look. She stood up slowly and walked to the open sliding glass door to find a breathtaking view of incredible colors mixing in every wave. She walked out onto the deck and leaned against the railing. There was nothing more beautiful than this to her. It's what miracles were made of.

"Incredible, isn't it?" Drew walked up beside her but kept his attention on the ocean. "It never fails to amaze me. It feels like God hangs a masterpiece just for me every time I'm here."

She was hypnotized by it, just as Drew seemed to be. They stood there in silence as the fire reds turned to deep pinks and purples. When the automatic porch light came on, it broke her trance. "Thank you for this. It was the perfect end to this day."

"Day's not over yet, lady. I haven't fed you yet." He turned his head to the side and made no secret of his assessment of her. "Are you up for eating, though? How do you feel?"

"I'm starving. I never ate lunch. It's still in my car. Oh God, my car. I need to move it and get my bag."

"Already done. I moved it while you were sleeping. I brought the bag in and put it in your room. The cooler was still full of ice, so all the food was still good. I put it in the fridge."

She stood there, blinking at him. "What else did you do while I was snoring, Cinderella?"

He laughed, "I told you I was good at fetching, and you only snore when you're on your back. I had a neighbor turn his hearing aids off and help me put a pillow behind you to keep you on your side. After that, it was quiet around here again." He winked at her, "Just trying to keep myself busy. I ordered dinner, it's in the oven, staying warm, but it's ready whenever you are. Let's eat out here, though. It's such a great night. That OK with you?"

She had never been catered to like this before. "Yes, it's a perfect night, but please let me help you. You've done so much already."

They went inside and found the only light was the moon. "I've been writing outside so I wouldn't bother you. Would you mind turning those lamps on while I get the food out?"

Millie walked around the living room, turning on lamps and looking at the house for the first time. Although there was a modern twist, the style was traditional at heart. Blues and greens were everywhere, set off by the white walls and furniture.

It looked like something from Southern Living magazine. It was absolutely beautiful but a comfortable place someone could live in. The pillows on the couch were the perfect color of blue but had clearly hosted several naps over the years. The art on the walls was beautiful but not pretentious and beachy without being over the top. The enormous table in the dining room was an antique and looked like it had seen generations of family dinners, but surrounded by modern tufted chairs, it made the whole room cozy and elegant.

She walked by a side table covered in framed pictures and couldn't help but laugh at the choices. There were no posed pictures, only funny family candids that gave her instant access to their connections and personalities.

The sheer number of frames piqued her curiosity, and she started counting faces. Drew came around the corner at number seventeen.

"Fairly motley crew, isn't it? No matter where I go, I can't shake them." He was joking, of course. She could see the love and pride in his eyes as he looked them over.

"Is this seriously all of your family?"

"Yep. Well, mostly. This is Aunt Lily, who by all southern standards is family, just not by blood."

"How many brothers and sisters do you have? I should know this, I guess, from the launch. I recognize most of the people from the party." She looked at him in awe, "They were all there that night, weren't they?"

"Of course. I know you had security there, but I would have loved to have seen them tell any one of these people they couldn't come into that party. Blood. Lots of blood."

"I just didn't realize they were *all* your family. Wow."

"Yeah, it's usually hard for people with small families to understand that many people in your business."

"Oh, I don't have a small family. It may not be twenty frames big, but we can fill a room."

Now, it was his turn to smile at her pride. "Let's get the plates and sit while we compare our craziest stories of big family chaos."

"Do you mind if I run to the bathroom first?"

"Oh sure, it's right through that door. I'll meet you out there. Take your time."

"I'll just be a sec."

Millie flipped the light switch on in the bathroom and fell in love with the marble heaven immediately. The room was white and bright with sparkling glass and Carrara marble. The windows were bare, allowing the moon over the ocean to be the perfect backdrop. It was serene, luxurious, and absolutely enormous.

She couldn't help herself and walked into the open shower. Her entire bathroom could fit into this shower. She touched the marbled walls delicately and began dreaming of a day when something like this was hers. Stepping out of the shower, she ran a hand over the edge of the claw-foot bathtub and sighed. It had been years since she had taken a bath. Her apartment only had a small shower. How rude would it be if she made herself at home in here for the rest of the night?

Millie walked to the sink to wash her hands, still under the marble's magical spell, when she caught her image in the mirror. Oh, the horror! How long had she looked like this? Her hair was everywhere. Everywhere! The rubber band she thought was an ally had given up on the idea of a messy bun and allowed flyaways to fall in every direction, including up.

She didn't have any makeup on, which always made her look "tired" to people, so she pinched her cheeks and hoped some color would stay put. Without a brush to tame the beast, she did her best to get a ponytail in place, which gave her a clear view of her bandaged eyebrow. She hadn't seen it before now and was struck at how swollen she was. The bruising had already started spreading around her eye. "You came to the beach for some color. You got it." She muttered.

Completely deflated, she tapped the light switch and headed outside. She was about to offer her sincere apologies and request a road map to her bedroom for the night when she stepped through the open sliding doors to find a table full of food and a small bouquet of flowers in the center.

"Hey there. I didn't know what you liked, so I just ordered a little bit of everything. I see now that I may have gone a little overboard, but most of this will reheat for lunch, so I consider it an investment."

Millie just stood there, looking at the table and this man who was jumping through hoops to make her comfortable in his home. It should be awkward, she thought. This whole day should have been laced with uncomfortable pauses in conversation, especially considering their time in the emergency room, but it had been … nice. She was comfortable with him.

"Millie, you don't have to eat if you don't want to. I can pack it all up, and we can call it a night."

That snapped her back into the moment. "Drew, I don't know how to thank you. You didn't have to do all of this. I'm starting to feel guilty for taking all of this hospitality."

He pushed his chair back and walked to her, closer than he had been all day. "A guy's gotta eat. I'm grateful you're here to eat with me. I'm sorry it took stitches to get you here, though. Maybe next time, I'll just call you."

She laughed out loud, which swept the black cloud of self-pity away. "You're very debonair when you want to be, you know. I'm starting to see what the magazine was talking about."

"Nah, I'm too simple for debonair. Come sit. You need to eat a little before you waste away, and I have to explain to that doctor why I'm carrying you back into the urgent care."

He pulled the chair back for her and waited until she was settled before he started shooting off the menu options. Three restaurants were represented at the table, with at least three or four items from each place. Millie was in heaven.

"You can't know this about me," she said as he filled their plates with the first wave of dinner, "but I have the eating habits of a frat boy. There is no rhyme or reason for what I eat. I mix and match things that no sane person would ever put together."

"So, this table is…"

"My heaven."

"Good! I was worried you would ask me for a side salad with light dressing and no croutons."

"I'll take it if you have it, but pass the croutons. They are the best part of a salad. What is that?"

"That would be chicken quesadillas. Over there is chicken Marsala. We have hamburgers. This is shrimp scampi. These enchiladas are awesome."

"Other than Chinese, you just named most of my favorite foods. Well done, sir."

"Ugh! I was going to order Chinese! Next time." She laughed, "This is perfect! Which of these are your favorites?"

"Depends on the mood, but they're all on the shortlist."

"Why wasn't any of this at the launch? We should have had your shortlist that night."

"Everyone seemed to have the whole thing planned out before I got there. With everything I had going on before the party, it was just easier to go along with it. It was all good stuff, so no complaints here."

Millie put her fork down to let that sink in. She was the new event director, but she never wanted anyone to feel bulldozed by her decisions, especially at their own party.

"I'm so sorry you felt that way, Drew. That was never our intention, but that doesn't make it okay. I'll do better in the future. Your next launch will have all your favorites."

Drew rolled his eyes with a moan and a mouth full, "I don't know when that will be. I'm completely blocked, but thank you. And what do you mean you'll do better? That party was amazing, Millie—all of it. I couldn't have asked for more. I should have thanked you before now for it."

"You thanked me plenty, and you're welcome, but if there are better ways to personalize a launch, we should do it. I have a lot of organizing to do, but we'll get there."

"You mentioned a new job in the sewing room. Are you leaving Grant?"

Millie's eyebrow hiked up in confusion. "The sewing room?"

Drew smiled mischievously, "Your room in the ER where they stitched you up."

Millie laughed into her tea and nearly spilled it everywhere. "You're twisted."

"Woman, you have no idea. So, new job?"

"That's actually why I'm here, at the beach, I mean. I got a big promotion yesterday. I'm the new Director of Events, I start Monday. Well, I'll be honest, I don't know when I stop with the old and start with the new, but I'm already thinking of ways to improve our events. Personalization is at the top of the list now."

"That's incredible, Millie! Congratulations! Wow! Cheers to you!" He held up his Styrofoam cup and waited for her cup to tap it. "To all the potential they saw and all the pizazz they have yet to see. Congratulations."

He pulled his cup away to take a sip. "Wait!" Millie held her cup up and waited for his tap. "To a man with all the right words. May the movie translate all of those beautiful words into equally powerful images. Congratulations."

They smiled at each other for a minute, both appreciating the next step they were taking professionally and that they had someone to celebrate with. Drew dove back into the enchiladas, "You know, I think it's interesting that all of this happened."

"You mean the movie?"

"I'm still blown away that the movie is even a thought, but I mean all of this." He pointed to the two of them, "I mean today. I saw you on the beach long before I decided to play pin the Frisbee on your face. I just didn't know it was *you*. The guys were giving me tips on how to pick you up."

Millie put her folk down on the plate. "And their best tip was a frontal assault, huh? I'd say you need new wingmen."

Drew laughed into his last bite of enchiladas. "Fair. Jeez, I could eat a thousand of those. Have you tried them? No pressure, but in about ten minutes, I'll probably go in for round three on that last one."

"It's all yours. I'm trying to be a lady and not shovel this whole quesadilla in my mouth. This is the best quesadilla I've ever had. It's all good, but this is awesome."

"It's my favorite restaurant around here. I know the owner and go in a lot. I can attest to every item on the menu being awesome. Literally."

"Did the awesome food and constant ordering introduce you to the owner, or did the owner introduce you to the awesome food and Mexican addiction?"

"The owner married a cousin of mine. He's in one of the frames on the table inside. He makes everything from scratch like his family did when he was young. His grandmother came to visit a few years ago and inspected everything he was doing in the kitchen. Then she blessed it so every meal made in there would be muy delicioso."

"Well, God bless grandma." Millie hesitated a bit. She wasn't sure she wanted to know the answer to the question jumping around in her head. "Can we go back a little to the wingmen?" She pushed the last bites of pico de gallo around on her plate. "You should be celebrating with them tonight."

Drew cocked his head to the side and put his hand over his heart like he was in pain. "Are you tired of me already? This usually doesn't happen until the second or third date."

She chuckled, "I wish this were a date. It would be the easiest first date ever."

In his best slow southern drawl, he sat up straight in his chair and said, "What do you mean 'easy'? I am a gentleman, madam."

This time, he got a belly laugh out of her. She smacked his leg playfully, "Not *easy* like that, Drew, good Lord!"

He laughed as he leaned back in his chair and put a hand on his full belly. "And why can't this be the easiest and best first date ever? We'll tell our grandchildren one day how Pappy had to knock Memaw out before she agreed to go out with him, and she hasn't stopped complaining of a headache since."

She smiled at him as he talked about their lives together as grandparents, all the sugar they would feed their grandbabies when their parents weren't watching, and the spoiling they would save for the little monsters. By the end of the story, she was as wrapped up in it as he was.

"The children will complain that we never let them do what we let their children do."

"So what!" He exclaimed. "We'll babysit for free every weekend so they can have their own *easy* dates. They can't complain too much."

For the first time that day, an awkward silence washed over them. Millie looked out over the water and wondered if she had ever been with a man she felt this comfortable with this quickly.

"Can I ask you a question, Millie?"

His question broke her train of thought, but she wasn't ready to look at him yet. She needed a minute to get her thoughts together. "God, it's beautiful here. How do you leave on Sundays? I love Raleigh, but I'm not sure I could leave if I had this to come home to."

"This is my family's home, not mine, but I agree. It's hard to leave." He put his elbows on the table and leaned a little closer to her. "Millie, I won't ask you to share anything you don't want to. I haven't been in the game very long and have never been good at playing it. I was just wondering why you weren't here celebrating your promotion with anyone."

Millie took a deep breath but kept her gaze on the moon. "Because I fought with the only person who knows about the new job." She hadn't meant to be so honest, but fate had presented her with a new trusted friend, and she didn't have the heart to lie to him. Just the idea of Taylor brought back all the angst and aggravation from yesterday's argument and made her tired.

"Drew, it's probably time for me to go to bed. It's been a long day."

"Please don't leave." He put his hand on hers before she could stand up. "I didn't mean to pry, truly. I won't push. It's just that even with the guilt of having caused that cut, this has been one of the best days I've had in a while. I…" He rubbed his thumb over her hand like he had in the doctor's office. "I like you, Millie. I've liked you since we met in the conference room at Grant."

He pulled his hand away and rubbed it on his thigh nervously. "I'm sorry. I just said I wouldn't push. I wasn't kidding when I said I wasn't good at the game." He scoffed at himself, "That implies I know how to play at all. I'm sorry, I'll let you go to bed. Don't worry about the food. I'll pack it up."

He stood up quickly and reached for a to-go box, knocking over her tea and spilling it all over the food. "Aw, hell! Could I be any worse at this?"

This was her fault. She had ruined what had been a pretty perfect dinner, all things considered, all because of … nothing. A fling, as Taylor had called it. She looked up at Drew, who was leaning over the table and trying to catch the spill with napkins. He had been nothing short of wonderful all day. Even now, as frustrated as he was, she knew she could trust him to be kind.

She stood up next to Drew and put her hand on his. "Stop."

"I'm sorry. I'll show you your room and then finish up down here."

"Stop."

"No burgers for breakfast now. I'll go out in the morning and pick something up.

"Drew."

He looked down at her pale, delicate hand on his. She was beautiful. He was average. She was young and energetic. He was shy and a homebody. She obviously had someone in Raleigh waiting for her, and he had to respect that.

When he looked into her eyes to say all of that out loud, the arrow struck him. He had never believed in love at first sight before, and although he had been drawn to her from their first meeting many months ago, he knew at that moment that Cupid had worked his magic. He was a goner.

The way he looked at her made her uncomfortable. Not because it scared her but because she knew he was looking into the future. She could see herself in his eyes and didn't think she could measure up to the pedestal he had put her on.

The breeze blew between them, but they didn't move. The tea was still dripping off the table, but they ignored it. Her hair blew across her face, but she kept her eyes on his. Drew used a finger to tuck the strands behind her ear, and as gently as he could, he rubbed the back of his fingers across her cheek.

He had to clear his throat to speak because, in just one touch, his mouth had gone completely dry. "Your skin is like velvet."

Millie didn't know what to say. She was confused but felt safe with him. She wasn't electrified like she had been around Taylor. There was a different kind of pull inside for Drew. Was different good? Was she attracted to him? How could she be head over heels for someone one day and interested in someone else the next? It just didn't work this way. Or did it? She didn't have much experience in the game department either. She needed to clear her head.

"It's such a perfect night. Want to take a walk? I'll help you clean up when we get back."

Drew didn't want to move away from her but was grateful for the extra time the walk would give them. His heart had been broken not that long ago, and he knew he needed to wrap his head around his feelings before he shared any of them with Millie.

"You're not too tired?"

She shook her head. "No, I'm sorry about that. I'd love a walk."

"Give me one second." He backed up slowly and walked into the house. A minute later, he walked out with a jacket. "The wind kicks up on the beach. You may want to put this on."

He held it open, and she turned around to slip her arms through. "Thank you." She pulled the open jacket across her and sighed into the collar.

"You OK?"

She nodded this time. "It smells like you."

"Hopefully, I wore deodorant the last time I wore it."

She wrinkled her nose. "Unfortunately, not." She laughed out loud when his face dropped. "It smells great, Drew. Thank you."

"You're welcome... punk." He flashed a smile and led the way down to the sand.

They walked in silence for a few minutes, both looking out over the ocean and enjoying the air. Millie cuddled into the jacket. Drew was right. The breeze was a lot cooler on the beach. She zipped it up and pulled her hands into the long sleeves.

"Are you too cold without a jacket? We can go back."

"Nah, I'm a manly man. Always hot." Drew looked over at her. "We'll just walk a ways, then turn around." He zipped her jacket up to the top. "Snuggle up."

"You are something, you know that."

He started walking again, but not before he looped her arm through his. "I'm really not. I'm sorry for overreacting back there. It's frustrating to have endless novels in my head but not be able to throw a sentence together in real life. I'm much better on paper than in reality."

"Drew, that scene was my fault. And I disagree. I think you are incredibly charismatic on paper and in person. I'm sorry you don't see it."

"I definitely don't see it, but thank you."

They walked in silence again, but the ocean was no longer their focus. They were both more interested in what was happening between them. Neither knew what to say or think about it, which made the silence awkward instead of peaceful now. They spoke up at the same time and smiled at their effort to keep the walk casual and comfortable.

"You first." Drew smiled.

"No, mine wasn't very original. You go ahead."

"Ok, tell me more about the new job. I know your title, but what does that encompass? Every event at Grant? Soup to nuts? Or just the launch parties?"

"Every event.... I think. I was in a bit of a daze when she was offering it to me. I actually thought I was getting fired."

Drew laughed, "Why on Earth would Samantha fire you after everything you did for me and all the other authors?"

"Samantha didn't offer me the job. I got pulled down to HR with a mysteriously ominous email. I was so shocked by the offer that the details kind of flew over my head. I walked out not knowing when I technically start, how much I'm making, or any of the key elements a sane person would listen for."

"Well, what does the former director focus his or her time on? You can get some of the details from them."

"There is no former director. They created the position for me."

Drew stopped walking and stared at Millie in awe. "Grant Publishing, a Fortune 500 company known for advancing authors' careers to an international level, has created a position for you out of thin air? Are you kidding me? Millie! That's amazing!"

He threw his arms around her and spun her around until she was dizzy and laughing hysterically. His reaction to her promotion was what she needed to finally get excited about it the way she should have been yesterday. It *was* amazing. She *should* be excited.

When he put her down, they held on to each other for a second for stability and were still smiling like goons. Drew saw happiness beaming in her eyes, and it made her all the more breathtaking and irresistible. He put his hand behind her neck and pulled her close.

"I have wanted to make you smile like that since the second I met you."

The whispered sweetness of his comment took her breath away. She looked into his eyes and saw sincerity and kindness, but she also saw passion. It was the first time Millie had looked at him as a man – a handsome, potentially lovable man. She had never in her life been this confused, but she knew Drew would offer her the kind of relationship Taylor would never be able to.

"Drew, I…"

"I won't kiss you, Millie. I can see there is something or someone holding you back right now." He put his forehead to hers, "I want to, but I won't."

She felt a wave of disappointment that confused her even more. What was holding her back from moving on with someone as wonderful as Drew? Taylor made it extremely clear that he didn't want to be with her, not in a real relationship, anyway. Anything she had hoped for with Taylor wasn't an option. Was she willing to ruin her chance at happiness because she wasn't done moping over someone who didn't want her?

"There was someone, but he recently made it clear that he wants someone else. I'm playing catch-up to that. I can't say that I don't want you to kiss me right now, but I want to be fair to you. I don't know that I'm ready to start something yet."

Millie wasn't a fan of talking about her feelings, but she always tried to be honest with people. This level of raw, honest vulnerability was new to her. "Can you be patient with me?"

Without raising his head away from hers, Drew sighed. "Millie, you captivated me from the moment we met." He pulled back to look her in the eyes. "Take your time. I'll be here when you're ready."

He traced her cheek again, but this time, she felt his tenderness and knew she wanted to know more about him. There was no awkwardness now, only hope.

"Can I be honest with you?"

"Always be honest with me, Millie. Please."

She sensed that please was more than him being polite. He had been hurt as well.

"I promise." And she did. In her heart of hearts, she vowed to always give him that respect, no matter what happened between them. "Until now, I've never looked at you this way. You were the client that I needed to make happy. Now, I'm looking at the man. I need a minute to adjust my thinking."

She stood up on her toes, put her arms around his neck, and gave him a hug. "I'm sorry for ruining a perfect moment."

He wrapped his arms tightly around her and rocked back and forth. "You made the moment perfect, Millie. There's no way you could ruin it."

She sank into the hug even more with that. "You really do have all the right words, don't you?"

She felt his smile on her neck, "I think you're being easy on me."

They stood there for what seemed like minutes, just holding one another, and the longer they did, the more attracted she was to him. She couldn't say there was lust, but there was definitely a growing curiosity about what a kiss from him would be like.

Drew squeezed a little tighter and breathed her in. God, she smelled great. He decided he didn't care how warm it was tomorrow. He was going to wear that jacket. She leaned into the hug just a little more and stirred something inside him that he knew she wasn't ready for.

"Millie, I love holding you, but even I'm getting cold. Do you mind if we head back?" She pulled away slowly with apologies and a sweet smile.

They started walking back towards the house slowly. He had been given the privilege of holding her and now couldn't stand the thought of not touching her, even in the smallest of ways. "May I hold your hand?"

She rested her head on his shoulder, their fingers intertwined. They walked back to the house as slowly as they could, in the comfort of silence and understanding.

chapter eight

MILLIE WOKE UP the next morning with a splitting headache. She knew if she opened her eyes, her head would explode. She moaned into her pillow and wished to God she had a go-go-gadget arm to reach into her purse for any pill she could find. She forgot to take any ibuprofen before she fell asleep and was paying the price now.

The memory of last night flashed in her mind and made her grin. If she weren't hurting so badly, she would jump out of bed to see if Drew was up yet. They talked for hours about nothing and everything in front of the fireplace. He told her about his family and all the personalities that helped him write his first book. She told him about growing up in the Army and all the places she lived. She felt like she knew him better than some of her friends at this point.

Her friends! She hadn't checked her phone all day yesterday. They were probably worried sick. She had cried to them all night and then left town, never to be heard from again. She knew she would get yelled at for breaking their cardinal rule – no unnecessary drama. A disappearing act after a crying binge would definitely go against that rule, not to mention coming home with a swollen, scarred face.

She moaned again at the thought of getting up but knew she needed to take something if she was going to function as a human being. She sat up just as Drew knocked on the door and peeked in.

"I heard you moaning in here and didn't think it was a good sign." He walked in carrying a cup of coffee and a bottle of Advil. "I didn't know how you like your coffee, so I put a little sugar and creamer in it."

He handed her the coffee mug so he could open the pill bottle. Millie sipped the coffee and waited for the caffeine to work its magic. "Thank you, Drew." She swallowed the pills and prayed for relief. "I forgot to take anything last night. Stupid."

"It's my fault. I had doctor's orders to remind you. Can I get you anything? Some ice?"

"Ice would be great, actually. I'll meet you downstairs in a second."

"I'll be in the kitchen when you're ready. Take your time."

Drew shut the door behind him to give her some privacy. He had looked at her for hours last night, but in the light of the fire, he hadn't seen how badly she was bruised. Guilt and worry filled him. He stood in the hallway for a minute debating on whether to call the doctor's office or not when he heard her yell, "Oh my God!"

He opened the bedroom door, afraid she had fallen, but found her in the bathroom, looking at her reflection. "Good God, Drew, was it this swollen last night? I look like Quasimodo!" She touched her eyebrow gently to see if it was hot and looked for any signs of infection like the doctor had warned her of.

"No, honey, it wasn't. Do you want me to call the doctor's office and make an appointment? Or just ask them if this is normal?"

She stopped for a second to turn to him. "Honey, huh?" She watched Drew's face turn from a very normal tan to a very embarrassed fire engine red. She wanted to keep a straight face but just couldn't hold back the laughter, which caused a lightning bolt of pain to shoot through her head.

"When you feel better, I'm going to tell you that's what you get. For now, I'll get you that ice while you get back into bed."

He started to guide her out of the bathroom, but she put her head on his chest. "Can I just stand here for a second? I'm sorry to be such a baby about this, but it's really pounding."

He leaned against the counter and put his arms around her to pull her a little closer. "Just try to relax. The medicine will kick in soon."

He rubbed her back in long, slow strokes that sent goosebumps all over her body. She felt safe again. She was surprised at how much that eased her. She lifted her arms to wrap around his waist.

"Good morning, by the way."

"Good morning, Millie." He kissed the top of her head.

"Did I mention last night that I'll do just about anything for someone who rubs my back?"

"Hmm. I'll have to remember that. What does ten minutes get me?"

"I may make you breakfast."

"Yum. And fifteen?"

"With coffee."

"I already made coffee."

"Chocolate milk, then. With a crazy straw."

Drew chuckled, "I do love a good crazy straw. How do I get dinner?"

"That will take more massage than rub and at least twenty minutes."

"I see. Did I mention last night that I give the best massages on the planet? I don't want to brag, but people come from far and wide to feel these weapons on their shoulders."

"Are you telling me that I spent all night talking to the master of massages and didn't get one knot out?"

He was glad to hear some energy back in her voice. "It's a Clark Kent situation. I can't tell just anyone that I'm Superman."

She giggled into his chest before raising her head to look at him. "Well, Clark, you can holster those weapons for now, but I'm going to need proof of Superman sometime."

"Name the date, and I'm yours." He tucked her hair behind her ear to get a better look at her. "I can't believe I did this to you. Millie, I am so sorry. If you don't mind, I'd like to call the doctor to make sure this kind of swelling is normal."

"I thought the same thing, but we don't need to call the doctor. I'll call my mom, she's a doctor. Might as well give her a head's up that her daughter looks like she's been in a bar fight. By the way, thanks so much for not arguing with me earlier when I said I looked like Quasimodo," she said sarcastically. "You could have thrown me a bone and said, 'Oh no, you don't look *that* bad'."

"Oh no, you don't look *that* bad." He drew out every word to make it sound as insincere as possible. "How was that?"

"Too late, Clark. Chime in sooner next time." She patted him on the shoulder and stepped away from him. "Do you mind if we get that ice now?"

Drew set her up on the couch with her coffee and phone all within reach and the ice pack on her head. He lifted her feet and sat where they had been, putting them in his lap. "What else do you need? Are you hungry?"

"I probably do need to get something in my stomach after taking those pills." She moaned a little too loudly when he started rubbing her feet. "Good Lord, Superman. That feels good." She closed her eyes to enjoy the spoiling. "I don't want to make you cook, though. I can just have a piece of bread. No need to go crazy and make your famous toast."

"You are seriously underestimating my toast-making capabilities. How about pancakes with strawberries?"

She opened her good eye to glare at him. "Your specialty is toast but you're going to whip up pancakes with strawberries?"

"Don't be crazy, woman. I'm going to run and pick it up. There is a great place just up the beach that serves breakfast all day. Want anything else?"

"You've spent a fortune feeding me this weekend. Please let me order it."

"I'll make you a deal. Let me spoil you this weekend, and you can fatten me up next weekend." He said it to be funny, but he held his breath, waiting for her answer.

"No deal."

His heart sank.

She lifted her head and opened her eyes. "I'd rather have dinner tonight if you're up for it?"

His head shot up, "Tonight?"

"I don't think it would be a good idea to go into the office like this tomorrow, and looking at a computer screen is bound to make my head hurt worse. You mentioned staying one more night last night, so I was thinking we could have dinner before I leave for Raleigh."

"Why would you go to Raleigh if you're not going to work tomorrow? Stay with me here."

She felt herself getting shy, her cheeks flushing. "I don't want to impose. You've already let me stay one night. Besides, I don't have any clean clothes."

"You can borrow something of mine while we wash what you've got." He put her hand in his and watched how easily their hands fit together. "Please stay."

"Are you sure? Don't you have anything you need to do? I've taken up your whole weekend."

"Please stay." He whispered the words, making the request so sweetly intimate. She nodded in response. She liked being here. She liked being with him. As she looked into his eyes, she knew she liked being the person who made his eyes light up like this.

"I want you to call your Mom while I'm gone. Make sure there isn't something we should be doing to help the swelling."

"Will do."

"Is there anything you want me to grab while I'm out? Favorite drink?"

"You have sweet tea and coffee. That's all I need to be happy in life."

He leaned over to pick up her phone from the coffee table. "I'm calling my number. Now you have it if you think of something you need while I'm gone."

She heard his phone ring in the kitchen to the tune of "Free Fallin" by Tom Petty and the Heartbreakers. "Nice," she laughed.

"Call me if you think of anything." He squeezed her foot one more time and put her feet back on the couch. "I'll be about thirty minutes."

He reached the foyer before she called out, "Thanks, honey." He popped his head around the corner to give her a wink before he left.

Millie sat there for a minute in the silence. So much had happened in the last twenty-four hours. It was hard to believe that around this time yesterday, she was on her way to the beach for a relaxing weekend. Little did she know her whole life would hit a plot twist.

What was happening between the two of them was real. She could feel it in her bones. Last night's marathon talk gave her an insight into a person with integrity, drive, and a love for life. He impressed her unintentionally while talking about his "crazy" family. It was endearing how much he loved and cherished them. She knew if she got to know them, she would like them immediately.

She took a deep breath and picked up her phone. She sent a short text to the girls so they knew she was alright. The news of the Frisbee attack would wait until later, though. Her headache was easing, but it still hurt enough that she needed to call her mom. The phone rang a few times before she heard the familiar voice on the other end: "Hey, honey, I was just thinking about you."

Honey. It made her think of Drew now.

"Hey Mama, what are you doing?"

"I'm at the computer working. You wouldn't believe how behind I am. You're worthy of a break, though. What are you doing?"

"I'm actually at the beach. I drove up yesterday for a relaxing day on the sand."

"Well, good honey, I'm glad you got away. You work too hard. Are you on your way home now?"

"No, I'm going to stay another night and call in sick tomorrow."

"Playing hooky, huh? Is everything alright at work?"

"Everything's fine. But I do have a medical question for you."

"Shoot."

Millie told her Mom all about the Frisbee hit, the stitches, the swelling, and Drew's help. It was better to be blunt and get the real scoop on what to do than sugarcoat it. After a full interrogation and the threat of driving to the beach to get her, she told Millie what to do and what to look out for.

"Are you sure you don't want me to come get you, Mil? I can be there in a couple of hours."

"How would I get my car home? I'm fine, Mom, I promise. I am minutes away from the doctor's office. I have someone here to watch me and an amazing view that makes me happy. I'm good here, but I promise to come see you tomorrow when I get home so you can check me out."

"You better, young lady. You worry the crap out of me, you know that?"

"It's my job."

"Tell me about this friend of yours. Have I met him?"

"No, he's one of our authors. Remember the big llama farm launch party?"

"Of course. I bought that book because of all the fuss you were making over that launch. He's a great writer. I loved the book. Is he really taking care of you? Watching the swelling?"

"He's hovering as much as you would."

"And you'll call me if you need anything?"

"I promise."

"Give him a hug for me and thank him for taking care of my baby."

"I will not."

"Well, tell him I owe him dinner for letting you stay there."

"Better. I need to get some ice on this head. The ice is melting, and I think my bag has a leak. I'll call you if I need anything." She knew her Mom had just said it, but she also knew she was still worried. *That's what good moms do*, as Mom always said.

"I love you, honey."

"I love you too. Bye."

She got up, grateful that the pain was slipping away quickly now. She walked to the kitchen for ice. "If I were a Ziploc bag, where would I be?" She looked through a few drawers and opened a few cabinets but couldn't find anything. "Alright, if I were a cup, where would I be?"

"Cabinet to the left."

Millie screamed and turned with a jolt to see a man standing in the doorway of the kitchen. "You scared me to death!"

"That will happen when you're sneaking around kitchens stealing drinkware. Should I call the cops?"

"I'm a friend of Drew's. We got here yesterday."

Millie took her first full breath since screaming. *He's not a psychopath. He's just the brother. You met him at the launch*, she thought. "My name is Millie. Drew ran out to get breakfast but should be back in a bit."

"Good, so I don't have to call the police and tell them a girl half my size scared the piss out of me." He ran his hands over his face and gave her a timid smile. "I'm sorry for scaring you. Can we call it even?"

She smiled nervously at him, "Sure."

"Can I help you find something in here?"

"I was looking for a Ziploc bag for ice, but a cup would do."

"No problem, it's harder to drink out of a plastic baggie, though." He walked past her to a drawer with sandwich bags, foil, and plastic wrap. He picked one out of the box to hand it to her and saw her eye completely for the first time. "Oh my God, are you OK? What in the hell happened? Do you need a doctor? No, you've already been to a doctor from the looks of that bandage. Sorry, you just caught me off guard. Your hair was covering it when I walked in."

"So I guess it still looks as bad as it feels."

"Hell, yes, it must. Let me get that ice for you." He filled the bag with crushed ice and wrapped the bag in a towel. "Do you want to sit somewhere? Or lay down, maybe?"

"I was on the couch before, but we can sit here if you want." She took the towel and put it to her head. "Thank you."

"My pleasure. I'm Drew's handsome younger brother Carson. Nice to meet you." He stuck his hand out to shake hers but saw it was busy holding the ice. "Let's get you back on the couch. Drew will kill me if he thinks I gave you a hard time."

"Scared of him, are you?"

"What! No way! But he never brings girls here, so I imagine we all better be on our best behavior."

She laughed a little at his defensiveness, but as she sat on the couch, his words sunk in. "We *all?*"

"The family. Everyone is meeting here today for linner."

"Linner?"

"It's a stupid word we created. It's a blend of lunch and dinner because we eat a little too late for lunch but a little too early for dinner. Linner."

"I see. And everyone is coming here? Drew didn't mention it."

"I'm sure he forgot. It looks like he's been distracted. Were you in a car accident?"

"No, nothing that dramatic. I was..."

"Honey, I'm home." Drew walked into the house and brought the fun energy back into it. She was embarrassed to admit that she had missed him. "I hope you're hungry. I may have gone overboard again."

"Thanks, lamb chop. I'm starving." Carson put on a megawatt smile as Drew came around the corner slowly.

"What are you doing here? I thought you were in Pinehurst."

"Change of plans. And aren't I lucky for it? Otherwise, I never would have met the magnificent Millie here."

Drew looked at Millie apologetically, "He didn't try to put the moves on you, did he? I'll give him an eye to match yours."

Millie giggled at him but laughed out loud when she saw Carson's pleading eyes. She could see the brotherly love but also the threat of wedgies and noogies of their past in his expression. "No, we scared each other pretty good. But there were no good moves."

"No *good* moves?" Drew put the bags of food down on the coffee table. "Come here, little brother, we're going to talk."

Carson leaped over the back of his chair before Drew could get anywhere near him. "Drew, stop it! I did not make a move on that woman! Millie, tell him!"

They played cat and mouse while Millie laughed hysterically. "You're just mean, woman! You two belong together! Just wait until the family gets here! Then I'll have reinforcements."

Drew stopped in his tracks. "The family?" Realization hit, "Shit. Linner."

Carson nodded his head slowly, a Cheshire cat grin on his face. "They're all coming, brother. Get ready."

Drew looked at Millie. "Are you up for this? I am so sorry. It never even crossed my mind after yesterday. We can leave right now and have you back in Raleigh to rest."

"What in the hell happened yesterday?" Carson cautiously sat back down on the chair. "I was just about to get the scoop when you walked in."

"Your brother made a move."

"*You* did this to her? And then got her to stay anyway?" Carson leaned towards her a little in his chair, "I don't know whether to bow at his feet or worry about your mental stability. How'd he do it? Is this a hostage situation? Blink twice if you're here against your will."

Millie giggled and looked at Drew, who was obviously uncomfortable and not ready to make light of the situation yet. She instantly felt guilty for joking about it and had the strong urge to hug him. Instead, she smiled at him under the towel-covered ice and gave him a wink.

"It was my fault. I wasn't paying attention. He rescued me and took me to the doctor." All of that was true technically. She just left out some of the details. She saw him look down in guilt, and this time, she couldn't help herself. She stood up and walked over to him. "He's my Superman." She wrapped her arms around his waist and snuggled into his chest.

Drew was taken aback by the sweetness of her hug. He wasn't prepared for what she could do to his heart. He wanted her in every sense of the word. He put his arms around her and kissed the top of her head. "Thank you, Miss Lane."

"Alright, it's getting too deep in here. What's in the bags? I'm hungry." Carson took the bags in the kitchen to give them a moment alone. He had never seen his brother look at anyone like he was looking at Millie. It was nice to see him happy again. Weird, but nice.

Drew kissed Millie's head again but kept his face in her hair to breathe her in. "How are you feeling? Has it eased up any?"

She kept close but looked up at him. "It's much better. I talked to Mom. She gave me some tips and then made me promise to tell you she owes you dinner for taking care of her baby."

He smiled down at her, "We seem to be meeting the family a little sooner than most. Of course, you have already met most of mine. Speaking of which, remind me to give Carson a hard time for not remembering you from the launch."

"You two crack me up. Were you always like this?"

"He's been my best friend and a pain in my ass since the day they brought him home. Are you hungry? If you want to eat, we should go in there and snag whatever we can before he eats through it all."

"Do you want me to go home, Drew? Be honest."

"Millie, I don't want you to leave this hug, much less this house. Please stay, but only if you want to. If you're not up to it, I'll take you home right now."

"You're sure no one will mind?"

"They will love you."

"I'm going to need some clothes. I don't want to meet everybody looking like this."

"We'll eat, then we'll shop."

She took a deep breath and laid her head back on his chest, "You make life seem so easy."

He hugged her tighter because he didn't have the words to tell her how much this moment was affecting him. He was definitely a goner.

"Let's get some food before our spree." He kissed her head one more time and let her go, but he kept her hand in his to preserve some of the moment.

They walked into the kitchen to find Carson helping himself to pancakes and French toast. "Carson! Save some for us, man!"

The three of them sat at the kitchen table, sampling all the options and talking like old friends. It was unexpectedly casual, and she was surprised at how at home she felt.

Millie wiped her face after her last bite of the most delicious French toast she had ever had. "You should know something about me before we go shopping." She saw the brothers look at each other with the dread of being pulled into a dozen stores. "I hate shopping."

"Are you kidding?" Drew looked at her puzzled, as if it were against nature for a girl to hate shopping.

"No, I'm not. I hate it, especially clothes shopping. I like to go in, pick something, and get out. I get grumpy when I'm shopping. Just a fair warning."

"Where did you come from, and where can I find your twin?" Carson held her hand on the table and batted his eyelashes obnoxiously. "You're the girl of my dreams."

"Back off or taste fist, Carson." They had that look in their eyes again like they had in the living room. Love masquerading as a challenge on the playground.

"Before the chasing kicks back up, I'm going to take a quick shower so we can go. I won't be too long, but I'm going to have to work around this," she pointed to her bandage, "so it may be minute."

"Take your time. It will give me a minute to drill the Drewzer here on how you two met and why I haven't had the pleasure of your company before today."

"Oh, well then, I'm sorry I didn't make a more lasting impression on you at the launch. Be back in a minute."

She smiled at Drew and watched him smack his brother on the back in victory. "I'll be right back to explain why you're a dumbass." He walked towards Millie, "I'll show you where everything is."

They walked upstairs in silence to the bedroom she had slept in when it dawned on her that a large number of people were coming soon. "Drew, this house is beautiful and definitely has a lot of space for your big family, but where will everyone sleep tonight? Maybe it really would be better if I got a hotel room or just went home."

He guided her into the room, his hand on the small of her back, to the dresser near the window. "Did you see this picture? That was me at four catching my first fish." He opened one of the dresser drawers. "Do you see these trunks? I wore these a few weeks ago when I stepped on a jellyfish in the surf." He pointed to the bathroom, "The shampoo and soap are in the shower because they are my favorites."

Drew looked at her pleadingly, "My things are in this room because this is *my* room. No matter what family comes today, or any day really, this is my room. It's your room today, though. It can be a place to rest if you need it or a place to escape if you need that." He dipped his head to the side like he had earlier and whispered, "Most of the family won't sleep here, and there is plenty of room for the ones that are. Please stay."

"It's official. I'm going to be spoiled rotten by the time I get back to Raleigh." She crossed her arms to keep herself from touching him.

"Millie, you haven't seen spoiling yet." He opened the closet and showed her where the towels were. "Do you need anything else?"

She was embarrassed to admit how thoughtless she had been in coming to the beach. "I should be fine. I'll just wear this again since we're going shopping anyway."

"Oh, that's right, you need a shirt." He turned to his dresser again to pull a t-shirt from the drawer. "This will be too big for you, but it's the smallest one I've got."

"Thank you."

They stood there again, looking at each other for the hundredth time. The talk the night before had bonded them. Moments like this seemed to lure them. She wondered what would happen if she stepped closer to him. He seemed practically perfect in every way, quirks and all, but it felt like both of them were holding back. She didn't know his reason, but she decided that hers wasn't good enough.

She was just about to step forward and kiss this wonderfully kind man when he spoke up. "I better let you get ready. They will start arriving soon, and I'd rather Carson not be the one to tell them all about you. There is no telling what story he'll come up with to explain that eye. Why I'm the storyteller in the family is beyond me, he's full of... stories. Have everything you need? Good."

He was so nervous and rushed that he backed out of the room, knocking into a chair on his way out. When he closed the door, she stood there for a second, looking at it, wondering what had happened in his head to tie him up like that.

On the other side of the door, Drew stood with one hand on the knob and the other across his forehead. *What in the hell was that?* he thought. It was the perfect moment to kiss her, the perfect moment to show her how much he wanted her to be in his life, and he blew it.

No one had ever made him this nervous and relaxed, all at the same time. He was a bundle of nerves right now, though, and couldn't decide whether going in and confessing his love was better than going downstairs and facing his brother's interrogation. He put his head to the door and listened for the water to kick on. If it was on, he would take that as the sign to go downstairs.

"What in God's name are you doing?" Drew jumped back a foot to find Carson leaning on his bedroom door frame, sipping coffee like he had watched the whole show.

"Make some damn noise, Carson!" Drew raced past him and headed downstairs. Carson, of course, followed but took his time to give his brother a minute to cool down.

He had never seen him like this and knew any teasing had to be done skillfully.

"Explain to me, big brother, why you aren't washing that beautiful woman's back in the shower right now." He made himself comfortable in a chair and kept sipping his coffee while Drew paced the kitchen.

"Carson, I'm in trouble here. Big trouble. I've been crazy about her since we met. Now that I really know her, I'm toast." Drew kept pacing but poured a cup of coffee out of habit. "I don't know what to do. I know what I *want* to do, but she's not ready for that. At least, I don't think she's ready. Am I ready? What if I'm just building this whole thing up in my head? Maybe it's just attraction. But it's not, though; I love listening to her. She's smart, you know? She's the whole package."

"Can I ask a question, or do you want to keep rambling to your mug?"

Drew walked to the table and plopped into the chair next to Carson. "What?"

"Forget how long you've known her. Forget trying to figure out where she's at in this. If you think you're ready to even think about a future with her, that's a big deal. Have you told her anything about Laine?"

Drew took a deep breath and put his head in his hands. "No. We talked all night, and I thought about telling her, but I didn't want her to look at me differently. I don't want her to give me the poor guy head tilt that everyone does when they see me. Even you." He looked at his brother, "Yep, you're doing it right now."

Carson scoffed, "I'm not thinking 'poor guy'. I'm thinking I don't have a woman, and I'm way better looking than you are. Makes no sense."

Drew laughed, "That you are, wee one, yet here we sit. Carson, I don't know what to do."

"My advice, since you didn't ask. Don't make a move until you're sure, but tell her about Laine so she doesn't misinterpret why you're waiting."

Drew nodded but put his head back in his hands, thinking. He needed to do some good thinking.

Carson hated seeing him like this but really hated that there was no real way to help him. He could surely take his mind off it for a few minutes, though. "Did you see the game last night? I told you they would tank."

"What! You're on crack. I told you they couldn't pull off a win against the Nats."

The discussion escalated, each of them trying to talk over the other. That is how Millie found them, reliving college days and reciting baseball stats. She stood there watching them, fascinated at the male mind in its natural habitat. She loved baseball, but to sit around screaming about it? Nope.

She walked into the room expecting to need a hose to get their attention, but both men stood when she entered. "I can't wait to meet the mother of men who rise when a girl walks in a room. I thought that was a myth."

"We're doing it because we know she's coming. We also know the sting of that wooden spoon over there if we *don't* do it. It's been a while for Drew, but I got a smack just a few weeks ago. Mom is stronger than she looks."

They all laughed as Carson rubbed his rear end. "I'm sure you had it coming for more than one reason."

"Fair." Carson smiled and shrugged. "So, where are you two love birds headed?"

"The best shop in town, but we won't be gone too long. It won't take much to make this girl gorgeous." Drew put his wallet in his back pocket and grabbed his keys. "You ready?"

"Not true, but thank you. And yes, I'm ready. See you later, Carson. Should I introduce myself to you again when I get back, or will you remember me this time?"

Drew nearly spit out his sip of coffee, and Carson just stood there grinning ear to ear. "Oh, so she's a funny one? I've got my eye on you, Millie. Well played, well played."

She patted his arm and smiled up at him. "Just trying to keep up. See you in a bit."

Carson watched as they walked out the back door and wondered how long it would be before he called her his sister.

chapter nine

DREW OPENED THE door of the store for Millie. "Thank you, sir." She did a quick sweep to see if anything caught her eye when a woman walked up to them, arms open.

"Hey there! What a surprise! What are you doing here? Are you pulling bystanders in off the street to help business?"

Drew gave her a big bear hug and kept his arm around her. "Millie, this is my beautiful and business-savvy sister, Ally. Ally, this is my Millie. I mean Millie, this is Millie. You met her at the launch party. She set the whole thing up."

"Oh, right! Lady with the clipboard. You were amazing that night. I can't believe you planned all that. We're all still talking about it."

"Thank you, Ally. It's nice to see you again."

"Millie came to the beach for a relaxing weekend and got hit with a Frisbee instead. She's going to stay at the house tonight and needs a few things."

Ally looked horrified. "That happened to you on the beach? Good grief, did they at least arrest the jackass that did it to you?"

Millie put on the most serious face she could muster. "No, if you can believe it. They just let the guy walk free without even a warning."

"Well, I think he should have some kind of penalty. Drew, you need to help her file a complaint or something!"

"That may be hard. My attacker seemed very clever. I'll bet he's long gone by now." Millie couldn't keep a straight face any longer. She chuckled at Drew. "I'm sorry. Too soon?"

"Carson was right. You are a funny one." He stepped closer to her and rubbed her cheek again.

"I try."

"Wait. *You* did this to her? Drew!" Ally smacked his arm hard.

"Ow! It was an accident, Ally, damn."

"He's done a great job playing nurse. I'm going to play hooky tomorrow to give the swelling a day to go down, though." She wanted to take the focus off her injury before Ally began the payback burning in her eyes. "I just didn't plan on being here one more day. And I definitely didn't expect to meet the family like this. Do you have anything that could downplay this," she pointed to her eye, "and upplay other things?"

Ally laughed, "You've got a darling little figure. You'd look great in anything. Let's walk over this way, and I'll show you some new stuff that just came in." She cocked an eyebrow at Drew, "You stay put. There are some marshmallow krispie treats in the back if you want one."

"You're in great hands, Millie." Drew darted across the store and headed behind the counter.

"Typical. They are his favorite." Ally looked back at Millie. "You up for trying things on, or do you just want to pick and pay?"

"Ally, I won't lie to you. I'm not a big shopper, and with this," she pointed to her eye again, "just pick something out for me, and I'll try it on."

Ally clapped her hands together. "You are my favorite customer today! Go to that dressing room, and I'll bring everything to you. Quick question first. Favorite color?"

"Blues and greens. Sometimes red."

"Good. Sundress or shorts?"

"Open to both."

"Excellent. Last question. Do you want me to take him down for that eye? I can do it. He won't admit it, but I can drop him in a hot minute."

Millie laughed at the seriousness of the question. "I have no doubt that you could, but he's a good one. Let's let him keep his pride for a while. But if it happens again…"

"If it happens again, he'll have the whole family pounding on him." Ally folded her arms and stared at Millie for a second. "I like you. Give me just a second to collect some things."

She turned with a mission and left a speechless Millie in the dressing room. She was meeting his family, one by one, and liked them all. She wasn't trying to fit in. It all just seemed to fit naturally. She had never really met the family before in past relationships. Was it always this easy, or were the niceties at play until the real personalities came out? She didn't think so. They all seemed so authentically kind. Protective and playful, with a deep love and understanding for one another.

She walked into the dressing room and started to take her clothes off but stopped to look in the mirror. She was wearing Drew's shirt, and even though it was too big and looked silly on her, she hated having to take it off. She liked being this close to him and the smell of him.

She raised the shirt to her nose and took a deep breath. Comfort shot through her system. It wasn't a lightning bolt, but it was just as energizing. Would he miss this shirt if it accidentally fell into her bag and went home with her?

"Millie? You ready?"

She jerked the shirt away from her face. "Yep."

"I'll throw the first few over the door. Let me know how they fit or if you need a different size. It will help decide what else I bring you."

In the end, the girls agreed she had to take the sundress, shorts, and top but were still up in the air about the others.

"We'll take them all. If you decide you don't want them, I'll bring them back."

Ally kissed her brother's cheek. "Now, *you* are my favorite customer."

She rang up the sale and handed the bag to Millie. "It was so nice to meet you away from the others. I'll see you guys later tonight. Leave some linner for me."

Drew held the door open for Millie to walk outside. "You look beautiful, Millie, but if I'm being honest, I kind of liked you wearing my shirt better. That just became my favorite shirt, you know."

"That's such a shame because it became mine as well, and I was planning on stealing it."

"That is a shame. I'll just have to make you wear another shirt tomorrow and keep that one."

"You don't care that I'm stealing it?"

"Nope. I have a clear visual of you wearing it. It never looked that good on me." He grinned at her, "Plus, now you'll have to come let me visit it."

"Visitation rights, huh? We'll have to set up a schedule. It's only fair."

Drew stopped at the car. "Do you mind if we just walk for a while?"

"A walk on the beach with a handsome man? I think I could stand it."

He opened the car door to put the bags and her purse inside. "Do you want some sunglasses?"

"I have mine, thanks though."

Drew locked the door. He held out his hand and waited for her fingers to fall into place. "Let's walk."

They walked hand in hand, people-watching and enjoying the sun. "How's your head feeling?"

"It's much better now. I usually get a headache while I'm shopping. This time, it seems to have taken it away."

"A girl who doesn't like to shop. I'm beginning to think you're too good to be true."

"I like baseball too."

"Well, now you're either lying, or you've ruined me for all other women."

Millie giggled. "I really liked your sister."

"Ally is great. Stubborn, but great."

"She seems so young to already own her own store. Are all the children in your family over-achievers? Isn't there anyone who has a regular job?"

"Hmm. Well, I have a cousin who works at a pizza joint nearby."

"He doesn't own it?"

"No, no. He's only sixteen."

They laughed, and Millie rolled her eyes, "I'm sure he'll own it one day."

"Success never meant much to any of us. Doing what we love means everything. My parents taught us to find our passion and jump in with both feet. We were luckier than most. We had them to fall back on if we needed help." He shrugged at her, "That makes jumping a hell of a lot less scary."

"So you always knew you wanted to be a writer?"

"Always. I started telling stories before I could write them down. When I truly started writing, I couldn't finish one story before another one would pop into my head."

"What is your favorite genre to read?"

"Dramas, with a twist of comedic brilliance, of course. My turn. Were you an event planner from the start?"

"Wait, one more. At the end of this book, you left everyone on a major cliffhanger, but at the launch, you said you didn't have plans for a sequel quite yet."

"All true."

"Is that because you haven't figured out how the twist ends, or are you just holding out on us?"

Drew laughed out loud, "I'm going with option A, but honestly, it's a little of both. It hasn't made sense in my head yet. I still have some details to figure out."

"So you haven't even started writing it yet?"

"Not on paper, nope. One day, I'll do something completely random, and the plot will hit me. I'll stop whatever I'm doing and write like a maniac for as long as it takes to type it all out."

"Just like that, huh?"

"I'm afraid so. It's a blessing and a curse." He stopped for a second to look at her. "Can I write about you in the next book?"

"Yeah, right. I'll be the klutzy secret agent that solves a decades-old government mystery while posing as an event planner for a publishing company three hundred miles away from DC?"

He brushed the hair away from her cheek. "It could happen."

"Will you give me a great operative spy name that strikes fear in the hearts of the bad guys?"

"Absolutely."

"And I want to be tan."

He laughed out loud again. "Millie, you have beautiful skin."

"Nope. Tan or no deal."

He stepped back a little and looked at her so intensely that it made her self-conscious.

"Her fair complexion shone in the southern sun like a strand of white pearls around the neck of an aristocrat. She was an erotic beacon of elegance, intelligence, innocence, and tenacity that could bring the strongest of men to their knees. She held the power but was completely unaware of it, making her seduction that much more alluring and her heart that much more worth winning."

Millie blinked at him for a minute, completely caught off guard by his description of her, or at least the character of her in his head. She had never been described in that way, or any way, really. She was cute. She hated that word but had accepted it many years ago, but what Drew described was far from cute.

He brushed her cheek again. He was curious why a few sentences had her looking at him in such awe and confusion. He wondered why no one had told her all of this before or why she had never accepted it. He promised himself that he would compliment her every chance he got, no matter what happened after the fairy tale weekend ended.

"I don't know what to say to that."

"Millie, you are incredibly beautiful. You don't have to say anything. I just want you to believe it."

His sincerity and kindness overwhelmed her. "Thank you," she whispered. She didn't quite believe what he said, but she could see that he did, and that was enough to touch her heart.

Millie stepped closer to him and put her hands on his chest. She lifted up on her toes and pressed her lips softly to his. "Thank you." She kissed him again, just as softly, but lingered until she felt his arms wrap around her.

Drew pulled her close but didn't deepen the kiss. He was in heaven and wouldn't do anything to change such a perfect moment. She raised her hands to slide around his neck, allowing him to pull her even closer. And there they stood on the beach, oblivious to the world around them.

Taylor watched the two of them in agony. He had wanted one more run before heading back to Raleigh to feel the wind on his face and wrap his mind around a plan. Now he stood there, the breeze on his face and the wind knocked right out of him. He wanted to hate her. He wanted to scream at her, but he just stood there with a front-row seat to heartbreak.

He saw the sweetness in their kiss and was furious that he had never given her that. He saw the serenity and hated himself for bringing so much turmoil to their relationship. He saw a life that he couldn't give her and locked his jaw at his defeat. She would be better off in that world than in his.

He turned around and started running as fast as he could until his lungs burned. He wouldn't let himself look back. The image of her with someone else was too much to bear again. He had lost her, pushed her away into someone else's arms, and every hope he felt earlier that morning went gray.

He stopped with a jolt to put his hands on his knees and give his lungs a second to fill. He pulled his cell from his pocket with frustration and resignation. "Jimmy, it's Taylor. I'll take the job. Yep, me too. I'll call you later to go over the details."

He wished for a landline he could slam down or a door to slam shut but settled for putting the fire back in his lungs. He kept running, far past the house, until he collapsed on the sand, breathless. He had lost her. His shot at happiness was now someone else's bliss. He let the bitterness of the last few years break free and gave up on his happiness for the first time in his life.

The kiss was something out of a fairytale. The kind of first kiss that you dream of having, but as Millie pulled away from Drew, she was certain of two things. She could trust him in a way she had never trusted any man before, and that a piece of Taylor was still in her heart.

She wanted his kiss to knock all doubt from her, but that wasn't fair to Drew. Their kiss showed her what she already knew. Her heart was preoccupied by someone who didn't love her—who couldn't love her. Her head was spinning, at war with the romantic and practical within her.

Drew brushed her cheek again, "It feels like I've been waiting forever to kiss you. If I wasn't already under your spell, that definitely did the trick. I hate that I have to share you with everyone now."

Oh, good Lord, his family. She had forgotten about his sweet family and the day she was about to spend with them. Her head began to ache from it all. How would she sort through all of this with his family asking questions and wanting to get to know her? All of a sudden, she felt trapped. She smiled at Drew, hoping he couldn't see the tension behind her sunglasses.

"We better start heading back." They walked, hand in hand, while Drew told her more about the personalities she was about to meet. She asked questions to keep him talking, hoping that would distract him from the way she had pulled away. She doubted it but hoped.

Drew turned the air conditioning on full blast as soon as they got in the car. "Nothing like a black car in the heat. It should cool down soon. Do you mind if we make a quick stop on the way? I want to pick up some cannolis at my dad's favorite bakery."

"Of course not. I've never had a cannoli before. Cheesecake is my nemesis. I have no control."

"I'll get you one of each and see what you think."

They pulled into traffic before he reached over to hold her hand. This man was so perfect on paper. Why did she feel this way? Thoroughly frustrated with herself, she rubbed her head out of habit.

"It's hurting again, isn't it? Would you rather go straight back?"

"No, no, it's fine. I mean, yes, it is hurting a little," an honest statement, "but let's go to the bakery. Do you mind if I wait in the car, though?"

"You sure? He can live without the sweets."

"No way. I'll be fine with the AC blowing."

"I'm such an idiot. I should have thought about what the heat would do to your head. I'll get a tea for you while I'm in there unless you want something else?"

"A tea would be great, Drew, thank you."

He parked in front of a little hole-in-the-wall shop that looked more eroded than edible. He laughed at the way she was looking at the store. "Don't let the exterior fool you. Sunshine and deliciousness await inside. I'll be five minutes."

She watched him rush in the front door of the shop before putting her head in her hands. One tear fell before she put her face in front of the vent to blow the rest away. She couldn't lead him on this way but didn't know how to tell him what was going on inside her head. She couldn't even figure it out. There was no way she could explain it to someone else.

She needed an escape, a chance to clear her head before making any decisions. She pulled out her phone and sent a group text to her girls.

I promise I'm OK, but need
a favor. Please call in one
hour with an emergency.
Dealer's choice, but you
need me to come home.
Meet at my house ~ 4p.

It was the coward's way out, and she knew it. She watched as the replies came in with thumbs up, hearts, and kissy face emojis. She put her phone back in her purse and closed her eyes. When had she become a coward? Why couldn't she tell Drew the truth?

He got back in the car a few minutes later with a box of sweets and a large sweet tea. She took a bigger sip than she meant to. Maybe she was a little dehydrated. "This is the best sweet tea I've ever had!"

"I'm tellin' ya, sunshine and deliciousness. Wait until you try the food. It will put anything you've had to shame. Mind sharing some of that tea?"

"I don't know. It's really good." She smiled at him and handed over the tea, already wanting another sip.

When they walked in the door, the house was bustling. Carson was telling a story in the kitchen that had everyone in stitches. He had quite a personality, and she wondered if he was seeing anyone. Audrey could use a character in her life. She made a mental note to ask Drew later.

She met a handful of cousins who introduced themselves like the von Trapp family in stair-step order and then split like pool balls after a good break. Everyone was on their best behavior, but in all honesty, she didn't feel like they were acting. She watched them and saw the kind of genuine bonds that only come with a lifetime spent loving and arguing with each other.

There was that feeling again. She had been welcomed into the incredible family of a man who was practically perfect in every way, and she hated that Taylor had crept into her thoughts to confuse her. She rubbed her heart, hoping it would help revive it to the present. *Forty-five minutes. Just hold on for forty-five minutes, and your phone will ring*, she thought.

Drew walked up behind her and slid his arms around her waist, putting his head in whispering distance of her ear.

"You're a hit. I've been told that our children will be beautiful and that they will choose you over me if this goes south."

He hugged her a little tighter and kissed the top of her head. "Come with me. I want to show you something."

He guided her to the kitchen, where his father was sitting down with the pastry box. "Dad, you should be ashamed of yourself. No dessert before linner."

"Oh shut up and grab me a fork so I can eat this. Millie, I don't know if Drew told you, but I have a horrible sweet tooth. I'm fairly good at home, but I figure when I'm here, I'm on vacation and deserve a little treat."

He didn't waste any time when Drew handed him the fork. Millie smiled as she watched this burly and brawny man moan from the mouthful of cannoli. "Mmmmm, that man is a genius. Do you want a bite?"

Drew sat beside Millie. "I'm sorry, I had to sit down. Did you just offer up a bite of your cannoli without being tricked or threatened?"

"Is he always this sassy with you, Millie? Don't hesitate to pop him on the back of the head if he talks to you like that. I would do it now if I could reach him." His words were stern, but the love in his eyes took any sting away as he smiled at his son.

"No, thank you, Mr. Arthur; I wouldn't dare take a drop away from you after that moan. You enjoy."

"Please, Millie, call me Pete. 'Mr. Arthur' is for the girlfriends I don't like. I've already decided that I like you."

"Dad! You made Paul call you 'Mr. Arthur' until after Ruthie was born."

"That was different."

"How?"

"I just like messing with him. He's so easy to mess with." He looked at Millie, "Honestly, I kind of forgot about it until I was trying to figure out what my grandpa name would be." He let out a deep, throaty laugh. "Yeah, that was my bad."

"That's awful and so hilarious." Millie laughed. "I like you more for it, though."

Drew watched as they laughed together and the new bond that was building between them. His heart was on his sleeve, and it terrified him, but as he sat there listening to them get to know each other, he felt more of a rush than actual terror—the kind you feel as the roller coaster clicks up the rail and then plummets into the ride. He smiled at Millie and let the thrill wash over him.

Millie was utterly at home, sitting at the kitchen table talking with Pete, learning about their family, and hearing some of Drew's embarrassing stories. The kind that a parent stores in their vault until the perfect moment. She was a people person and could create conversations with nearly anyone, but she rarely clicked with people like this. She felt like she had known Pete for years and was just catching up on what she had missed since their last "linner".

She didn't hear her phone until the fourth ring. She answered it while laughing about two-year-old Drew's obsession with taking his diaper off in public places.

"Hey chick, I have quite the story to tell you the next time I see you." She smiled at Drew, who gave her a grinning scowl.

"Millie, you need to come home. Where are you?"

She knew she had told them to call, but the tone of Rory's voice made the hair on the back of her neck stand up. She wasn't laughing anymore.

"I'm still at the beach. What's the matter?"

"Sweetie, your Mom is in the hospital. She was taken by an ambulance about an hour ago to…"

"An hour ago! Why didn't you call me?"

The room was silent now. She didn't know how he moved so quickly, but Drew was already kneeling next to her when she looked up.

"I just found out, Mil. I called you the second I hung up."

"What the hell happened?" She held her breath and waited for whatever blow was next.

"I don't have a lot of details. All I know is that she was having a hard time breathing and called 911. She's at UNC. They are running tests and have her on oxygen. Which beach are you at?"

"Sunset. Who is with her?" There was silence.

"Rory! Who is with her!"

"No one yet, but I'm on my way there now. How fast can you get here?"

"I'm leaving in five. Stay with her, do you hear me? You tell those nurses you are her daughter. You stay with her. I'll be there as fast as I can."

"She's going to be fine, Mil. I've got the prayer chain activated. Sinners all over North Carolina will be on their knees for her within the hour. Do you want me to call Brooks?"

Her brother was working on his master's and was at the tail end of a major project. "No. Call me with an update once you get there. I'll call him then."

"I love you, Mil. Be safe."

"I love you too."

She hung up the phone, staring at it in a daze. This feeling. She had never felt this before. The fear was actually painful. She felt like someone was twisting her heart from the inside out. The whole conversation was surreal. She stared at the phone, waiting for Rory to text, saying that it was just an act, just a response to her text. Nothing.

"Millie, what's going on? You're shaking. What happened?" He was rubbing her arm, but she could barely feel his touch.

"My mom. She's in the hospital. She couldn't breathe. She… She needs me. I'm hours away, and she needs me. I have to go."

Pete came around the table and took her hand. "Drew is going to drive you. You don't need to be behind the wheel right now. Get her keys, leave her stuff here. I'll send someone to Raleigh with it. Is that alright with you, Millie?"

Millie nodded without even thinking about what she was leaving behind.

"Meet me at the back door." Drew flew out of the room, causing a million questions along the way.

Pete helped her out of her chair and walked her towards the door. She knew everyone was watching but didn't have it in her to make eye contact with anyone.

"When was the last time you took something for your head? I'll bet it's spinning right about now."

"In the car, after the bakery."

"You didn't take anything in the car, Millie, but I have some medicine right here. Carson, go get us some drinks."

"Oh wait, my purse."

"I've got that too. Let's go." Drew gave his dad a big hug. "I'll call you later. I love you."

"I love you too, buddy. You drive safe. Millie, we'll be praying, honey."

Pete put his big arms around her and squeezed softly. "You just take a deep breath and remember, faith gets us further than fear. She's a strong woman if her daughter is any indication. She's going to be alright."

She could only manage a whispered, "Thank you." Any other words were choked back with the sobbing she refused to let out.

"Drew, let us know."

"Promise." He took Millie's arm gently and was surprised by how cold it was. He felt her hand. She was freezing. "Someone get me a sweater or something."

Carson came sprinting out of the kitchen with drinks, "Got it. I'll grab something and meet you at the car."

"Come on, Mil. Let's get you in the car."

They had been in the car for two hours. Rory had called, saying they were admitting her mom, then a text with the room number. Other than that, the ride had been entirely silent. She felt terrible for being so distant, but she didn't have the energy for small talk, and she wasn't sure he could handle the weeping she wanted to let loose while driving ninety miles an hour. There was no doubt he would get them to the hospital in record time. She wasn't sure her car had ever gone this fast.

The silence was deafening, though, and she knew it was her fault. "I'm sorry."

Her voice sounded so small now. He ached to hold her and help somehow, but the silence allowed him to focus on getting them to Chapel Hill at warp speed without any accidents.

He slowed a bit and put his hand on hers. It was still ice cold. "There is nothing to be sorry about."

"She's my world. My whole world. What if…" Her voice cracked and nearly had him pulling over to comfort her. He lifted her hand to his lips and kissed her knuckles, then laid it on his leg with their fingers intertwined.

"Tell me about her. You said she was the good kind of crazy. What's one of the craziest things she's done?"

"Drew, I don't want to..."

"Please. I want to know her a little before I run into the hospital like a lunatic, demanding answers for you."

Millie laid her head back but couldn't take her eyes off of him. He was too good to be true. "Why couldn't I have met you a year ago?"

"You weren't ready for all this awesomeness." He winked at her and stared for an extra second. "Truth is, I probably wasn't ready for yours."

He touched her heart so many times over the last two days in ways no one ever had. She squeezed her eyes shut and cursed herself for being careless with his feelings. She needed to tell him about Taylor. She needed to tell him that even though he was the man of her dreams, her reality was currently spoken for.

"Drew, I need to tell you something. This weekend seems like years have gone by in a breeze."

"Hey, that's a great line. Can I use that?"

She grinned because she could see he wasn't kidding. "It's yours. I've never been seen the way you see me. It's like you only see the good." She looked at their hands on his leg. "You're offering me a future before you even know the bad."

"I'm sure you'll annoy me eventually, Millie." He winked at her again and squeezed her hand.

"But how can you jump in like this without knowing me? The real me, I mean?"

"I'm just as scared as you are, honestly. I just choose not to let fear rule my life anymore."

She was a coward. One hundred percent, bona fide, grade-A coward. "Drew, I really need to tell you…"

The phone rang, cutting her off and sending her focus back to her mom. "Cate, what's the matter? Where are Mom and Rory?"

He listened to her end of the conversation but couldn't tell what the update was. There were no tears or signs of panic, though, so he was hopeful. He took a deep breath, grateful for the interruption. He didn't know what she was trying to tell him, but he could feel it wouldn't be a confession of undying love.

He saw the sign for Raleigh and hoped he could keep her distracted long enough to get to Chapel Hill. If they could just get to the hospital, she would see how strong he was and how much she could depend on him. The fear of losing her swept through him again, but he ignored it. He kissed her hand again and sped up. He knew he was racing the clock in more ways than one.

chapter ten

AS THEY PULLED into the parking deck, Millie felt every nerve in her body radiating energy. She felt completely alert and numb at the same time. Drew walked around the car to open her door. Every ounce of her wanted to sprint inside to hold her mom's hand and see for herself that she was all right, but her legs betrayed her. She sat still, looking down at her feet, willing them to move.

"She's going to be alright, Millie, but take all the deep breaths you need to before we go in."

Millie shook her head, "I've never been this scared before."

Drew shimmied down to sit beside her feet. "I threw up."

She looked at him, stunned. "Just now?"

He shook his head and looked across the aisle at the other cars. "I got a call from Ally a few years ago telling me that dad was in a car accident and was being rushed to the hospital. I was in college, two hundred and fifty miles away, with no car. There was literally nothing I could do but wait and pray."

He looked down with the pain still in his eyes from that day. "I made them call me with updates every five minutes until he was out of surgery and could tell me himself that he was fine." He took a deep breath, looking up at her. "Scariest day of my life. There is no comparison to anything else – until we have our children, I've heard."

She looked down at her legs. Drew was rubbing her knee, but she still felt numb. She focused on his hand until she could feel his touch. To his credit, he didn't throw any cheerleader clichés at her or try to push. He was quiet and let her decide when she was ready.

"Once we get in there, the girls will surround me and be my strength until I find it." She felt him tense and saw the hurt. She took his hand as he started to pull away. "I'm saying that because I don't want you to let go."

She put her other hand on their joined hands. "This sounds stupid, but will you hold my hand in there?"

Drew smiled at the rush of love he felt for her. She was taking baby steps, but letting him know how she wanted him to support her was a big step in the right direction. "I won't let go of your hand until you are using it to hold your mom's." He kissed her palm and sent waves of peace through her. "You ready?"

They walked through the parking deck towards the elevator in silence. He couldn't tell if she was praying or preparing herself for what was inside, but either deserved her focus. The elevator doors opened to a woman crying with her husband holding her. The couple walked past them, their quiet sobs sending a shiver through Millie.

"I've got you," he whispered. He led her into the hospital elevator, pushed the button, and pulled her in close when the doors closed. "You didn't ask for a hug, but I could use one."

She wrapped her arms around his waist and sunk into his chest. How did he know what she needed before she did? "What's wrong with you?"

"What's *wrong* with me?"

"You can't be this perfect."

"Millie, I assure you there is not an ounce of perfection in me."

She leaned back a little, "Got nothin', huh? Not one little scrap for me to hold on to?"

He brushed her cheek in the way she was growing to want. "I drink from the milk carton on a regular basis."

"You're a monster."

"I knew I should have hidden my ugly side a little longer, but you pushed."

She smiled at him for the first time in hours, a genuine smile that made him proud. They were smiling at each other when the doors opened to a whirlwind of people. Cate and Audrey saw that moment between Millie and Drew and looked at each other in surprise. They didn't know much about Taylor, but they had done enough internet stalking over the last two days to know that wasn't him.

"Audrey has been stalking the window. She saw you walking in. Come here." Cate gave Millie a tight hug that left her breathless. "I'm so sorry you had to race back like this… what in the hell happened to your head?"

Cate practically jumped into the elevator to hug her. "Audrey, come look at her!"

Audrey walked up to Millie in her soft, sincere way. "I'll check this out after you see mom, but are you in any pain?"

"I'm fine. Just a nasty cut from a vindictive Frisbee."

"A Frisbee did this to you?" Cate looked at her doubtfully. Audrey put a hand on Cate's arm to keep her from peppering Millie with questions.

"I promise I'm fine. I'll tell you the whole story later. How is Mom? Is Rory with her? Which way is her room?"

Audrey let one arm go for another. "She's in room 602 with Rory. She just got back from having some tests. The results haven't come back yet."

"What tests? They should have done the EKG hours ago!"

"This was an echocardiogram. They're getting a good look at her heart and blood vessels to rule out anything serious."

Audrey rubbed both of Millie's arms when she saw the chill of reality run through her friend. "They are being cautious, Millie. It's a good thing. She's tired, though. All of this has worn her out."

Millie shook her head while letting everything sink in. "602?"

"Yes, you want us to go with you?"

Millie shook her head again. She needed them around her now. She didn't know what to expect in 602 but knew it would require more strength than she had to face it.

"OK then, let's go." Cate took her arm and started to lead her down the hallway. When she didn't feel Drew near her, she stopped and turned to see him walking behind them. Millie walked back to him and put her hand in his.

"I need all of you with me." She turned to the girls. "Audrey. Cate. Meet Drew."

"Nice to meet you, ladies."

"Drew was the person who took me to the doctor and helped me through all of this." She pointed to her eye and smiled at him. "He's a good one to have around in hours of need."

Audrey stepped forward first. "It's nice to meet you, Drew."

Cate shot an eyebrow up at Millie but smiled at Drew. "Thanks for taking care of our girl."

"You can get to know each other later, but I want him in the room and the loop." The girls nodded in understanding. "Let's go see Mom."

Mille held Drew's hand tightly as they followed Audrey and Cate to the hospital room. Millie stopped at the open door and took a breath. She felt the shaking coming back and cursed herself for being so weak.

Drew turned her to him when he saw her hesitation. "You have a whole room of people to get you through this and be strong for you. You have all the strength you need. Depend on ours until you find yours."

Millie took a deep breath, staring at him until she trusted herself to keep it together. "Okay, I'm ready."

Audrey patted Drew's arm and gave him an approving smile. "Well said."

The sight of her mother in a hospital bed was like a swift kick to the gut and left her breathless. She felt Drew squeeze her hand before she let go to hug Rory.

"Hello, love."

"Hi."

"She's been sleeping for about twenty minutes. She's not hurting, just tired."

Millie sat slowly on the side of the bed to take in the scene. She reminded herself that none of the wires or machines were keeping her alive. She was doing that all on her own. Millie watched her chest rise and fall, relaxing a little with the simple rhythm of it.

"It's about time you got here. Please tell me you brought a Diet Mountain Dew with you. I'm going through withdrawals."

"You're crazy, Mom. They told me you were sick, but I think you're faking it. I'm here to say the joke's gone too far."

Her Mom patted her hand, and just like that, some strength returned to both of them. They had a connection that would never be defined as simply mother and daughter. They were kindred spirits and needed each other as much as the breaths the machines were monitoring.

"So? Hit me with it."

"I know you've been getting updates. There's no news yet."

"My spies have been working hard, but I want it from the horse's mouth. Details. All of them."

"You first. How's the head?"

"It's fine. I'll have Audrey look at it later. I'm sure it will scar, but that will just help me fit in at the biker bars."

"Oh Lord, don't say things like that to your mother!"

"Why not, Mom? You should come with me! We'll find you a Hells Angel named 'Big Daddy' to ride into the sunset with."

"You are the crazy one, child. And you're making a terrible first impression of me to Drew."

Drew smiled through the surprise of her knowing him by name. "Don't be silly, Ms. Sullivan. I know you're a wonderful mother. Why else would you have her name tattooed across your backside?"

The entire room went completely silent and then erupted in laughter, earning Millie a smack on the hand from her mom.

"Thank you for that, Drew. We needed a good laugh. And please, call me Mary."

"Yes, ma'am. Can I get you anything, Mary? Anyone?"

"No, thank you, but will everyone please sit down? You're making me nervous."

"There aren't enough chairs, Ms. Mary," Rory said as she propped herself against the window sill.

"I'll go find some." Drew left on a mission, leaving the girls with their own.

"Okay, Sullivan. Spill. Who is this knight in shining armor, and why didn't you tell us about him?"

"No way! We are talking about Mom first. I want details, woman. You scared the sh… crap out of me. I talked to you this morning, and you seemed fine. What happened?"

Mary was wrapping up the day's events and all the tests she had gone through so far when Drew came back with an orderly and four chairs.

"Excuse the interruption, ladies, but we have to get these in here before the cafeteria manager catches us. You wouldn't think she'd miss four little chairs."

Drew got them in place and took a deep breath, "I'm man enough to say that she scares me a little. Thanks for being my accomplice, Joe."

"No problem, man. Just let me know when you want to sneak them back in."

The girls were still laughing when Rory took her seat next to Drew and gave Millie a wicked smile. "You have perfect timing, Drew. Millie was just about to tell us how she got that cut."

"Oh, well, maybe I should go while I'm ahead." He smiled at Millie, letting everyone see their connection and affection for each other.

Cate was watching them both like a hawk and caught the innuendo first, "Wait, you did this to her?"

"I'm very sorry to say I did."

"I deserved it. I was lying on the beach in my bathing suit, blinding the pedestrians walking by with my paleness. He was afraid for the children, so he took matters into his own hands."

"That is not true. I saw a mosquito land on your forehead. I was just trying to keep it from biting you."

"Alright, you two." Mary rolled her eyes in delight at seeing her daughter's smile. "Tell them what really happened."

Millie and Drew corrected each other and laughed all the way through the story, like an old married couple reliving their young and carefree days. Everyone was laughing with them and could see how well they got along. He was warm and caring but matched her wit and challenged her in a way they had never seen anyone else do before.

By the time the story was finished, the girls were convinced that this random trip and rogue Frisbee may have been the twist of fate Millie needed in her life. Cate leaned over to whisper in Audrey's ear. "Forget what's his name. Drew here has my vote."

Over the next few hours, the test results came in slowly. Although it wasn't a heart attack, the chest x-ray came back a little worrisome, which was going to keep her in the hospital for observation. She had gotten several calls from friends and family, and a basket of tulips had already arrived from her brother, Brooks. He was going to pick up Mary's best friend on the way to Chapel Hill but couldn't get there until sometime in the morning.

"It's getting late. I'm staying here tonight," Mary groaned, "but you guys should go home and get some rest. I'll call you if I need anything. Will someone go home for me, though, and bring a change of clothes for tomorrow?"

"I can stay with you," Audrey said, yawning. "I have to be here by six anyway."

"No, you need to go home and get some sleep. You, of all people, need to be on your A game at work."

"Fine, but I'm going to check in with you bright and early. Oh, and I'm going to look at Mil's cut before I go. Let me get some fresh gauze. I'll be right back."

"Mil will text me and let me know if you think of anything else you need, alright?" Cate gave Millie a big hug, whispering, "Girl, we need to talk. Call me," before bending down to kiss Mary on the head. "I'll see you tomorrow, Ms. Mary."

Rory followed that kiss with a big hug. "You take care of yourself. No more scares for a while, please. You've hit quota for the next few years."

Mary held her hand, and for the first time since Millie arrived, she saw her mother let her guard down and show the emotion of the day. "Sweet girl, I can't tell you how much it meant to me to have you here through all of this. Thank you for coming. I'm so sorry I scared you. No more scares, I promise. I love you."

They hugged, tears rolling down their faces. Millie couldn't keep a tear from falling but was determined to keep it together until she was alone. Drew walked up behind her and wrapped his arms around her shoulders. "Don't mind me. I've been wanting to hold you for hours."

"Thank you for being here. I don't think I could have driven home, certainly couldn't have gotten here as quickly."

Drew chuckled in her ear. "It was my honor."

He hugged her tight but didn't let go. She hadn't realized she needed a hug and let herself relax a little in his arms. "I know you're exhausted. You should get some rest. Have you called your family?"

"I talked to them a few hours ago. They all send their love and are also sending some linner leftovers to Raleigh with Carson if he doesn't eat them on the way home. I can bring them here if you want, but it might be best to put them in your fridge. Speaking of food, you didn't eat much of that cafeteria food Cate brought up. Do you want me to get you something?"

"No, thank you, I'm not very hungry. Nerves go straight to my stomach and shoulders."

"Well, if I can't help the stomach, I'll aim for the shoulders." He started using his thumbs on the boulders in her shoulders. "You weren't kidding. These are serious knots. When does your brother get here tomorrow?"

"I think around eleven."

"I'll be here around noon to pick you up then. I'll take you home for a shower, a change of clothes, maybe some food. I promise to bring you back to the hospital right after. Deal?"

"Deal. I'll text Cate so she knows not to stop."

Rory walked up to them and wrapped her arms around both of them. "I'm so glad you're alright. I love you."

"I love you too. Thank you for being here when I couldn't be." Millie's voice cracked.

"It was the only place I wanted to be. Call me if you need anything. Thank you, Drew. You've been stamped and approved in our books. Good luck keeping this one in line."

"It was really nice to meet you, Rory. Can I walk you out to your car?"

"That would be great, thanks."

Drew walked away from Millie to say goodbye to Mary. Once she was free, she hugged Rory with every ounce of love in her body. "I don't know how to thank you, but I wouldn't have trusted anyone else with her. You were our hero today."

"She's going to be okay, Mil. I've been begging and making deals with God all day. He's listening. Make sure you talk to Him."

"I'm planning a whopper of a talk once Mom falls asleep. I hope He's ready."

"And you better call me. We need to talk about Mr. Dreamy over there." The girls giggled and wiped away tears as they hugged one last goodbye.

Drew walked up to them, and Rory smiled at how much she already liked him. "Let me know if you need anything."

"I promise."

The awkwardness of having their goodbye in front of an audience was laughable. Millie put her hand on his cheek and whispered, "Thank you."

He kissed the palm of that hand, "I'll see you soon. Get some rest."

When she closed the door and turned around, she was completely caught off guard by her mother's tears. "Hey, hey. What's the matter? I know Rory is your new favorite daughter, but I'm here too."

She knew jokes were not the answer right now, but she couldn't lose it when her Mom needed her. She lay next to her and cuddled her close. "This didn't just scare the hell out of *us*, did it?"

Mary shook her head into Millie's chest.

"Well, you just cry it out, and when you're done, we'll order some ice cream and watch a movie."

Mary cried for what felt like hours until she wore herself out and fell asleep on Millie's tear-soaked chest. She lay there looking down at her mother, knowing this moment would be etched in her memory forever.

It wasn't often she was able to take care of her mom. She was a kind soul, and she always thanked Millie for being a good daughter, but she knew she would be lost without her mom—completely lost.

She waited as long as she could to keep the tears under control. Millie slid out of bed, careful not to wake Mary, and closed the bathroom door behind her. She looked in the mirror for the first time in hours and was surprised by her surprise. "I almost forgot about you." She touched the new bandage Audrey had added tenderly. The swelling wasn't any worse, but the bruising had gotten so much more colorful. "Lovely."

What a day. She thought about all of the highs and lows while she splashed cold water on her face. She felt so much better now that she was here and could see her Mom with her own eyes, ask questions, and hear the answers herself.

The problem was that the answers weren't coming fast enough, and that worried her more than anything. Her heart was in great shape, her blood pressure was good, no anemia, and thank God, no cancer. So what was it?

She tip-toed into the room and sat in the chair closest to the end of the bed. What was going on, and when were the doctors going to figure it out? Her fear came from the unknown, and it was almost too much to bear. She felt like an elephant was sitting on her chest.

Millie put her head in her hands and wept silently. She wept for the fear, the uncertainty, and the idea of facing a world without her Mom in it.

She heard the door open but couldn't hold back the tears. The nurse would just have to work around the scene she was causing because the rush of emotions was too much to contain now.

She heard a chair move and felt him before she looked up. There were no words to be said, no reason to explain, just acceptance of the need to release some of what she had been holding in. She laid her head in his lap and cried while he rubbed her hair back and whispered that everything would be okay.

When she had given all she had, she felt herself doze off, wondering how in the world Taylor had known where to find her and confused about the feelings that he had.

She slept in his lap, trusting and peaceful. He watched her breathing while his own breaths were heavy. How had he screwed this up so badly?

On his way back to Raleigh, he had planned to go home and continue life as it was, but when he saw the exit to her apartment, he felt the pull again and decided to talk everything out with her. He sat at her door for hours, watching and hoping that she would be alone so he could convince her to start fresh.

As he drifted off, Cate arrived at Millie's door to leave her favorite muffins inside. After an intense session of begging, she finally told him Millie was at the hospital.

Taylor kept rubbing her hair, careful not to touch the bandages. It kept the fact that he was holding her again real.

He needed this to last as long as possible because he was deathly afraid she wouldn't take him back. He didn't know how he would do it or how long it would take, but he was determined to win her trust and heart again.

"I'm sorry to interrupt the moment you are having over there, but who are you?" Mary wasn't afraid but absolutely confused, which worried her considering her current un-diagnosis.

Taylor's glance shot up to Mary's, but his voice was tender and soft. "I beg your pardon, Ms. Sullivan. My name is Taylor Fitzpatrick. I work with Millie at Grant. I am a friend, ma'am. I'm sorry if I startled you."

"Well, you did, but I'll forgive it. She's worn out. I told her to go home and get some sleep, but she's stubborn. In all honesty, I'm glad she didn't listen."

Mary looked at her daughter's swollen face. "She's been crying."

"Yes, ma'am. She was pretty upset when I got here. She just needed to get some of the fear out. I think you gave her a good scare."

"Indeed. She's so much stronger than she gives herself credit for. Tears are a weakness to her. I can't convince her that it's quite the opposite."

She looked at Taylor again. He had resumed rubbing Millie's hair. She saw the worry in his eyes and the love in his touch. "On the other hand, some show their strength through tenderness."

Taylor smiled but didn't take his eyes off Millie. "Ma'am, you should know that I am in love with your daughter. A fact that she probably doesn't believe now. I had a shot at her heart and blew it, but she has mine if she'll take it."

Mary took a deep breath. She didn't know how Millie felt about Taylor and certainly didn't understand how Drew fit in the picture, but she did know a hurting soul when she saw one.

"Taylor, tell me this. Do you know her well enough to love her?"

"Yes. Yes, ma'am, I think I do."

"Does my Millie know that you feel this way?"

Taylor winced at the question and the memory of their argument at Grant. "No, ma'am."

"Hmm. Well, it seems to me that if she didn't care for you, she wouldn't have trusted you to hold her while she cried. I can say with certainty that she doesn't let people in easily. If you are worried you have blown your chance, keep in mind that she let you hold her in her weakest moment. She's a phenomenal actress, my Amelia. She can hide her pain from anyone, including me."

Taylor smiled to himself at hearing her whole name and thought back to their late-night conversation at the launch party. He rubbed her cheek. "May I ask you a question, Ms. Sullivan?"

"You can ask me anything, but call me Mary."

"How do I win her back? I am terrified to move because if she wakes up and looks at me like… like she did… I hate that I hurt her." He sniffed back the burn of tears that were threatening to fall. "I'm so sorry, ma'am. Here you are in the hospital, and I'm keeping you up with my blubbering."

"It's Mary, not ma'am, and watching you love my daughter is warming my heart. I can't tell you what will happen when she wakes up. I won't persuade her to do anything. Only she can decide who to love. I will say this, though. She needs to hear everything you've told me and more. It's not going to be easy. As I mentioned, my girl is quite stubborn. Make her listen, make her hear you." Mary tilted her head, debating on how much to say. "One more piece of advice. Do it soon. You'll lose her if you wait."

Taylor knew what she was referring to but appreciated her discretion. "Thank you, ma'am. I'm sorry. Thank you, Mary."

"While you're trapped here, do you mind if I ask you a question?"

"You can ask me anything."

"What do you do at Grant?"

Two hours later, that one question had turned into an in-depth conversation. They had gotten to know each other in a way that left him bonded to Mary and more in love with Millie than ever. Mary asked about his family, and he told her about his trouble with Carrie and their failed marriage.

They laughed at Millie's childhood adventures, and she told him about some of the pains in her past that shaped who Millie was today. Now he sat there watching these two amazing women sleep, and he was more confident than ever that he wanted them as family.

He rubbed her cheek again, desperately wishing he could kiss it, surprised at how soft her skin was. She moved a little at his touch and gave him a better look at her face. He saw the bandage on her eye at the beach but was free to stare now and inspect the damage. Mary was right. She was so much stronger than she gave herself credit for.

He closed his eyes and hoped that he would have the right words when she woke up. He opened his eyes a few minutes later when he felt her stir and found her looking up at him.

"How long have I been out?" Millie whispered.

"A few hours." He smoothed hair away from her face. "You must be sore, sitting here like a pillow for so long." She started to get up, but he gently put his hand on her shoulder.

"It was my pleasure to be your pillow, Millie. I loved it."

She grinned at him and felt that rush of wanting bolt through her. "Good Lord, you are gorgeous. It's the middle of the night. Most people look ragged, how I must look, but here you sit. Gorgeous. It's infuriating."

She put her hand on his leg to push up and look at her mom. "I'm glad she's still sleeping."

"Mary and I had a long talk."

Millie looked at him, disbelieving. "When?"

"She woke up and saw her daughter lying in a stranger's lap. It was a great conversation starter."

She chuckled, "I'll bet."

"She's quite a lady. I see where you get it from."

"Get what?"

"Your spunk and your heart."

Millie looked at her Mom and chuckled again, "That pretty much nails it. She's much nicer than I am, though."

She stood up stiffly and slowly walked to the window. The sun wasn't up yet, but she could hear the birds starting to sing and knew sunrise wasn't far away.

Taylor walked to her side, and without even thinking, she rested her head on his shoulder. "What are you doing here, Taylor? How did you know I was here?"

"I went to your apartment and ran into Cate. She told me you were here."

Millie scoffed, "I can only imagine how that conversation went. Wait," she stepped away from him when the fling conversation came flooding back to her. "Why were you at my apartment? I think you said it all at the office. I'm not interested in being your fling." She saw him tense up but wanted to understand why he was there.

"I deserve that. And so much more. Millie, I am so sorry for... well, for all of it. I have done nothing to earn your trust, but I need you to believe I never meant to hurt you." He closed the space she had put between them, "I'm so sorry, Mil."

She felt herself weakening and looked away from him before she lost herself again. "Thank you, Taylor. I appreciate that, but too much has happened to go back now. I can't. But Taylor, more importantly, *you* can't."

"I know it seems that way, but there is too much chemistry between us to throw it away." He turned her to him so he could look her in the eye. "What I said that day was wrong on so many levels. I didn't mean it the way it sounded. Honest. I meant that I wouldn't think of leaving my marriage for anything less than what I feel for you. That is certainly not the way it came out, and I can't blame you for being hurt. I'm so, so sorry. It's stupid, and I hate that I said what I said. I was dying to hold you. Instead, I acted like a child and threw a tantrum."

"You may not have meant to say it, but it came from somewhere in you, Taylor."

"God, Millie, it was an awful position to put you in, and it's been eating me alive since. This kind of connection doesn't exist for me, and it scared the hell out of me. Still does, but only because I know I could lose it. Lose you."

Taylor rubbed his forehead like he did when he was frustrated. "I'm in sales. I should be better at this. You unhinge me, Millie. I've never felt like this before. I want you. Only you."

"You want me? What happens after you get me? I don't see sunset walks on the beach in our future, Taylor."

"I don't know what happens next. I just know I want you with me."

"Stop saying that!" Millie had to remind herself to keep her voice in a whisper.

"What?"

"You wanting me. You can't. *We* can't."

There was a moment when all she could hear was the monitor beeping and the birds chirping. She found the contrast of them strangely comforting and closed her eyes to listen for a second.

In a strained whisper, she heard his voice crack. "Millie, please don't give up on me. I need you. I'm a better person when I'm around you, despite all the evidence to the contrary. I want to be someone you are proud to spend your life with."

She opened her eyes in time to see the plea in his. She started to put a hand on his cheek but stopped halfway. "What about Carrie? Where does she fit into all of this? You said…"

"I know what I said. She is miserable. We both are. It's time to admit it and move on."

"I want to believe you, Taylor. I do, but I just…"

"I've done everything wrong. You have watched me spinning in circles, and you're dizzy from my carelessness. That stops now. I told your mother that I'm falling in love with you." He watched her eyes widen in shock. "Do you know what she said?"

Millie shook her head.

"She said it won't be easy, but I should keep trying until you hear me. So when I say I want you, I mean I want all of you. From your stubbornness to your sweetness and everything in between. Those are Mary's words, not mine, by the way. Please let me show you. Let me in, Millie."

Millie would have bet the farm that her tear supply was dry for the rest of the year, but she felt them falling and, this time, didn't try to hide her face. "I don't know, Taylor. I don't trust myself with you."

Taylor took a deep breath. "I won't push you, but I would love the chance to earn you."

"I'm scared to love you."

"I know. It's scary for me, too." He rubbed her cheek with his finger. "Fate brought you to me. I don't plan on letting you go. May I kiss you, Millie?"

He pulled her closer and slowly lowered his mouth to hers to savor every second. It was a kiss full of sincerity and promise. Millie wrapped her arms around his waist to pull him closer, but they kept the kiss soft and slow.

When Taylor pulled away, she put her head on his chest and exhaled some of the hurt he caused in their last conversation. They stood at the window, watching the sun rise with all the hope and color they felt inside. Like many of her moments with Taylor, she knew this would be a cherished memory, but this time, she wondered how long the feeling would last. She hugged him tighter and took in the scent of him.

Mary woke and watched them standing by the window. She wasn't sure what was in her daughter's heart, but she worried about her. She closed her eyes to give them some privacy and said a small prayer of peace for her baby girl.

chapter eleven

MARY ROLLED OVER in her hospital bed with a groan and gave an Oscar-winning wake-up so Millie and Taylor wouldn't suspect she had overheard their conversation.

"Mom, are you OK?"

"I'm fine, honey, just getting comfortable. You should go home and get some sleep, though. You'll never be able to get any good rest in that chair. I don't care how comfortable Taylor's lap is. Brooks and Jane are coming in a few hours. I'll be asleep most of that time."

"Not a chance, old woman, I'm not leaving."

"Millie, don't be stubborn. You've got to rest if you're going to take care of all my demands when we get home. I'm thinking of getting a bell."

Taylor laughed and got a swift smack to the shoulder. "Don't encourage her," Millie grinned.

Mary sighed, "I just want to sleep. I know you want to help, but I can't sleep well with you watching me. It's unnerving."

Millie sat on the side of the bed and held her mom's hand. "I'm scared to leave. What if you need me and I'm not here? Again."

Mary sat up and gave her sweet daughter a big hug. "You can pray from your apartment just as easily as you can here, and that's all I need right now. I'm so sorry I scared you, honey, but I'm going to be fine. They have ruled out anything too serious and are just keeping me here to run some tests that will make a little more money for the new wing of the hospital."

Millie laughed and hugged her mom. "You promise you'll call if you need anything?"

"You'll be my first call."

"I'll bring you something to eat when I come back. Text me and let me know what you're craving."

"If you come back without a Diet Mountain Dew, I'll tell everyone in this hospital about that time you peed your pants in third grade."

"Mom!"

Taylor chuckled, "I'll go find a machine that has them right now if I can hear that story."

"You get my sweet girl home safely and make her eat, and I'll tell you either way."

"Yes, ma'am. Sorry, Ms. Mary."

"I hate both of you right now." Millie crossed her arms in a pretend pout.

Mary rubbed Millie's hand and smiled, "Nah, you love us."

They shared a look that only lasted a second but spoke volumes. "I really do," Millie whispered.

"I know you do, honey. I love you right back."

One more hug and a little rearranging to make sure everything was within Mary's reach, and they were headed to the elevator.

"Have you had anything to eat since you got here?"

"The girls brought dinner up from the cafeteria."

"Mil, have you eaten?"

She put her head on his shoulder and sighed, "No."

"I doubt much is open this early. Let's stop at the grocery store and pick something up. I make a mean omelet."

"I'm not really hungry, Taylor. Can we just go home?"

"I'll make you a deal. We'll find a drive-through and take it home." He kissed the top of her head, "You need to eat something, Millie, even just a bite."

"A bite."

They walked onto the elevator without Millie's head leaving Taylor's shoulder. "Taylor, what is wrong with her? Why haven't they figured it out yet?" She turned her face into his arm, "I can't lose her. I'm not ready."

Taylor wrapped his arms around her to let her rest on his chest. "She's strong, Millie. Letting her sleep this morning will only make her stronger. She isn't going anywhere."

She looked up at him and felt the vulnerability that she generally hated. "I need you to keep telling me that."

"I just need you." He bent his head down and gave her a light kiss.

The elevator doors opened to a bright lobby made gray by so many people waiting for news and holding on to hope. It made her hold his hand tighter.

"Do you want to wait here? I can get the car and pick you up."

"No, no, don't be silly. I can go with you. I could use the walk. I haven't had any fresh air since yesterday."

"I'm not too far then, just down that aisle."

They walked in silence for a second, allowing Millie to appreciate the cool breeze. She was disappointed that they reached the car so quickly. "Do you mind if I roll my window down? I love this weather."

"Sure, we'll roll them both down."

"Have you noticed that time seems to be picking up its pace the older we get? It seems like yesterday I was sitting in the park eating ice cream."

"You do that a lot. I used to look out the window and try to figure out what you were thinking about."

Millie turned in her chair to look at him, "Chances are, I was thinking about you."

Taylor lifted her hand to his mouth and gave it a gentle kiss. "Chances are, on any given day, I was thinking about you too."

"What a pair we are."

"Great minds."

Taylor stopped at a red light and let his head fall back on the headrest. It wasn't until that second that she realized how exhausted he must be. She put a hand on his knee to get his attention.

"Let's go home and sleep. Then we'll eat, I promise. You've been up all night, Taylor. You need rest just as much as I do."

"I wasn't tired until now." He turned to look at her, "I'm sorry. I know you have gone through…"

"You went through most of it with me last night. Please, let's just go home."

When the light turned green, he pulled into the next lane to head towards Millie's apartment. When they pulled into the parking lot of her apartment, Taylor parked next to her car. She noticed a note on her windshield but was too tired to think. Reality would wait a bit. Right now, she just wanted to lie down.

She unlocked her apartment door and suddenly realized it was Taylor's first time in her home. It was a mess. She immediately started making excuses and cleaning up. Taylor didn't notice the mess or the fuss she was making. He was simply thrilled to be in her space.

He put his keys, phone, and wallet on the counter. "You know, I have pictured this in my head for a long time."

"What? Me running around like a chicken trying to hide my crazy."

He stepped up behind her and put his hands on her shoulders to stop her from picking anything else up. She leaned her head back on his chest, putting their mouths just a breath apart.

"Please stop cleaning. I like it the way it is." He kissed her gently, "I just want to hold you."

Millie couldn't help herself. She turned into him, wrapped her arms around his neck, and kissed him. It wasn't as gentle as he had been, but she had lived a roller coaster over the last few days and just needed the contact.

"Millie, if we keep this up, we won't get any rest. I can only be a gentleman for so long."

Millie giggled and dropped down from her tiptoes. "We do need rest. Come this way."

She led him to her bedroom and the disaster that it was. "Good grief, I never saw myself as a slob before today, but I'm thinking I may be their poster child right now."

"The bed is all I'm concerned with, and look, it's already turned down and waiting for me."

Taylor slipped his shoes off and plopped into the bed with a deep sigh. She couldn't get over the sight of him lying on her pillow, getting comfortable in her sheets, pulling the covers back for her.

"This is so surreal. You can't imagine how many nights I spent wishing for this." She climbed into bed but didn't lie down. "You know, you're lying on my side."

"I can tell. It smells like you. Come down here."

He pulled her close and hugged her back to his stomach. "I'm going to fall asleep in a second, but don't think for a minute that my thoughts or dreams will be virtuous with you this close." He kissed the back of her neck, "You are intoxicating, Millie. You have no idea how amazing you are to me."

She cuddled into him, wanting to be as close as possible. "Taylor."

"Hmmm."

"Sweet dreams."

She felt his arm tense against her in an effort to hug her, but he was already dozing off. She closed her eyes, enjoying every second of him holding her.

She woke up to a buzzing noise she didn't recognize. Neither of them had moved an inch, which made her think she had nodded off for a few minutes. She lifted her head to see her alarm clock and blinked at it until she was sure she was reading it correctly. They had been asleep for three hours.

Millie slid off the bed, careful not to wake Taylor up. He had held her last night and given her a few hours of sleep, but *he* hadn't slept at all. He looked so peaceful and young lying there.

She watched him pull her pillow to him and curl into it. Even in sleep, he wanted to be near her. It made her want to lay back down to be close to him for as long as possible, but she needed to get up. Hopefully, Brooks was close to the hospital by now, but she wanted to check on her Mom just in case.

She walked into the kitchen and opened the fridge. "Hmmm. Slim pickin's." She closed the door and looked at the first love of her life. Coffee was her breakfast of champions on most days, and this coffee maker had seen her through a lot.

Millie put the water and grounds in the machine and turned it on, waiting for the pot to fill. She poured a cup of water while she waited for the coffee and then put her elbows on the counter and her face in her hands. "Please, let her be alright. Let me keep her a while longer."

The buzzing came again, much louder now, and startled her. She looked across the kitchen at Taylor's phone vibrating wildly and caught it just before it fell off the counter. She didn't need to look to know it was Carrie, but she turned it over anyway and saw her picture on the screen.

When the voicemail picked up and the screen went to its homepage, she saw that he had missed thirteen calls. He got calls all the time for work. Surely, Carrie hadn't called that many times. She was debating on whether to wake him when her phone rang to the tune of "I'm Too Sexy". Brooks hated that as his ringtone, but that only made her keep it.

"Hey, little brother, you here?"

"Yep, got here about fifteen minutes ago. I've been catching up with Mom and Jane. These two are nuts, by the way. They are planning a trip to Moldova, wherever the hell that is."

"Good grief, I feel bad for the doctors now. They are a force of nature together."

Brooks chuckled, "Why are you whispering? Where are you?"

"I'm at home, just woke up. I haven't had my coffee yet. It was a long night."

"I'll bet. I'm sorry I couldn't get here sooner. Do you want me to pick you up? Mom said you were coming later with food. I want in on that order, so we can get it together if you want."

"No, you stay there and be with her. She was missing us yesterday. Text me what everyone wants, and I'll bring it." She looked at the stove. "Geez, it's already 10:30 a.m. I need a shower big time. I'll be there around 12:30 p.m. Does that work?"

"No. I'm a growing boy. I need food."

"Shut up. I'll be there as soon as I can. Text me your order, and make sure she's eaten something for breakfast from the cafeteria." She took a deep breath. "How does she look to you?"

"She looks good, like herself. I kind of expected the worst, so she looks like a movie star to me." He lowered his voice, obviously not wanting Mary to hear the rest. "She's tired, she looks worried."

"Has anyone been in to update her?"

"Not that I know of, but we haven't been here long. Just get here when you can. I'll text you about lunch."

"Brooks, I'm glad you're here."

"Me too, sis. See you in a bit."

She hung up, relieved. Her Mom would be stronger with her "babies" together, and Lord knew Aunt Jane would be probing the doctors and nurses as soon as she could find one. Everything was going to be fine. She leaned over the counter again, trying to focus on the good news and letting some of the fear melt away.

"Shit." She had forgotten about Drew and his offer to pick her up at the hospital. "Shit." She texted him as quickly as she could, knowing there were too many misspellings to count, thanks in part to her rush and autocorrect.

Good morning
I made in home and am completely exhausted.
Going to sleep for a wheel before I go back.
I'm sorry for the short novice,
time seems to be out of my comprehension right now.
Thanks again for everything,
well talk when I'm out of my puma.
M

She put the phone down and her head back in her hands. What in the world was she doing? Reality had waited, but only a few hours. She jumped when her phone buzzed with Drew's reply.

You really must be exhausted.
Reread your text when you've slept
a few hours. I laughed out loud at you
being in a puma, hoping that meant coma.
Seems an odd thing to hope for though.
I'm going to try to write for a while,
but let me know if you need anything.
I'll keep my phone close.
I miss you.

"Shit." This whole situation was headed for the Jerry Springer Show. She had an incredible man who missed her and wanted to be with her. Then there was this beautiful, complicated man in her bed who made her insides turn in circles. She knew Drew was who she should want, but Taylor had already invaded her heart. What she didn't know was how they would ever make it work.

"Waking up in your bed without you in it is a travesty. How long have I been snuggling that pillow?"

She didn't move, only turned her head to see him walking towards her, sleepy-eyed and beautiful. "Good Lord, you're gorgeous."

"Pah! I'll bet." He drug his hands through his hair. "I can feel the Flock of Seagulls action happening up here."

"Want some coffee?" Millie reached to get a mug, but the feel of Taylor behind her stopped her cold.

"I do want some coffee. Thank you."

"How do you take it?" She asked breathlessly.

Taylor bent down and kissed the back of her neck. "Hot."

With that simple kiss, he sent shock waves down her body, making her shiver to her core. "How did you sleep?"

"Mmmmm." He kissed the back of her neck again and leaned against the counter beside her. "Like a rock. It's been a minute since I've pulled an all-nighter."

"Thank you for coming to the hospital, Taylor. I'm sorry I kept you up all night."

"Millie, I was honored to be there and help you, even if it wasn't particularly helpful. I just wanted to give you a moment of peace."

She couldn't help herself around him. Having him all to herself, she couldn't get enough of him. She put the mugs down to wrap her arms around his neck for a hug. "It was very helpful. Thank you."

"I would do anything for you, Millie." He kissed her before she could thank him again. "Please continue, don't let me interrupt."

"I... I just... Um..." She sighed, exasperated. She looked at his mouth and licked her lips, "I ..."

"The I's have it." He kissed her gently, wanting to show her tenderness.

Every inch of her wanted to pull him into her bedroom and take full advantage of having every inch of him to herself. As the kiss grew deeper, his moan snapped her back to reality. He wasn't hers to have. She knew if they were going to have any chance at a real future, they had to take it slow. She pulled back, doing her best to breathe but feeling the burn in her chest.

"Taylor, I'm not strong enough to tell you to stop."

He bent his head down to her shoulder to catch his breath. "Millie, if you want me to stop, I will. I'll never push you." He looked up sincerely, "I want you, Millie, all of you, in every way, every day. You saying no now won't change that." He hugged her as platonically as he could manage in his current state.

She didn't want him to let go but knew she needed to keep her distance. She felt like a child who couldn't make up her mind. Talking about feelings was difficult for her. Talking about *her* feelings was nearly impossible.

She buried her face in her hands, "I'm sorry."

"Our time will come. If it's not today, then I look forward to tomorrow. Or the next day. Or the week after that. If your heart isn't in it, I don't want..."

"My heart is completely in this. That's the problem!" She hated that the tears burned her eyes. It made her want to hide.

"Hey, talk to me. Whatever it is, it's how you feel, so I want to hear. Millie, I love you. Do you hear me?" He pushed her shoulders back just enough to see her face and look into her eyes. "I love you."

A tear fell down her cheek. He loved her. "I love you too," she whispered. She looked down and took a breath. "Carrie called before you woke up."

"Did you talk to her?"

Millie shook her head but didn't look up.

Taylor sighed, "I need you to believe me, Millie. I know I have put us in this mess, but please, please believe me."

Millie put her hands on his face and brought his mouth to hers for a kiss to calm their fears. "I believe you. Honestly, I do, but that doesn't make you any less married. She's calling because she loves you, and I know you love her."

Taylor started to object, but she put her hand over his mouth. "Taylor, stop. I would be disappointed in you if you didn't. You're better than that. She's your family."

He pulled her hand from his mouth and put it on his heart. "You are the most amazing woman I have ever met."

"No, I'm not. I just know how important family is." She looked down again. "That's why I can't do this, as much as I want to. As much as I want to tear every stitch of clothing off you right now. I can't, while you're still… I just can't."

"Then we wait. And as much as I want to tear every stitch of clothing off *you* right now, you're worth waiting for, Mil."

She fell into his arms again, completely at war with herself.

After a minute of holding each other, Millie giggled in his ear.

"What's so funny?"

"I don't know what to do now. I literally can't think of anything else I want to do with you."

"Ha! Gee, thanks."

"No, no, I'm sorry, I didn't mean it like that. I just have to get you being naked out of my mind."

"Well, don't let it go completely. I'm not." He gave her a wicked smile and kissed her nose. "Do you trust me?"

"I'm not sure after that grin."

"Do you trust me?"

"Are we about to do the falling trust exercise?"

He took a deep breath and looked into her eyes for an honest answer. "Do you trust me?"

The room was sparking again, but she knew he wouldn't push her. "I trust you."

"Good, come with me." He pulled her to him and carried her to the bedroom with her laugh in his ear.

"Where is your bathrobe?"

"On the back of the bedroom door."

"Change into your robe and meet me in the bathroom in five minutes."

"You'll need to put me down first."

"That is the only flaw with this plan. Come here." He kissed her again, very sweetly, "Five minutes."

He put her down and kissed her quickly. When he closed the door behind him, she was left alone, smiling like a loon. She took her old robe off the hook and wondered how undressed she should get when she heard the bath start running. "That answered that."

Her heart was racing. Being this close to him in just a robe was sending ripples of excitement through her. Millie looked in the mirror and cinched the belt a little tighter. "There is just no way to look sexy in this old thing." She stood behind the door, waiting for the remaining three minutes to pass. She listened for any sounds, but the running water washed out any hints she might hear.

After what seemed like an eternity, Taylor knocked on the door softly. "Are you decent?"

She opened the door slowly and saw this gorgeous man standing at the door with a small bouquet of roses in hand.

"Where in the world did you get those? I was only in there a few minutes."

"It's smooth, right? Sometimes I amaze myself." He held out the roses. "A beautiful lady should always be surrounded by beautiful flowers."

Millie reached out to take them, awestruck by this man and the unbelievable scene she found herself in. She took the roses with both hands to smell the petals, and both hands managed to hit thorns the size of push pins. "Ouch!" The flowers dropped to the ground, and the blood covered her palms almost immediately.

"Oh my God, Millie! I'm so sorry! I was rushing to get back up here. They are from your neighbor's yard. I saw them last night when I was waiting for you. I didn't think… I'm so sorry! Come into the bathroom. Let's rinse them off."

Her hands hurt, but she couldn't stop the belly laugh that came from watching Mr. Smooth's face go from charming to panic at the sight of the blood. "Taylor, it's fine. I'm sorry I'm laughing, but you should see your face right now."

Taylor pursed his lips together and tried to ignore the laughter and the blood. He never had a strong stomach when it came to blood. He hadn't tested that reflex in a while, but he was already feeling woozy. "I need to sit down."

He fell back against the bathroom cabinet before Millie could catch him. She struggled to lay him on the floor but wanted to make sure he was safe before she checked him out. Being a doctor's daughter had provided gruesomely detailed dinnertime stories and enough common-sense medical knowledge to get her by in an emergency.

"Good grief, you're out cold. Taylor, talk to me. How hard did you hit your head?" Millie massaged his head a little to feel for bumps but didn't find any. She propped his feet up on the counter to keep the blood flowing to the "hot spots," as her Mom would say, and rolled a towel up as a pillow. She got nervous for a second. Whenever she had any sort of medical question, she would call her mom, but with everything going on, she didn't feel like she could do that now.

"Taylor, talk to me. Tell me where you are. Tell me your name. Tell me something."

Taylor's moan sent relief pouring through her. "Taylor, you better talk to me, or I'm going to get that thorn stick you stole and stab you with it."

Taylor grinned, "I should have gone for the mums out front. They are a safer flower."

Millie laughed while she draped a cold, wet washcloth across his forehead, "I find safer flowers incredibly romantic, but then I would have missed the show."

Taylor scoffed and threw his arm over his eyes. "In all the years I have been courting women, I have never in my life been more embarrassed than I am right now. Except maybe when I tried to kiss Lauren Henson in eighth grade, and she told the teacher I was trying to French her in front of the whole class. This ties with that, I think."

"Don't be embarrassed. When I tell and retell this story, I promise to make it a very manly faint."

He moved his arm to look at her with one eye. "I want a blood oath right now that you give me a year before you tell it. Give me time to build my manhood back up."

"Is a blood oath really a good idea? I'm already bleeding. Do you really want to chance adding yours to the mix? I guess since you're already lying down, it might be safe."

"Oh, you're so funny!" He grabbed her around the waist to pull her to him. "Let me see those hands. Are you OK?" He hadn't focused on her robe until then, or rather, what wasn't underneath the robe. Now she was laying on top of him, and it was all he could think of. He traced his fingertips up and down her back. "I'm sorry I ruined this."

"You didn't ruin anything. You made it possible. That water isn't cold yet, and if it is, we'll warm it up."

"We?"

Her face blushed bright red at the idea.

His hand kept running up and down her back, but she could feel the bolts of lightning down to her toes. "Do you feel like you can stand up?"

"I have a gorgeous woman on top of me. Why on Earth would I stand up?"

He lifted his head and kissed her gently. He respected her need to wait, but he couldn't help himself. For just a second, he let himself go and kissed her with all the passion he felt for her. When he squeezed her into him, her moan nearly sent him to the edge of sanity. He rolled her to her back to look at this beautiful woman who made him feel like a teenager.

She was breathless again, a natural reaction when he was near, but he was intoxicating and made her light-headed. Everything in her wanted to give herself to him. Everything in her wanted to pull him closer. She wrapped her leg around him and kissed him.

"Millie. Millie, I need to… Mmmmm, Millie, we have to stop before I can't…" He rolled over to his back to give them a second to think, both feeling fire in their lungs and aching in their core.

"I know, I know. I can't get enough of you."

He looked over at her, still overcome with need but doing his best not to push her. "I want you to say that to me again one day. Over and over again."

"One day, I plan to."

"I'm thinking the bath is definitely cold now. How about we head back to the bedroom? The bathroom floor has lost its appeal."

"Can I be honest with you?"

He pulled her hand to his mouth and kissed it sweetly. "Come here." She curled up next to him with her head on his chest and smiled at how rapidly his heart was still beating. "Always be honest with me. I want to make you happy, Mil, and I don't want any secrets with you."

She kissed his chest and pulled into him tighter. "I could stay in this spot forever."

"Surely there is a more comfy spot you can think of." Her giggle made him want to hold her forever. "Tell me what you are thinking."

"I'm thinking that at this point, if you get in the bed with me, there is no way we're getting out without…"

"Agreed. You're pretty much killing me right now in that robe, and I haven't seen anything yet."

She propped her head up on her hand to look at him. "Another question."

"You need to stop announcing them. You make me nervous." He tucked a hair behind her ear, "Anything."

"It's awkward, and you don't have to answer if you don't want to. I just can't imagine not wanting to be with you. What happened that was so terrible to make you give up? I'm sorry to phrase it that way, but that's what you told me. I just, I… she's amazing. If you can't make it work with her, I don't know how I could…"

"Millie, don't do that. Don't sell yourself short like that. Carrie is amazing in every sense of the word. And I… it breaks my heart that we couldn't make a family or make it work, but I can't keep playing house with someone I'm not in love with and who isn't in love with me. I love her so much. I want to always love her, but I feel like every month that passes, I'm starting to resent her more and more, and the same for her. We put our focus on having a baby and forgot that it should be on each other. It's not her fault it didn't work. It's not mine. It just didn't."

"I know, but…"

"You want to know if something happened that clarified the whole thing for me."

"No," she took a long breath. "I want to know that it wasn't me."

"Oh baby, no. That's not what this is." He sat up and pulled her onto his lap. "I want you to really listen to me, but I'll tell you as many times as you need to hear it until you believe me. My marriage has been ending for years. I just haven't been brave enough to admit it. I've been holding on to it to avoid hurting everyone, me included. One person can't hold on for both. If we had been blessed with children, things might have been easier between us, but I still think our need for it outweighed the reasons we were staying together. It's just time to end it and try to be happy again."

"If there were no me, would you still leave?"

"Eventually, yes. Millie, I swear, this is not your doing. You gave me a reason to hope for happiness again. You make me feel alive again. You make me feel wanted again. But I wouldn't leave if I genuinely thought I could make her happy."

"I'm sorry for you both."

"I don't want to hurt her. She's been through so much pain already. I don't know where I'll go now, but I don't want to prolong it for either of our sakes."

"Your networking skills are unparalleled. Surely, you know someone who can help you find a place you like."

"Well, thank you, but I mean, which city."

Millie sat up with a jolt, digging her tailbone right into Taylor's thigh, making him squeal in pain. "Damn, that's sharp. We've got to get you something to eat and pad that thing up."

"You're moving?"

"I don't know what I'm doing anymore," still rubbing his thigh.

"Don't be coy, Taylor. Where are you going?"

"Please don't pull away from me. Come here." He stood up and held out a hand to help her up. He held her hand and walked to the bedroom.

"When you told me you had taken another job, I went a little nuts. Well, a lotta nuts. I kept Hank talking until the wee hours of the morning about the direction my life was taking, or lack thereof, and what I needed to do to regain control to show you I was worthy. We went to the beach for the weekend. I put a deposit down on a house on the water and accepted a job with a friend who runs sailing tours."

"You did what?" She jumped off the bed to pace. "Good God, Taylor, you changed your world because I got a raise? What happens if they make me a vice president one day? Will you move across the Atlantic?"

"What raise? You said you took a new job."

"It *is* a new job. They've created a position for me. Director of Events. I should have started today, but I called Samantha and told her about my eye. We agreed I would take the day off."

"Are you telling me that I quit Grant and agreed to sail tourists around the coast because you won't be at the same desk you were at last week?" Taylor was struggling to keep his cool. He had no one to be mad at but himself, but the rage was there regardless. "Damn it!"

Millie sat back down on the bed with shaky legs. "You've already quit?"

"I couldn't bear the thought of being there without you, of not seeing you there but still feeling you everywhere, every day. It was rash, but I needed to start fresh." He took a deep breath, "I saw you at the gazebo on Saturday, looking out at the ocean. You took my breath away. I wanted to apologize and beg you to forgive me, but I wasn't ready. I needed to get my head on straight. The next day, I went for a run on the beach. I saw you kiss the author, and the idea that you could be happy with someone else nearly broke me in half. I called Jimmy and accepted the job almost on the spot."

"I saw you," Millie whispered. "On the beach. I saw you walking away, but I thought it was my imagination. I wanted to run to you, but thought I was crazy for thinking you would be there." She looked up at him in awe, "I saw you."

Taylor laid down beside her and pulled her to him. "I'm such an idiot. I've made such a mess of everything. Millie, I don't know how to fix this, but I will. I can't lose you now."

She lay on his chest with all these details running through her head. The woulda, coulda, shoulda's were torturous, so she shut them out, but the reality of everything wasn't much better.

"I don't know how to fix this either, but none of that matters until you are sure of what you want. Pretend you are talking to your old pal Millie for a second, no strings, no pressure. What do *you* want?"

She propped her head up on her hand to look at him. "Taylor, that's all that matters right now. I want to be with you, but I'll never ask you to leave her. I'll never push you to come to me. You have to make that choice on your own. It's the same for the job. If you want to live at the beach, then you should move. I won't tell you to stay. You have to make the choice. No matter what, though, I will support your decision."

Taylor tried not to read anything into what she was saying. She had already told him that she loved him, but a small part of him wanted her to ask him to stay with her. It was the coward's way out, and he refused to put her in that position again.

"I want to be with you. I want to build a future with you. I need to get my life in order first, though. I know you have the author to think about, too. Were you two serious?"

Millie got defensive so quickly. She didn't know where it came from or why, but she could feel herself pulling away. "No, not yet. What you saw was a thank you for being incredibly kind during a traumatic experience." She gently touched her eye.

She knew she was downplaying their weekend together, but it didn't make sense to go into detail now.

"How is your eye today, by the way? Your Mom told me what happened. That must have taken the fun out of your weekend, huh?"

Millie closed her eyes. "Actually, it was a pretty great weekend, all things considered. Being at the beach is my favorite thing."

"It's the same for me. It's why I bought the beach house."

Taylor let out an exasperated sigh. "I have a beach house. I've always wanted a beach house. Now I can't wait to get rid of it."

"Me too," she played with his shirt absently. "I've always wanted a beach house, I mean. Actually, that's what I was thinking about when you saw me on the gazebo. Where it would be, what it would look like, how peaceful it would be."

"Mmmmm, I agree. I'm never as relaxed as I am on the beach." He kissed her sweetly, "Well, at least we know where we'll retire. Everything else is semantics."

Millie smiled but knew there were so many obstacles in their way. She was exhausted again and laid her head on Taylor's chest, feeling like the weight of their world was too heavy for her to carry. "I need to get back to the hospital. Everyone will be hungry soon, and I'm their meal ticket."

She started to sit up, but he held her tight. "Can we just lay here for one more minute, please? I know you need to go, and your Mom is the most important thing right now. I just don't want to leave feeling like this. I want you to believe in me, in us. I have managed to screw up *again*. I can feel you pulling away, and I get it. I really do. I just want you to know that I love you before you get up."

As she lay there looking into his troubled eyes, she thought again how surreal the last few days had been. She rubbed the beard he had grown overnight, which made all his features rugged.

Good Lord, he was gorgeous. And he loved her.

"I'm sorry. I'm trying not to, but I'm still afraid to trust this. It was complicated from the beginning, but we have somehow doubled that. It will take me a minute to catch up to you." She hugged him tightly, "I love you too."

Taylor left Millie's apartment with the determination of ten men. He was going to get his job back at Grant and put his life in motion again. He felt like he had been at a standstill for years, going through the motions of a happy life but knowing it was an award-worthy performance. Millie had given him the resolve to want more for himself, and for Carrie.

He thought of how their life used to be when they couldn't imagine anything more important than each other. How had they let having a baby take that away from them? He drove home on autopilot, trying to remember when they had put any energy into their relationship when it didn't revolve around a baby. He honestly couldn't remember.

He took the responsibility for that. He should have tried sooner, pushed harder, and taken her away from reality more often. She would be hurt when he left, but he genuinely thought she would be happier in the long run. They had been together for too many years for him to misinterpret the feelings behind the looks she was giving him lately. She was miserable, and he was desperate for her not to hate him.

He pulled into the driveway and was surprised to see her car there. He knew there would never be a good time to break all of this to her, but he hadn't wrapped his head around doing it now. He lowered his head to the steering wheel.

He felt like such a disappointment to her. He wanted to make it right. He had prayed for many things over the years but asked for guidance through the conversation they were about to have, it could only help things.

He searched for the courage to say the right thing and reassure Carrie that he was truly thinking of both their futures and happiness.

He opened the front door to a quiet house. It used to be filled with such incredible energy. The air had a life to it that made him feel invincible. They used to run to each other when they got home, eager to hear about their days and grateful to be near each other again. That was years ago. Now, the air was dull, like someone had let the air out of the balloon. He would find her when he got home and ask how her day was, but the interest had waned to polite conversation. That was one of the things that hurt Taylor the most: how cold and polite they had become.

He walked down the hall to his bedroom to change his clothes but saw Carrie sitting on the end of the bed in the master bedroom. She had been crying again, another stab to his heart. He hated that he could never seem to take her sadness away. She deserved to be happy. She deserved to love someone who could make her happy.

He sat down next to her but was afraid to touch her. He never knew what kind of response he would get. She pulled away more often than not, and it hurt him more each time she did. He put his hands on his knees, "Do you want to talk about it?"

She hadn't made eye contact with him yet, but he could see that she had something on her mind. He would give anything to be able to talk the way they used to.

"I was going to leave you today."

The words were soft, but the meaning held a punch. Of all the things he had expected, that was nowhere on his radar. He tried not to be hurt, considering what he had planned to tell her, but the hurt crept in anyway.

"My bags are packed. I have an appointment to look at an apartment this afternoon."

He slowly slid his elbows to his knees. How awful was it that they had gotten to this place of no return, and how ironic was it that it had happened on the same day?

"I looked in the mirror last night and just accepted that a family was not in the cards for me."

She had been saying that for months, and it sliced into his heart deeper each time. "Carrie, you have a family. I am your family. I'm sorry that's not good enough for you, but you have a family."

"It wasn't enough…"

That broke any control of the emotions he was trying his best to keep inside. "Wow! You finally said it! I'm not enough." He stood up to give himself some space from her. "I hope it feels good to get that off your chest. You wouldn't even consider adoption or surrogacy or anything other than you having a baby." He felt his voice crack with grief, "If you had just thought about it, any of it, we could be listening to our children laughing right now instead of talking about leaving each other."

Taylor sighed as he regained control of his frustration. He sat back down next to her to confess his sins when she put a hand on his leg. "Please let me finish, Taylor." She so rarely touched him anymore that it caught him off guard. He nodded to let her go first.

"It wasn't enough, and I'm sorry for that. I don't know why I took it out on you that we couldn't get pregnant, but it was easier than accepting the blame." Taylor started to argue, but she shook her head, "I know you don't blame me, but *I* blamed me. *I* failed over and over again. *I* put us in debt because I wouldn't take no for an answer." Her voice was so deep with grief, "*I* took our relationship for granted and just assumed you would be able to read my mind and know what I needed. Whenever you did something sweet to show me you loved me, it felt like a consolation prize for failing."

Carrie covered her face with her hands. "It all sounds crazy now. I know I've been acting crazy, Taylor. I've been furious for so long, I didn't even see what I was doing to you. Until one night a few weeks ago, you came home happy. You were humming in the kitchen like you used to, and I watched, hiding behind the doorway, smiling at you." She wiped a tear from her cheek. "I knew I hadn't done anything to make you smile in months, and it made me sick to my stomach. I've been taking all my hurt and frustrations out on you, and you've been the only one to stand by me through it all."

She turned to him, needing him to see her. "I am very sorry, Taylor. Not having children is one thing, but this, us, it's all my fault."

"Don't say that. This is not your fault. It's nobody's fault. I just want you to be happy, Carrie. It's your turn to be happy."

"I think we both deserve a chance at that."

"I'm sorry for not trying harder. I should have taken you away from all this and started fresh somewhere."

"The beach."

He laughed at the irony, "Yeah, the beach."

His phone buzzed, but he silenced it and threw it on the bed behind them.

"So it does work."

"What?"

"I've been calling you all morning. When you didn't answer, I thought something was wrong."

"I'm sorry, I was up late last night and put it on silent so I could sleep in this morning. I want to talk to you about that actually…"

"Did you open the picture I sent?"

"Picture? No, I didn't see a picture." He got up to get his phone and scrolled through half a dozen texts from Hank, a text from Jimmy asking when he would be able to talk about the new job and a text from Millie. He skipped over them all for now, but seeing her name sent a wave of love through him. He was already missing her, but he needed to keep his thoughts on the conversation he was about to have with Carrie.

He opened Carrie's text and laughed. "What does that mean?"

She stood up to face him. "What do you see?"

"I see a text that says, *'Will you get fat with me?'*. You couldn't get fat if you wanted to. You eat like a bird."

"True, I need to eat more. Open the picture."

Taylor clicked on the picture and zoomed in to get a better look at it. He blinked at his phone in silence, barely breathing. "Is that a…"

"Yep."

"And it says you're…"

"It does."

"So we're going to…"

"Finally."

He pulled her into a hug before she had time to react. Tears poured down his cheeks. There was no holding back this feeling. He was going to be a father. He was going to have a baby of his own to spoil, love, teach, and adore. He pledged right then in his heart of hearts that he would be a great dad to this child and put all his hope and energy into creating an amazing life for him or her.

Carrie held him tightly, relieved by his reaction. After everything she had put them through, she was deathly afraid he would feel trapped or angry. As her tears fell, she felt the anger and frustrations of the last few years melt away. In that second, she was filled with joy for him. There were new fears, of course, but they were centered around a baby. Their baby.

"I'm so sorry for it all, Taylor."

"Shhh, don't concentrate on that now. When did you find out? How do you feel? Have you seen the doctor? Here, sit down."

She giggled at his misguided chivalry, "I'm fine, I feel fine," but she sat with him anyway to enjoy the moment. "I took the test this morning. I was packing a bag of toiletries and found one last pregnancy test in the box. I don't even know why I took it, really. I just couldn't throw it away. I haven't seen the doctor yet, but I left a voicemail at the office just before you got home."

"Last one in the box." Taylor smiled, "She's our hail Mary."

Carrie beamed at him, "So, it's a *she*, huh?"

"Of course, and she's a daddy's girl."

"Most men want a boy, don't they?"

He looked at her stomach and already felt so much love for this tiny little bean of a baby. "I don't care what's in there. I'm wrapped around all ten of their fingers already."

They sat together awkwardly. Taylor put his elbows to his knees and took a deep breath. He was at war with himself again. He got to the house knowing exactly what he wanted and was finally ready to make a move towards a happier life. Now he sat next to the wife he would always love but knew he was not in love with, who was carrying the baby that he was completely in love with. He had a choice to make, but he needed all the facts first.

"You said you were leaving me today."

Carrie knew they had a lot to work out before any kind of real happiness would be permanently welcomed back into their home again. She wasn't prepared to stay in a marriage of convenience, but the idea of attempting the next eight months alone, not to mention the next eighteen years, scared her to death.

"I thought we had put each other through enough." She looked down in embarrassment, "I thought I had put you through enough."

"Why today? What happened?"

"You didn't come home last night, so I called Hank. When he said you were alright but sleeping at his apartment, I was relieved."

Taylor's stomach twisted in shame. Hank covered for him without question or judgment and must have been texting all night. He would have to see him later and apologize for worrying him.

"I'm sorry I worried you, I just…"

"No, you misunderstand." She paused, debating on how honest to be. If there was any hope of keeping him, though, she needed him to know. "I was relieved… you weren't coming home."

Taylor turned his head slowly to look at her. He didn't know how to react to her indifference anymore. He walked across the room to get a little distance, but it didn't bring any perspective. "Is living with me so awful? I'm serious. I really want to know. Is there something about me that repulses you now? I have seen it in your face for months, no, more than that. For over a year, I have been miserably aware that you don't want me around. I would just like to know why."

"You don't understand. I'm not explaining this well at all."

"Well, do elaborate, Carrie, because I'm here now, much to your regret. I've tried to give you everything you need. You needed time, so we put everything on hold. You wanted to start trying again, so we put everything in motion. You needed space, so I moved into another damn bedroom. You needed your family, so they lived with us for weeks. Just once, just *once*, I wanted you to need me. I was there, ready and waiting and wanting to help. Not once in the last three years have you come to me, needed me, or hell, just given me the time of day."

"Taylor, I'm sorry…"

"I was hurting, too, you know! You weren't going through this alone, whether you secluded yourself or not. It was crushing to go through this God-awful roller coaster, only to be told 'no' over and over again, knowing there was nothing I could do to make it better for us except to start the whole damn process again.

I jumped on that roller coaster, hoping and wishing all over again every single time you did. I was right there in the back seat, crying just as hard when we lost our babies.

I needed someone to tell me everything would be alright. I needed to know you didn't think this was all my fault and that even through this shitty hand we were dealt, you loved me enough to stay with me even if I couldn't give you a baby. I needed to know I was enough for you. I needed any sign that there was love in this house. Now the test is positive, and all I can think is how much I love that child and how disappointing it is that we are its parents."

She lost her breath from the blow of his words. She knew she had been difficult over the last few years, intolerable even, but she hadn't seen his pain until now. She could see the anger behind his words, but the agony of it all was front and center.

She stood up and walked to him slowly. He was facing the window and doing his best to regain control, but she knew it was his turn to be comforted. She had done this to him, and it would be a lifetime before she would forgive herself for it. For now, she could start with a small gesture.

She touched his back and felt the muscles tense. She ran her hand across his shoulders, back and forth, the way she used to do when he was stressed about work. "Taylor, none of this is your fault. It never dawned on me that you would think that. I've been taking the blame so long, I didn't see what it was doing to you."

She kept rubbing until she thought he would accept more. She stepped closer and pulled him into a hug, whispering, "I'm sorry," over and over again.

Taylor unraveled from his very core. He grabbed Carrie into a hug and wept. All the years of disappointments and trying to be strong crashed into pieces inside him. He cried for the loss of their hope, the death of the babies he would never hold, the fear of losing this baby, and the shell of a marriage he had been in for far too long. He hated that he was breaking apart like this, but there was no holding it in now.

Carrie walked him to the bed so she could hold him and take as much of the burden away from him as she could. He deserved to be held, to be loved. She couldn't remember the last time she had wanted to hold him. She held his head at her chest and rubbed his hair while he let some of the torture of infertility, loss, and heartache escape.

Utterly exhausted, he fell asleep listening to the beat of Carrie's heart and a hand on her stomach.

chapter twelve

TAYLOR FELT HER fingers combing through his hair. She had the most incredible touch. It left pins and needles in its path. She was rubbing his head so gently, but it was waking every part of him. He felt the wanting spread through him and grinned at the way his control evaporated when she was near. He loved her. He loved how she loved him. They were going to make each other so happy.

He lifted his head to reach her neck. He loved the spot just under her jaw. It was so soft and always made her moan. Her moans sent shockwaves through him, and he was ready for the next wave to hit. He stretched a little further and caught a scent from his past. That wasn't Millie's perfume. He had given it to Carrie to wear on their wedding day, and she had worn it ever since.

Taylor bolted up and out of what he saw now as a dream. Carrie lay next to him nervously, smiling, worry surrounding her eyes. "It's alright, Taylor. You just fell asleep."

He looked down as her hand covered his, and her thumb rubbed his knuckles. "Hey, everything is going to be alright."

The shock of seeing her instead of Millie was the worst form of guilty torture. He pulled his hand out from underneath hers to rub his face. Surely, this was all a bad dream he was about to wake from. "How long was I out?"

"A little less than an hour. You must have needed to escape for a while." She looked at him apprehensively. She hoped he would wake up rejuvenated and excited for their future, but she saw the opposite now that he was up. "How's your head? When I cry that hard, I always have a raging headache afterward."

"Yeah. It's pretty fierce."

"There is some medicine in the bathroom. I'll get it."

"I can get it."

Taylor walked into the bathroom they used to share and barely recognized it. She hadn't done much to it, he didn't think, but it had been over a year since he had been in this room. How was that possible? How did he live in this house but not know the rooms within it?

He looked in the mirror and saw a ghost of the man he once was. Being in this house for a few hours had stolen the lighthearted, happy person he had been with Millie. He couldn't live here anymore. The walls were like prison bars now, and no matter how hard he fought to see their blessings, this house wasn't one for them any longer.

He splashed water on his face to clear away the confusion and sighed deeply, "Guess that only works in the movies."

What was he going to do? He walked in the door today, ready to leave. Hell, Carrie was even ready to quit. This baby, this perfect little creature, changed the game completely. Was he willing to sacrifice his happiness for the child he had prayed for so many times?

He looked in the mirror again, only this time he saw himself grin. He was a father. This baby girl would count on him to love her and keep her safe. He was a dad. His grin turned into a full smile. He could see them playing together, building sandcastles together, walking to school together, and cuddling up while he told her how beautiful she was. He was positive it was a girl, and for whatever reason, he was positive this time would be different. This time, he was going to hold his baby.

The decision to stay would hurt in many ways, but this child was his ultimate blessing. The impact of his prayers over the years hit his body like a thunderbolt. *"Show us a way to make our lives a blessing rather than a burden."* He had prayed to God for a blessing, and although it wasn't what he had in mind now, they had been provided a blessing nonetheless. There was no way he could turn his back now.

He walked out of the bathroom to find Carrie on the phone. He sat beside her and recognized the voice on the other end of the line. Brittany Carroll had been with them from the beginning and was an incredible doctor, and friend, at this point. He laughed when he heard her squeal, "We're having a baby!"

Dr. Carroll heard him laugh, "Is that Taylor?"

"Yes, ma'am," Carrie smiled at him.

"Put that fine husband of yours on the phone for a minute."

"You've done it now." She laughed as she handed Taylor the phone.

"Dr. Carroll, so good to hear from you. How is the prettiest MD in Raleigh doing today?"

"Oooh, you are terrible! Don't you start that flirting in front of your pregnant wife. Women get crazy when they're pregnant, son, don't say I didn't warn you."

"Yes, ma'am. I'll watch for it."

"You think I'm kidding? You just wait until she's crying over her cucumbers because they aren't pickles, even though she hated pickles yesterday."

"No cucumbers. Got it."

"Now, when are you going to come see me? I'm making room for you at 1 p.m."

"Today?"

"Yes, today! We need to check our girl out, make sure everything is doin' what it needs to be doin'. Has she been taking those vitamins I gave her?"

Carrie nodded her head. She could hear most of the conversation, even on the other side of the room.

"Yes, ma'am, she has. She was hoping you have some that are just a little bit bigger, though. These vitamins are only an inch long. Where's the challenge in that?"

"I'm gonna pop you when you get here if you keep that up."

He looked up at Carrie, who stood near the window, smiling. "What did she say?"

"The good doctor said she will pop you if you don't take those vitamins."

"Boy! I will drive over there and do it now if you don't stop it."

"You know we love you, Brittany. You think this one is the one?"

"Honey, no one deserves this more than the two of you. You be here at 1 p.m. and tell her to drink something before she comes. One day, I'm going to discover a way to test hormone levels without making these poor women pee in a cup every time they see me. That isn't anybody's good day. I'll see you later."

"Bye, doc."

He ended the call and shook his head at the phone. "That woman is a fruitcake. You know she will be the first one over here when she finds out this kid has scraped her knee. She'll bandage her up, then slap the shit out of us for letting it happen."

"I'm so glad we found her. She never gave up, even when we did."

"She's a keeper. She wants to see you at 1 p.m. It wasn't really up for discussion."

"I heard. That work for you?"

"Yep, I just need to make some phone calls." Taylor walked out of the room, wondering how things could be so different but feel the same. He knew for certain now they weren't in love with each other anymore, but there was a comfort level between them that so many years together had awarded. He shook his head at the babies they were when they met and the grown-ups they were now. The grown-ups had ruined everything.

He closed the door of his office and sat at his desk. His father gave him this desk when they moved into the house. It had been his father's and grandfather's before that. When he sat at this desk, he felt pride, like years of men before him were there to support whatever he was working on. It gave him a sense of power that he didn't feel anywhere else.

He let his head fall back on his chair and closed his eyes. He needed to wrap his head around everything that was happening. He had to make a decision quickly. He tried to clear his head, but Millie's face haunted him. She deserved to know what was going on, but it wasn't fair to tell her everything until he had a plan. He rubbed his face with his hands in frustration. How could this be his life?

In one conversation, Carrie had told him she was leaving him and that they were having a baby. He wasn't sure what the next step was, but he felt robbed of the joy that a baby should bring. He needed a voice of reason to help him see things clearly, even if he didn't like what he heard. He dialed Hank's number, hoping for a few words of wisdom from his friend.

"Man! I've been worried about you. Where in the hell have you been? Carrie called last night looking for you."

"I know, I'm sorry. I'm at the house now, everything is fine. Thanks for covering for me."

"Do I even need to ask where you were?"

"It's not what you think, Hank. I went to her apartment and ran into a friend of hers who told me she was at the hospital."

"What happened? Is she alright?"

"She's fine. Her mother is sick, though. I walked into the hospital room and found her crying. She fell asleep on my lap. I stayed until she woke up this morning."

"You couldn't have texted me that and let me know you weren't dead somewhere. And where have you been since then?"

"I know; I'm sorry, Hank. Really. There's more, though."

"What more could you possibly pile on to all of this?"

"Carrie is pregnant."

Taylor felt shock in his silence. Hank cried right along with them through a lot of the heartbreak. "Are you sure?"

"She told me when I got here. We have a doctor's appointment this afternoon."

Hank let out a deep sigh and a somber "Congratulations."

"Thanks."

"How far along is she?"

"I don't know. I'll give you the details after the appointment."

The silence wasn't awkward. Both men were trying to think through the details, and they were good enough friends to know it. Taylor broke the silence first, "I can't believe this."

Another sigh from Hank let Taylor know he understood his full meaning. "It's a lot, that's for sure. You just found out about the baby. I wouldn't make any big decisions until you've had a minute to let that settle."

"Yeah."

"You were going to leave her, weren't you?"

"Yes. I was going to talk to her today, but she hit me with the news before I could. And in a dark twist to the story, I walked into the bedroom to find her bags packed. She was going to leave me until the test came back positive this morning."

"Shit. That throws a wrench in the celebration, doesn't it?"

"I don't know what to think anymore. I'm head over heels for this baby already. I want to be a great dad. It deserves the best life I can give it. Does that mean I stay in a marriage where both parents want out? Or do I leave and make a happier life for myself but risk not being with this child from the start?"

"The circumstances could be better, but T, they could be so much worse too. You said the appointment is this afternoon?"

"Yep." Taylor put his head back against his chair and closed his eyes again with a sigh.

"Hey. You'll know what to do when the time comes." He hated knowing his friend was in this kind of pain. "And if not, just pull out that Magic 8 Ball you used to have."

Taylor's chuckle felt sad. He knew Taylor and Carrie had been unhappy for a while, but he also knew they wanted a baby more than anything. He didn't envy the punishingly hard decision ahead of them.

"I need to get some work done. I've been... distracted and am behind. Thanks for everything, Hank."

"I'm always here, man. You'll let me know how the appointment goes?"

"Yeah. Bye." He let a minute of silence pass, willing the decision of his fate to present itself.

He opened his email and saw far too many unread messages. After reading several without retaining any information, he knew now was not the time for work.

Taylor looked at the phone in his hand, fearing and hoping Millie would call. He wanted to be with her, to love her, and to build a loving and adventurous life with her. What was worse, he truly believed they would be happy. If he chose to stay here, he wouldn't just be breaking her heart but his own as well. He could feel his stomach churning at the idea of hurting her and decided to call Jimmy to give the nausea a minute to pass.

Carrie walked into the office to see Taylor smiling, which she took as a good sign. She wanted him to be happy about the baby. She *needed* him to be happy about the baby because in the darkest depths of her heart, she wasn't sure she was, and that doubt was tearing her apart.

This child deserved to have two loving, devoted parents. They would always be devoted to the baby, but she wasn't sure she wanted that from Taylor.

She tapped her watch to let him know it was time to leave and quietly walked out of the room. She stood in front of the mirror at the front door and saw the reflection of someone she didn't recognize anymore. She knew it wasn't the fear of losing another baby that kept her from being excited. It was the fear of losing more of herself in whatever was next for her. For them.

"Sorry to keep you waiting. You ready?"

Carrie looked at Taylor in the mirror behind her. He used to thrill her every time he walked into the room. She wondered if that feeling would ever return. Comfort had replaced that thrill a long time ago, and it crushed her to realize she hadn't missed it. "Ready."

They were completely silent on the way to the appointment. Neither of them had the energy for small talk. There was too much at stake, too many big questions that needed answers. So, they looked out at the city passing by, feeling more alone and uncomfortable than ever before.

They maintained the silence up the elevator to the fourth floor. Oaks Ob/Gyn was a state-of-the-art practice in the heart of downtown Raleigh. For Taylor and Carrie, its walls were marked with memories of loss. This was the place their dreams had been crushed over and over again. They had walked in this very door seven times now with the hope of becoming parents. Today made eight.

"So, it's true! Come here and give me some sugar!" Ginny was the head nurse of the practice and had become the southern aunt they would always consider family.

"Dr. Carroll told me you were coming, but I didn't want to believe it. Now you're here, and I just want to squeeze you!" Never one to speak figuratively, she proceeded to squeeze the air from Carrie's lungs in a hug that would have sent a linebacker to his knees.

"You're next, hot shot. Come here!" Taylor, being second, had time to throw his arms around her waist to prevent the rib crushing. "You two go sit down. I'll check you in and tell her you're here. Lordy, lordy, I feel good about this one." She turned around and hurried through the door to find the doctor.

Taylor chuckled, "Do you realize we just had a full conversation with her without saying a word."

"She's excited. I think it's sweet." Carrie sat down in the colorful waiting room. "I should have brought a snack."

"We can get something on the way home if you want." Taylor sat down beside her, "Do you want me to wait here? When you go back, I mean."

"What? Why?"

"I just don't want to make you uncomfortable."

"Nothing about that foot-long wand is going to be comfortable. Just stay by my head."

"Carrie, I need to tell you something…"

"Alright, you two, she's ready for you." Ginny was beaming as she opened the door for them.

"My favorite couple is here at last! I can say that 'cause there's no one else here. Come here and hug me, handsome. It's been a minute!"

"Dr. Carroll, it always amazes me that you get more beautiful every time I see you. Does your husband know how lucky he is?"

Taylor gave her a side hug and wasn't surprised when she wrapped both arms around him and held on.

"Oh yes, he does, son. I make sure to tell him every day. And how is our mommy-to-be doing?"

"She's fine," Carrie giggled. "But you better throw a beautiful my way, too. I'm feeling left out of the pretty people club."

"Honey, let me tell you something. I looked in the mirror the other day and thought, 'Who is this old woman?' You know what I did, I mean right then and there? I told myself I earned these grays, laughed these lines, and ate those cheesecakes, and I wouldn't change a thing. You're beautiful, just the way you are. Tell her."

Taylor was looking at his texts and wasn't ready for the blow to the arm. "Ouch! What in the world?"

"I said, tell this woman she is beautiful."

"She is extraordinary."

"That's better. Now come back here, and let's take a look at this beautiful baby we're having." She led them through the doors to the exam rooms. "We'll meet you in room two, honey, but I need you to head that way to the bathroom and fill up the cup."

When she heard the bathroom door close, Dr. Carroll rolled a stool to the chair near the exam table. "Have a seat, sir. I want to talk to you in private. I want to know where you two are at this point. The last time was rough. The worst one of the losses, I'd say. I want to know that you are going to be there for her, no matter what."

He took a deep breath and ran his hand through his hair. He had absolutely no idea how to answer.

"I see," she sighed.

"Each time has cracked us a little. Last time... last time broke us. Both of us."

"And yet, here we sit. With a baby that did not come from thin air and without my help, I might add."

Taylor thought back to that night. The only night in almost a year. "I think we were trying to fix something the easy way. You don't have to talk if you're... you know."

It pained her heart to see this strong man, once so full of life, so miserable. "The Lord certainly has a plan for each of us, you know that. I'm sorry this has been your journey. I'll never understand why such good people have had so much heartbreak. It's not for me to know, but I'll tell you this. She needs you. That baby needs you. You may feel broken, but the love of family can heal you in ways nothing else can. The love and trust of this child can make your family's heart whole again."

She put a hand on his knee, "Don't miss out on a future of such incredible love because the past was hard. Embrace that hurt, learn from it, and make the decision to give this baby a lifetime full of love so that when it's their turn to hurt, they know they can overcome anything because they have parents who will love them through it all."

Taylor was choking back tears. To Dr. Carroll, it was a sign that she had gotten through to him. To Taylor, it was a sign that his decision was made the second he found out about the baby. He wanted Millie with all his heart, but this baby was a part of him, and needed his love more.

"But that's just my opinion, and nobody asked me. It would be unethical for me to tell you what to do but think about it anyway. And here's our guest of honor. You ready to see that gorgeous little peanut?"

Back in the car, Taylor held the picture in his hands and saw the hopes, the fears, the excitement, and the future. It was all there in this little black-and-white picture. He was going to be a dad. They were already more than ten weeks along, which made it feel different this time. He could see this little girl playing in the ocean so clearly.

"Taylor, can you start the car? It's getting kind of stuffy in here."

"Oh, I'm sorry." But he couldn't take his eyes off the picture.

"Do you want me to drive so you can keep looking at the picture?"

"No, no. I'm... I just... it's different now. Do you feel it? Something is different."

"Let's hope."

"I talked to Jimmy. He wants me to come to Sunset and help him with the business. He wants to expand it and for me to be his partner." He didn't add that he had already accepted the job. He looked at Carrie with a mix of hope and fear. "He wants me to start as soon as possible."

"Oh. And you want to?"

"I do. I want a fresh start." The circumstances had changed, but it was the truth.

"I see." The tears stung her eyes, but she refused to guilt him into staying. "If that's what you want, I understand. We can sell the house. I can move in with my parents for a while until I get..."

"What? No! I'm asking if you want a fresh start with me?"

"You want me to come?"

"I want you both to come."

She didn't have any words to describe the tug of war in her heart, so she buried her head in his neck and wept.

He lifted her chin to look her in the eyes. "I can't promise it will all work out. I don't think it will be easy, but I love this baby and will do my best by her."

"You're so sure it's a she?"

Taylor smiled and looked at the picture again. "She's the most beautiful thing I've ever seen."

Laughing, Carrie smiled at the picture with him. "I think she's the size of a strawberry."

"A beautiful strawberry." Taylor looked up, determined to give the child in the picture the best life possible. "What do you think? Are we beach-bound?"

With tears streaming down her cheeks, she tried to kiss him like she used to, with passion, love, and partnership.

"Beach bound." She hugged him tight so he couldn't see the panic on her face. That kiss had proven that although she loved him dearly, the passion for him was no longer in her heart.

Taylor held her, accepting the commitment he just made and feeling his heartbreak. He would never hold Millie again. Never hear her laugh. Never feel the love she offered him so purely. What killed him, though, was that he would be the reason for her heartbreak. He would be the man who promised her the world and then stole it from her. He would be the cause of her loneliness. He held on to Carrie and hoped with all his heart that she could love him enough to make him forget.

MILLIE HURRIED AROUND GETTING ready, still smiling from the morning. She still felt him there even after he had kissed her goodbye. She wondered if there would ever be a time when she looked at her bed that she wouldn't see him in it. Her bathroom floor certainly would never be dull white tiles ever again. She stopped brushing her hair for a second to roll her eyes at the idea of having a gorgeous man in that position on the bathroom floor. "Only you."

She checked her phone to read through the food orders and rolled her eyes again at the sheer volume of food Brooks was ordering. "Growing boy, huh?" she muttered. She locked her apartment and passed the now infamous rosebush on her way to the car. Her hands were still sore from the thorns. Between her head and her hands, she was glad to be headed to the hospital, where doctors would be available if anything else went wrong.

Millie stopped at the car and saw the note on the windshield. She recognized Cate's handwriting right away.

*Let me know how Mom is doing tomorrow,
then call me so I can catch up with you on the
crazy train. I've met them both now. I'm ready
to pull my degrees out and diagnose.
You know I love you, C*

She smiled at the note and the grilling she knew Taylor must have gone through last night. And then there was Drew. In any other situation, she would have thought she had won the lottery. He was perfect. A part of her wished life had introduced them sooner, but she didn't feel like she had a choice. She loved Taylor, and waiting would only make telling Drew worse.

She got out her phone but thought he deserved to hear this in person. She refused to be a coward when it came to him. He deserved more than that. He deserved everything. She sent him a text asking him to meet her later that afternoon at the hospital.

She had barely gotten her seatbelt on before his reply popped up.

So glad you are out of your puma, those can be tough to escape from. Sounds like a plan. Let me know if you need me to bring anything to the hospital. I hope Mary is feeling better today.

She giggled at the puma comment and smiled at him wishing her Mom was alright. He had a great heart. She hated the idea of hurting him. As she put the phone in the cup holder, another message popped up. As soon as Millie saw Rory's name, she felt like scum.

I've texted you twice. Do I need to drive over there??? How is Mom?

She called her immediately to give her what little information she had and to apologize for not texting sooner. She wanted to tell Rory all about the last few hours, but when she asked about Drew, she couldn't bring herself to talk about it. She couldn't get to the hospital upset. Mom needed her to be strong and focused. They set up a dinner date, and Millie promised to give all the details then or get pounded. Only Rory could make that sound supportive.

She made it all the way to Mary's hospital door before nearly dropping the tray of drinks and bags of food. It was a lot for anyone to carry, but Millie wasn't exactly known for her grace. She kicked the door gently because trying to knock would have been an instant disaster.

Brooks answered her knock with a big hug and a great catch of two of the bags. "What are you doing, weirdo? Why didn't you call me to help you?"

"I didn't want you to eat everything before I got it up here. You owe me like fifty bucks for all this food, by the way. Don't you eat at school?"

"Of course I do, but I don't have a delivery girl as pretty as you to bring it to my door."

"You're full of sh…"

"Young lady, clean up that mouth. We have company."

"Sorry, Mom, but Aunt Jane doesn't count as company."

Jane laughed as she stood up to hug Millie, "Child, please. I've known this woman far longer than you two, and I can assure you that you learned that language from her. How's the head?"

The whole room had a belly laugh and made life feel normal for a second. "It's OK today. Thanks for driving up with him today, Jane."

"Well, my schedule was free, so I thought I'd see what the fuss was about. Plus, on the way here, I made Brooks stop at that nice thrift store off Glenwood Avenue. I found a picture frame for fifty cents and some solid brass candle sticks for two dollars. She wanted ten for them if you can believe it, but I handed them right back to her and said I only had two-fifty on me."

Jane was notorious for finding amazing deals at thrift shops all over the East Coast. She could walk into a store and, within minutes, spot a treasure that the rest of us would pass without thought. She owned an 8,000-square-foot home in a beautiful neighborhood that Millie was sure to have cost a fortune, and she was willing to bet everything she owned that Jane had decorated and furnished every inch of it for less than a thousand dollars. She was brilliant when it came to haggling and had a gift for making something used look brand new.

"That poor woman had no idea who she was dealing with."

"Nope. But she will. I'm adding that one to my list of stops." Jane winked.

"I look forward to seeing your finds. And what about you, gorgeous? How's the patient today?" Millie bent down to kiss her mother on the cheek. She felt warm again and looked so much better. Rested. Alive.

"Oh honey, I'm fine. I'm going home today."

"Says who?" Millie looked at Brooks accusingly, "I told you to text me with updates."

"No one," Mary smiled, "I just know it. You can't keep a healthy person in a hospital. I think I was just tired. I feel great now."

"Has the doctor been in at all today?"

Jane gave Millie the rundown of every nurse who had come in, any vitals taken, or bathroom breaks that had happened since she arrived. "That!" Mary raised her voice a little in a grin of sisterhood. "That right there is why I hated studying with you in college! You remember everything without even having to think about it. It's not natural. And leave my bathroom visits off the checklist, if you don't mind."

They laughed, ate, and told tales like they were at her Nannie's kitchen table when the doctor came in.

"What is going on in here? It seems I've found all the troublemakers in one room."

Everyone in the room chuckled at the familiar face. Dr. Brandon James was an old family friend who had worked with Mary for years. He was a tall man with broad shoulders and a deep southern drawl that had a soothing quality to it despite his size. Millie trusted him completely and felt immediately reassured when she stood up to hug him. Her mother was in the best hands.

"Young lady, what in the world has happened to you? Your mother worked hard making that head. You should take better care of it."

"I try, but things just kind of happen to me."

"I'll find a helmet you can wear when you leave the house. Maybe one with the Spice Girls on it."

"You're never going to let me live that down, are you?"

"That is still the best costume I've ever seen, darlin'. You sang that song a hundred times until you were hoarse. You wouldn't be interested in a quick performance, would you? I could use a good show."

Brooks chuckled, "Um, I could definitely use a good show and I think it would make Mom feel better."

"You people aren't hearing anything today," she lovingly swatted Dr. James on the arm. "I want to hear about Mom's results. Any news?"

He sat in the chair next to Mary and patted her hand. "How are you feeling?"

"I got some Diet Mountain Dew, so I'm doing much better."

"No doubt, thanks to the troublemakers here smuggling it in for you. And how is your breathing? Any trouble?"

"Give me the results, Brandon. I've known you for twenty years. I know when you are worried. You're making me worry. Just say it."

The group found chairs and were surrounding the bed, but Mary's admission of worry sent chills down their spines. Dr. James took a deep breath and patted Mary's hand again before sitting in the chair. "Sarcoidosis." He leaned forward again and spoke to his friend as a colleague. He wanted to distract her from the worry with her medical logic long enough to reassure her that she would be fine.

When they had gone through the technical jargon, Jane spoke up first. "You two are going to have to translate everything you just said. I'll be the first to admit that I'm no doctor. It sounds to me like you get paid to make up a whole lot of words."

Mary smiled at the three of them sitting around her bed. They were her favorite people in the world and were holding their breaths, waiting for the worst and hoping for the best. "Sarcoidosis. It's a growth of inflammatory cells in my lungs."

Millie shifted forward to put a hand on Mary's foot. Any breath that had been in her was replaced by an ache. All she could manage was a whisper, "Cancer?"

"No honey, not cancer. This is good news. I mean, I don't like that I have it, but the point is I can *live* with it."

Dr. James spoke up, "I didn't mean to scare you, Millie. Sarcoid is most commonly found in the lungs and lymph nodes. She works in a hospital every day, so there is no telling what she's been breathing in, but her body didn't like something, which sent her immune system into overdrive. It would explain why she's been coughing so much lately."

"It wasn't a cold?" Millie thought back to all the cough drops her Mom had been eating. "But wait, she couldn't breathe."

"It wasn't a cold. She couldn't breathe because Mary here also has bronchitis. We'll get her on antibiotics for that. I like it much better when my patients breathe well. Bottom line, most people live very healthy lives with little to no treatment."

Brooks didn't like the words 'most people.' "Doc, you know we're not most people. What about the other people?"

Dr. James looked him in the eye, "In many cases, it goes away on its own. In some cases, however, it can last for years. And then there are the few cases, it has been known to cause organ damage." He looked around the room, "Mary is healthy, she's active, and she's strong. I truly believe she will be fine. I wouldn't say it otherwise."

They had dozens of questions, and he stayed with them until everyone had a clear understanding of Mary's diagnosis. He received big bear hugs from everyone, including Mary, who was already out of bed and packing. "I'll have someone come in with discharge papers as soon as they are ready. Don't you go anywhere until you sign them, woman."

"Alright, but I can sign them tomorrow when I come in."

"Mary, no. You're taking a week off." He gave her the look of an impatient parent, and Millie nearly laughed out loud when she watched her mother concede.

"I'm going to get a drink and text the girls the news. Anyone need anything?"

"Nope, still have mine from lunch," Jane scoffed. "You know, sodas cost a dollar and fifty cents here. You need a loan just to buy a drink. Forget what they're about to charge you for a Tylenol. I brought some with me, by the way. I'll only charge half of what they're asking."

"Jane, it's on me," shaking her head with a giggle. "You want a refill?"

"No, thank you, sugar."

"Well, I do. Cherrywine, please, two of them." Brooks leaned back in his chair with a grin. "What? One for the road."

"You're a goober. I'll be right back."

Millie sat next to the vending machines to type an all-clear group text to her girls. It felt amazing to breathe again, full breaths without the worry, or at least as much of the worry. Her Mom was going to be alright. She closed her eyes and tilted her head back, "Amen and thank you," she whispered.

Not surprisingly, it took only seconds for the replies to start pouring in. The girls were just as relieved as she was, and she knew it. They loved Mary like a second mother, almost from the minute they met. She read through the texts smiling and was replying to their questions when Drew's text popped up.

Just thinking about you.
Hoping for good news…

He always knew the perfect thing to say. Simple, but perfect. She felt terrible again, but she needed to talk to him.

Just talked to the doctor.
Are you free?

She took a deep breath. She envied whoever was lucky enough to end up with him.

She looked for a text from Taylor but didn't see one. She had texted him earlier, but his plate was full today. She wished she could help him in some way but knew what he needed was time. She texted him again to share the good news about Mary.

Taylor was still holding the ultrasound picture when Millie's text came through. He was sitting at his desk holding everything he had ever dreamed of and knew at that moment, he was sure. He couldn't give Millie any hope. If this was going to work, they had to part ways forever. He didn't want this to be any more cruel than it already was for her. He would make her hate him so she could move on and find the happiness she deserved. His heart seized at the thought of her not loving him, but he wanted her to have a full and happy life.

She had just finished buying the drinks at the vending machine and was juggling everything when her phone rang. "Hello."

"Hi. Can you talk for a minute?"

"Taylor! Hey!" She nearly dropped everything at the sound of his voice. "How are you? Did you get my text? Mom's going to be fine, it's just …"

"I need to talk to you. Where are you?"

Caught off guard by the curtness, she walked towards the front door of the hospital. "I'm still at the hospital, walking outside. Taylor, what's the matter?"

"I've been doing a lot of thinking since this morning." His palms were sweating, his head was throbbing, and his heart was breaking. "I don't know what came over me. I mean, you're pretty and all, but I'm married. I have responsibilities here, and I can't let what I'm sure would be great sex ruin that."

Millie stood frozen in the sunshine of the hospital parking lot. Her blood was running ice cold. She felt her body numbing and heard her ears ringing. "Taylor… I…what are you saying? We just…"

"Thank God we didn't go too far. I have come to my senses, and I hope you do too. I won't be at Grant any longer, so the punishment of seeing you every day is gone." Now, he felt sick to his stomach. He wanted to hold her. "I'm sure you'll find someone new to charm soon. You're an amazing girl. I have to go. I'm taking Carrie out to dinner. I'm glad your Mom is alright. Bye, Millie."

Taylor hung up before he could beg her forgiveness. He was shaking when he put the phone down next to the picture. His stomach was churning enough that he headed to the bathroom, hoping to vomit all the vile words that he had just said to someone he knew he would love forever.

Millie stood with the dead phone at her ear. The whole conversation was so surreal. How could he have said those things to her? *He* had come to *her* last night. He had been so kind and loving. She told him how afraid she was to love him, but he held her and whispered all those fears away. Now she was left empty, dazed, and feeling ridiculous for ever allowing herself to love him.

She dropped the cans on the grass and sat on a bench, weeping at the pain of having her heart truly broken for the first time. She could feel herself changed forever. From now on, she would keep her heart for her own and allow others only glimpses of it. She felt the happily ever after fantasy drain from her. She wept harder at the rage she felt for this man she loved so much. He had shattered her in ways only he could have, and she hated him for it. No, worse than that, she hated that she couldn't hate him.

Drew spotted her from the parking deck and sprinted to hold her. Breathless and scared, he scooped her up and put her on his lap. He scared her at first, but when she saw that Drew had come to be with her, it only made her cry harder. This wonderful man had literally raced to be by her side, while the man she loved had broken her into pieces.

"What's happened, Mil? What did the doctor say? Whatever it is, I'm here. We'll get through this together. You're not alone."

She hadn't thought she could sob any harder, but his words were, once again, perfect. She tried to take deep breaths, but she wasn't able to just yet. "Mom's OK," is all she could get out.

"She's alright? She's going to be fine?"

Millie shook her head while making an effort to get control of herself.

"All you said in the text was that you had talked to the doctor and wanted to talk. Then I saw you crying... Girl! You scared the hell out of me!"

She saw this scene through his eyes for a second and sat up straight. "I'm so sorry. I didn't mean to scare you. I just... I wanted to talk to you about..." She started to sob again.

"No, no honey, it's alright. I was close by anyway, and I wanted to see you." He pulled her to him again and swayed back and forth while he brushed the hair from her tear-soaked cheek. "I know how strong you've been. Your strength is one of the things that amazes me about you, but you don't have to be strong with me. I'm here either way. I'm not going anywhere. Just take your time and let it all out."

She clung to him in that moment like a lifeline. She felt anything but strong but wanted to believe she would be alright again. Still tearful but gathering control, she sat up to look at him. "It looks like this shoulder went for a dip in the pool."

He looked at the tear-drenched shirt and chuckled. "That better be all tears." Her giggle bubbled up but came without a smile. "I guess this is why gentlemen carry handkerchiefs for damsels in distress. All I can offer is my sleeve. I can just roll it up when you've loaded it up."

"That's disgusting," but another giggle came with a grin that time. "I can't even imagine what my face looks like right now, but my head is killing me."

"Well, I imagine if we sweet talk someone in there, they may be able to find you a pill to fix that. As for your face," he stroked her cheek, "I've never seen anyone more beautiful. Your eyes are the most brilliant blue."

She would have scoffed at the beautiful comment, but she could feel he meant it. "Thank you."

"Your eyes are what love poems are written of. They are amazing. You are amazing."

"Drew, I need to…"

"Can I tell you something first? I'm sorry to interrupt, but if I don't say this now, I'll chicken out."

She nodded at him, "You're no chicken. Go ahead."

"I'm so incredibly grateful that your Mom is going to be alright. I want to hear more about that, by the way. I haven't stopped thinking about you since yesterday. Actually, since Saturday. Well, if I'm being honest, since the first book launch meeting months ago. For me, you have become an unattainable fantasy that somehow landed at the other end of my Frisbee." She rubbed her bandage and grinned. "This weekend was a dream for me. I hate how it happened, of course, but I can't in good faith tell you that I would take it back."

He put her hand in his. He was floundering, he was a writer, and he couldn't find the words. "I'm falling in love with you. The kind of gut-wrenching love that makes you stammer and stutter all over yourself when all you really want to say is 'I love you'."

She was dumbfounded that this perfect man could look at her in her current state and profess love for her. "Drew, I…"

"I know it's only been a short time for you, hell, a weekend. I don't expect you to say anything right now. I understand. Really. But I've been pacing all day, worried about you all day, and wanting to be with you all day, and I know it's because I love you. This isn't exactly the ideal time to tell you for the first time. But it's always a good time to hear you are loved, right? Now here I am, and I can't stop saying it like an idiot."

He sighed in defeat at the moment. He was up all night and spent most of his day rehearsing lovely lines to say to her when the right time presented itself. Now, here he sat, bumbling and making a fool of himself at the worst possible moment. The cat was out of the bag now, though, and he wouldn't take it back.

"There are so many more romantic ways I could have done this, but holding you, just being with you, is my dream come true. If you'll let me, I would really love to love you."

She hadn't noticed the tears streaming down her cheeks but felt the war inside her heart battling. She couldn't say she was in love with him. That wouldn't be fair. She sat next to him, looking into his eyes and replaying the kindnesses he had shown her over the weekend and throughout their many meetings for the party. He was a good man, an exceptional man, and she refused to hurt him in the way she had been.

"Drew, from the minute we met, I've thought how lucky any woman would be to be with you. You are unnervingly perfect. I…" she looked at his hand holding hers and sighed. "I am a mess right now. My world was flipped upside down. When I say those words, I want to know that it's really me saying them, not because of anything else going on." She looked up at him again to see the hope in his eyes. "Can you give me some time?"

It wasn't the scenario he had hoped for, but she was being honest with him, and that went a very long way. He kissed her hand and held their hands at his heart. "When you say it, I want it to mean something. If you don't mind, I'll keep telling you until then."

There were no words for how moved she was that he didn't pressure her. She threw her arms around him and wept again. How awful was it to have used her heart to trust Taylor when such an incredible man was offering his heart and soul to her? She vowed then and there to do right by Drew and never look back at what might have been with anyone else. She held on to Drew with everything she had and hoped with all her heart that he could love her enough to make her forget.

chapter thirteen

MILLIE CHECKED HER voicemail with a hitch in her breath. It had been almost a year since Mary was taken to the hospital, but the fear of that call never completely left her heart. They had always been close, but the whole experience had taken them to a new level of friendship.

> *"Hey honey, the checkup went fine. Dr. James says I'm in great shape and even said I could start running again. I told him I was only running if someone was chasing me. He said insurance probably doesn't pay for that, so there will be no running, but the point is I could. Anyway, I have some errands to run, then the clinic, which will be done by fourish, and then we can leave. The car is packed and ready to go. Can't wait to get out of here for a relaxing weekend. Oh, don't forget that bowl you brought back last time. Gosh, that was months ago. And I packed beach towels, but I don't have..."*

Glory, the woman could talk. She hung up the phone, grateful for the long message. It made her smile to hear her

Mom so excited. They were headed to the beach house to spend one last weekend as single girls before Rory's wedding in a few weeks, and they were all chomping at the bit to leave.

After the excitement had worn off, Rory pushed the wedding back when she realized how many details there were to plan and pay for, which gave the girls plenty of time to help and spoil her.

Her phone rang again with "The Wedding March," the tune Rory had set as her ringtone on all their phones.

"This ringtone has got to go. I'm going to replace it with a baby giggling."

"Don't you dare! If I had known I'd be getting the baby questions this whole time, I never would have agreed to wait a year to do this. Why do people do that? Like I don't have enough to think about? It's like they want me to have a breakdown."

"Please don't break down. I already bought your wedding present, and I look hot in the bridesmaid's dress. I can't wear that to work. Someone has to see me in it."

"I'll try to lock it up for you. Now tell me the plan. When and where?"

"My apartment, five o'clock. Everyone is coming straight from work, so it may be five thirty with traffic. I'm saying the last one that arrives, drives."

"I'll be there at four with a bottle of something then."

"See ya then, go on in if you beat me."

"Of course. Have you talked to her? How was the checkup?"

"All is well, she says. We can interrogate her in the car while she's trapped."

"Perfect. See you soon."

Millie hung up and dove into work. She was still learning, but she had established a solid foundation for the position and loved the responsibility it came with.

She worked harder this year than she ever had before, but it never felt like work because she loved every minute of it. She saw each day as a blessing and never took the freedoms they gave her for granted.

Before she knew it, the reminder on her phone buzzed.

"Got a hot date or afraid you'll fall asleep?" Pearce, the new salesman, stood at her door.

"Neither, it's my reminder that it's quitting time. I tend to get wrapped up."

"You work too hard. A bunch of us are headed to the bar up the street later. Want to join?"

Pearce had flirted with her from the day he was hired, and although he was nice enough, he only reminded Millie that Taylor wasn't here to do it properly.

"No thanks, I'm headed to the beach this weekend."

"Another time, then?"

"Sure. Have fun with Jake. He could probably use a night out after the audit."

"Poor guy, he's wound tight as a drum. Everyone knows he has an eye on every dime this company makes. It's going to take more than one night out to unwind all that. I'll do my best, though. Have fun at the beach."

"Thanks, Pearce."

Millie wrapped up the emails she needed to send and shut down her office. It still amazed her that this was all hers. She smiled as she closed the door and did a mental check of anything left to do before she drove away.

A few goodbyes, and she was off. The weekend couldn't start fast enough. She walked into her apartment to find

Rory and Cate on the floor, laughing at old pictures they had found in a middle school album.

"What in the hell were you thinking with these bangs? I mean, they are enormous. Even the eighties would say they are too much!" Cate was hysterical, and Rory was the culprit.

"You suck." Millie laughed.

"I didn't get them out this time," Rory said innocently. "I merely reminded her about the album marked 'never show anyone with a sense of sarcasm'. Besides, Cate needed a laugh. She had a hard day."

"Bullshit. You took the day off."

"Yes," Cate straightened up, "but they canceled my mani-pedi, so I couldn't get my nails done."

"You're the devil." Millie chuckled.

The girls burst into a new round of laughter as Millie walked past them to the fridge.

"I'm pouring a drink. Audrey's the last to arrive, so she drives."

"Nope, that's all you chick." Audrey walked out of the bathroom with a big smile on her face. "Those pictures are ridiculous, Mil. Why don't we get those out more often?"

"Like at parties," Rory giggled.

"Let me remind you, hyenas, that you each have pictures like this, and I am happy to find them. Especially considering we have the perfect party coming up with all our loved ones attending."

"You're not as mean as we are. You wouldn't dare." Cate grinned. "Except Audrey, you're definitely meaner than Audrey."

"Everybody's meaner than Audrey," Rory rolled her eyes. "Are you all packed up, hotshot? What kept you at work so long? I wanna leave town!"

Rory's excitement was palpable. She had worked so hard to plan a family-oriented wedding on a frugal budget without feeling like she was missing out on any of the good stuff. It had been a hard year for her friend, though. Planning a wedding without her Mom to share it with was miserable for her some days and tolerable on others, but always hard.

Millie lost count of the tears but marveled at the tenacity. Rory was determined to make the day fun and uplifting, with plenty of room for the mementos to keep her mother present in every aspect of the day.

Millie gave her a big hug. "It's starting to fly by. We're down to weeks."

"Can you believe it?"

"Ok, you two, I'll put some Celine Dion on for you to feel the love in the car." Cate was the queen of avoiding tearfully sentimental situations. "Are you packed? I want the surf at my feet and the salt in my drink."

"Are we back to your hard day? Need a margarita from all the napping, do you?"

"Shut up. I'm pitiful. Pack."

"I just lack the stuff I couldn't pack this morning. Give me five minutes."

Millie walked to her bathroom to load her essentials. In her hurry, she dropped her hairbrush on her foot. "Klutz."

She looked down at it and saw a flash of Taylor lying on the floor. She hadn't thought about him in a while. She was surprised by how clear the image was.

She was happy now. She was herself again. The girls consoled and cried with her while she wrapped her heart around what happened. They had given her a shoulder to cry on but also the kick in the butt she needed to see what was right in front of her. No one dismissed her pain, but they wouldn't let her wallow in it when there was someone wonderful showing her how much he loved her. Drew had proven himself to them with his patience and love for Millie. He was an incredible man, and she knew she was lucky to have him in her life. Everything happens for a reason was her motto this year.

In the quiet of the night, though, every once in a while, she would catch herself thinking about Taylor. She blinked away the image and pulled everything she needed from the cabinet. She may not have been able to chase the ghost away yet, but she'd be damned if she let it haunt her life anymore.

"Enough."

"THAT'S YOUR BOAT. CAN you say boat?" Taylor pointed to the boat he bought, or rather the bank bought, and would be accepting his payments until his mid-eighties, he thought. He held his daughter up to see her name on the stern.

"One day, when you're bigger, I'll teach you how to sail it, but for now, we better get you out of the wind. Your little cheeks are bright red, and this little river falling out of your nose is flowing a little too fast for daddy to keep up with."

Taylor checked his pockets for anything that could absorb the green stream without luck. He squeezed what he could from her nose without thinking and stood there staring at his snot-covered fingers. With a deep sigh, he wiped his fingers on the dock.

"I wouldn't do that for just anyone you know. In fact, you're the only soul on this Earth that could get me to wipe their snot with my own hands." He lifted her up to bite on her belly and make her laugh. "I love you. I do. Yes, I do."

He laughed at the sweet giggle his baby talk rewarded him and thought how silly he must sound to anyone listening and how little he cared what anyone thought. Charlotte captured his heart from the second she was born. He had fallen more in love with her every day.

As he kissed her little cheek, she sneezed a spray of gooey green that covered the side of his face. He had been coughed on, peed on, spit up on, but this was a first. Taylor drew his head back slowly, trying his best not to overreact, watching the string of snot that connected them grow longer like cheese on a hot pizza.

"Now that is nasty, brother. I understand now why you don't call me back." Hank stood a few feet away with his lips curled in an evil grin of disgust and amusement.

"Don't just stand there, man. Help me! I feel it sliding down my cheek."

"Isn't there a bag full of stuff somewhere to help you? Where's the bag?"

"Would you get the hell over here and hold her!"

"Language, dad. Language." Hank walked over to the baby to say hello, enjoying the moment without any intention of offering assistance. "Is this normal? That's a lot of slime, man. And what are the chunks? What did she have for lunch?"

"You suck. Take her." Taylor handed Charlotte to Hank before he could refuse. He played the cool uncle well, but his love for this sweet girl was hard to miss.

"You know, one day you're going to have one of these, and I'm going to stand by and laugh when you get hosed by something."

"I would expect nothing less, but I'll have the bag to mop it up. Won't I, sunshine? Let's go home and see what your mommy made for dinner. I'm hungry. You hungry?"

"What brings you to the sea? I know you didn't come to see me."

"Of course not. I came to see my girl." Charlotte curled up at Hank's neck and nearly made him wish for one of his own. "You missed me, didn't you, sweetheart? Watch the snail trail on the shirt there, cutie pie." Before he could redirect her little nose to a tissue, she smeared a patch of gooey goodness on his shoulder.

"For the love. Children are gross, but none are as pretty as you," he cooed. "Handoff."

Taylor took his girl and felt her forehead again. "It's hard to believe you have this much snot but no fever. Let's get you home."

He slid Charlotte into her car seat with the ease of a seasoned professional. Hank joined him in the front seat, grinning as he watched his friend living his dream come true.

"This suits you."

Taylor put the car in drive, "I hope so. It's been a hell of a year, but we're making progress."

"No. This." Hank winked at Charlotte and got a smile that made her eyes sparkle.

"Oh, yeah. She is the best thing I've ever done."

"No regrets?"

Taylor looked at his daughter in the rear-view mirror with the pride of a king. "Only that she didn't come along sooner. I can't imagine life without her now."

Hank looked out the window, wanting to phrase his thoughts carefully. "I know it's been hard. I'm proud of you."

"Thanks, Nancy. Want to braid each other's hair when we get home?"

"Go to hell." Hank popped him on the shoulder and laughed.

"What's going on with you?"

"Not a thing. I just haven't seen you this happy in a long time. Like I said, this suits you."

"Thanks, man." They grinned at each other with an unspoken appreciation. "So, tell me, what's happening in the publishing world? Any good books I need to be on the watch for?"

"She's doing well."

"Who's doing well?"

Hank cocked his head and waited for the sadness to flash over Taylor's eyes. He was as close as any brother could be to this man. He hadn't asked directly, but Hank knew that when it came to Millie, Taylor's heart would never let go.

"She's actually planning a gala for next month to show off all the new talent and raise money to buy books for local schools. It's a good cause, but I'll be forced to pull out the tux and behave."

"Remind me to write you a check."

"You could bring it to the dinner yourself, you know. Everyone would love to see you."

That familiar wave of excitement and sorrow washed through him at the thought of seeing Millie. Hank saw it and tightened his jaw at his carelessness. "I'll remind you to write the check."

They rode in silence. Taylor's mind was trapped on her face. Her smile. Her heart. He drove slowly, not seeing the familiar signs that usually guided him home. He drove by memory, only seeing her face. He knew she would never leave his heart and half hoped he would never leave hers.

"Taylor. Taylor. Taylor!"

"What! Sorry, what?"

"What in God's name is that smell, and how do you not notice it anymore?"

Taylor snapped out of his trance and caught his first whiff of what little Charlotte had blessed them with. He caught her eye in the mirror and saw a face of determination and strain. "Uh-oh, she's not done."

"What?! How can there be more? It's everywhere."

"What do you mean it's everywhere?" Taylor stopped at the red light and turned to see a red-faced baby smiling in a car seat full of brown goo that smelled like the devil's own creation. "For the love, Charlotte, you couldn't get that out before I changed you?"

Charlotte giggled and melted his heart all over again. "You think this is funny, don't you? You want Uncle Hank to clean you up, don't you?"

"Aw, hell no. I'll pay cash for whatever we're eating tonight. I'm not working for my supper with that on my hands."

When they pulled into an empty driveway, Taylor chuckled. "She's not home, so you're going to have to help me."

"I mean it, brother. I'll leave before I touch that. Let's call Carrie and tell her she needs to come home while you get the hose and spray this thing out. Or better yet, go run it through the car wash with the doors open. Hell, just burn it."

"Hank, you're helping. I'll lift her out. You get the seat out of the car and put it on the grass. Just hold it at the head. There's nothing up there."

"You owe me so big for this. You too, sunshine." Hank looked at Charlotte, still smiling and now spreading the evil gravy down the sides of the seat. "Thank you for being a precious, little, live-action birth control commercial for me."

Charlotte spoke to him in a language of her own that would have made him swoon a few minutes ago. "Not many could make this cute. Well done."

"Come here, baby, you're a mess." Taylor unbuckled her from her seat, careful not to touch the stickiest spots but unsuccessfully keeping his hands free from the mess. "If you had told me two years ago that I would have my hands in all this, I would have called you a liar to your face. I don't know what happens when they are born, but it's like a switch goes off. This just doesn't bother you anymore."

As the words of wisdom left Taylor's mouth, a river of poo slid from the gaping side of Charlotte's five-pound diaper. He watched the brown liquid lava run down her leg and splatter all over his legs and shoes. He felt his stomach roll. "Oh God, that's nasty. I'm gonna be sick."

"What happened to the switch? Flip the switch, man."

It was too late. Taylor sat the cooing baby on the lawn and leaned over the bushes to throw up any lunch he had left. "Watch her," was all he could manage between heaves.

"Man, come on. I can take the cute one, but I can't hear you throwing up or…" Hank threw up on the sidewalk before he could finish the warning.

When Carrie pulled into the driveway, it took a second for the scene to soak in. Her husband was covered in what she could only hope was mud and throwing up in the bushes.

Hank was losing his lunch in front of the house. There was a car seat completely covered in poop next to the car and a very merry Charlotte sitting in the grass and still wearing most of the mess. She tried her best but couldn't hold back the belly laugh. She was breathless by the time she got to Charlotte.

"Shut up." Hank wiped his mouth and spit.

"Yeah, shut up. You can't judge, you weren't there." Taylor sank on the front step to catch his breath.

"Oh, I'm not judging. I wish I were filming this, though. You three are quite a sight. What in the world, baby girl? You took down two grown men with your superpowers." Carrie looked at her men in pitiful concern. "Is everyone alright now? What happened?"

"Your kid blew up in the back seat. Your man said he could handle it but forgot to flip the switch. Your single friend can only take so much."

"That pretty much sums it up." Taylor stood up, "Can you handle her while I clean up a bit?"

"You people aren't going in my house like this. I'm getting the hose."

"Yeah, right. You're not going to hose me off in the front yard." Taylor started to move towards the front door when he heard his full name in the Mom tone Carrie had developed since Charlotte came along.

"Taylor Andrew Fitzpatrick, you stop right there. You're getting hosed, sir."

Hank laughed out loud at the about-face his friend made when given the order. Marriage definitely wasn't going to catch him any time soon.

In the end, Carrie only hosed down Taylor's legs and shoes before letting him go in to change. The car seat and baby were a more intensive soaking, but in true Charlotte form, she laughed through her warm outdoor bath while breaking a tooth on her favorite chew toy. After a change of clothes, a double shot of bourbon, and a few more laughs at their expense, Carrie kicked them out of the kitchen to make dinner.

"No argument here. I'm happy to obey the Hose Queen."

They chuckled their way out the back door to the water's edge. Taylor let out a deep sigh. "I still can't believe I live here."

"It's pretty amazing. Dream come true."

"To dreams coming true. Cheers."

They clinked glasses and sat back in the Adirondack chairs he had just painted gray. "I hate this color. I wish I had just stained them."

"Why didn't you?"

"Carrie wanted them gray, so they're gray."

"You didn't want to get the hose, I get it." Hank laughed into his drink and wondered again why a man would succumb to the restrictions of marriage unless that woman were Scarlett Johansson, of course. "So, really, how are things?"

"Things are good. The new boat is a great step towards…"

"I mean things here."

"Oh." Taylor took a long drink. "Things are good. We're friends again."

"Friends?"

"We lost that for a while. We've got it back now."

"That's a start. And the rest?"

"The rest will come between feedings, changings, work, and exhaustion." He took another long drink of his bourbon, draining the glass. "Charlotte is our focus right now. She's the best part of me. She needs me. I need her."

Taylor smiled at the view, thinking about this perfect creature he helped create. She was the part of his heart that had been missing his whole life. No one and nothing had ever been loved more by another person. He was sure of it. She was the most perfect thing he had ever done, and he would spend every day proving it to her.

In the corners of his mind, though, he could still see Millie, and in the quiet moments, he could hear her laugh. Some mornings, he would run towards the gazebo. The one that he saw her smiling on in another life. It was his reminder of the hurt he had caused. He would race home to the precious cuddles Charlotte gave him to remind him of the miracle he had been gifted.

"I need her…" Taylor whispered, but Hank couldn't tell which of his loves he was thinking about.

chapter fourteen

THE DRIVE TO the beach was easy, and with her women in the car, it was fun. Their road trip gave them almost three hours of uninterrupted conversation about the wedding, work, potential love interests, and of course, embarrassing stories of the past that would, Millie was sure, be passed down to their children.

She felt strong when they were all together and wondered what in the world she had ever done without them. "I love you guys."

Mary smiled at her from the driver's seat. "We love you too, sweet girl."

"Not me. I just like you for this beach house."

"Shut up, Cate. We love you too," Audrey said while patting Millie's knee. "What brought that on?"

"Just thinking. We've been through a lot this year, and I don't know what I would do without you. I'd like to raise my Chick-fil-A sweet tea to no more surprises, a wonderful wedding, and a lifetime of more girls' trips like this."

They pulled up to the beach house and each took a deep breath of ocean air.

"This is the life. Explain to me again why we don't live here." Cate was already walking towards the water to feel the sand in her toes.

"Because you haven't won the lottery yet. Hey, if you want to move in, come help with these bags!" Rory pulled the first bag out of the trunk and propped her sunglasses down on her nose. "She's not coming back to get this, is she?"

Audrey smiled, "We could hide it and convince her she forgot it."

"She would just use it as an excuse to steal our clothes. You know she's had her eye on those sandals since you bought them." Millie grabbed their bags and put her back into lifting Cate's up the steps. "Holy hell, she owes me for this. It's a weekend for crap's sake. What did she pack?"

They walked in the back door to the sound of yelling and the game playing as loudly as it would be at the field. Drew had Carson in a choke hold, their dad was high-fiving the groom-to-be, a few cousins were chest bumping, and the newest male member of the family was walking around without his diaper on. It was a sight.

The girls laughed out loud when Drew's distraction gave Carson the opportunity to reverse the headlock that landed them both on the couch. "Say it!"

"Fine!" Drew used a tactic only pulled during extreme measures. He tickled his little brother until he could get away. "Ha! Maybe next time!"

"Cheat!" Carson was still laughing, along with the whole room now, while Drew sauntered like a winner over to Millie. "Excuse me, men, while I welcome my woman properly." He put his arms around Mille and dipped her back for a kiss when she employed her own extreme measures and tickled his ribs. Drew squealed like a little girl and promptly dropped Millie to the floor.

"Oh my god, are you OK? I'm sorry!" He knelt to help her up.

"You know, I might believe you if you weren't laughing through the apology."

Still chuckling, he helped Millie up and into his arms. "I'm sorry, honey. Forgive me?"

"Better, but I may get you again later to call it even."

Carson piped up from the couch, "I want in on that. Just give me a wink."

Millie gave Carson a wicked wink and a high five as she hugged Drew.

"I missed you," Drew whispered into her hair before kissing the top of her head. "How was the drive?"

"I missed you too." She looked up at him with laughter and love in her eyes. "It was good. Mom flew us here."

"I was just trying to get around those cars," Mary smiled as she walked around the room, greeting everyone.

"All of them?" Cate laughed.

Millie rubbed Drew's arm to get his attention. "Can I talk to you for a minute upstairs?"

"Everything OK? Mary's appointment?" Instantly worried, Drew held her tighter without realizing he was gripping. She loved that he loved her.

"She's alright. We interrogated her in the car. Clean bill of health. She can even start running."

"I didn't know she was a runner." She felt him relax his grip.

"She's not, but she *could*." Millie gave his arm a squeeze before letting go. "I'll grab our bags and meet you up there."

"Have you learned nothing, woman? Give me those." Drew grabbed as many of the girls' bags as he could, only allowing Millie one small bag that wouldn't fit anywhere on him.

Millie looked around the room to see his family welcoming the loves of her life with open arms. Drew's mother, Gretchen, was already guiding Mary into the kitchen with his sisters, laughing at how cute "the kids" were together. Carson was catching Cate up on the game. Rory was getting a play-by-play of the seasoning Pete used on the ribs.

The families had met several times over the year. Millie was shocked at how much they had in common and the friends they shared. It seemed so easy for all of them to be together. She and Drew had talked about it several times, how lucky they were to have families that got along so well. The whole relationship felt like it was destined to happen in so many ways.

When she reached the top of the steps, Drew had already put the bags in the right rooms and was waiting for her at the door. "Come here. I missed you while you were gone." He pulled her to him and kissed her gently. "This working thing is getting in the way. I may have to quit."

Millie giggled, "Your book is becoming a movie. Let's not retire quite yet. Maybe stick with it until the premiere, then we'll talk." She kissed him as she used her foot to close the door. "I missed you too. A week is too long."

"I'm glad everyone could be here this weekend, but we should have told them to come tomorrow. I want you all to myself for a while." He intentionally kept his kisses gentle since it was definitely not the time to show her how much he really missed her, but they could both feel the need between them.

He pulled away first, begrudgingly, and plopped down on the bed. "I'm going to get us into trouble if I keep this up. What did you want to talk to me about?"

"Honestly, I just wanted a minute alone. Drew," she looked down, suddenly embarrassed, "I can't seem to get used to how much I need you." She walked to the bed where he was sitting and put her hands on his shoulders. "I really did miss you this week."

He put his hands on her hips and pulled her to him in a big hug. It was music to his ears. It had taken almost the entire year, but she finally told him that she loved him. Hearing that she needed him made him feel like he could fly. "That's it, I'm quitting. Let's sail away somewhere. We'll leave a note so no one worries."

She bent down to kiss the top of his head and whispered, "I love you."

It was still an arrow through his heart every time she said it. He looked up and put his hands on her face, "I love you too, honey. You have me, heart and soul."

She knelt and kissed him gratefully. He always had the perfect words to make her feel like she was his favorite person in the world. "You know, they're wondering where we are by now."

"They know exactly where we are. They're wondering what we're doing." He said it with a devilish grin that shot an unexpected lightning bolt through her. He saw her look behind him at the bed and knew where her mind had gone. He stood up and brushed her cheek with the back of his hand. "Can we go to bed early tonight? I want to hold you."

"It's a date." She lifted up on her toes to wrap her arms around his neck. "Just one more for the road."

That's how Carson found them when he opened the door. "I'd say get a room, but you're in it. You guys going to join us or stay up here for the weekend?"

"Staying, spread the word," Drew was still holding a giggling Millie. He gave her a big squeeze before looking up at his brother with a death stare. "It doesn't count as knocking if you open the door while you're doing it. We'll be locking the door in the future. Don't pick it."

"No need, sir, there's a house full of beautiful women to entertain me."

"They're off-limits, Carson. Keep the flirting to a minimum."

"Not true, big brother. Mary is as single as they get. Isn't that right, Mil?"

"Very true. Go get her, tiger, but if you could wait to lay it on thick until I get down there to watch, that would be awesome. We'll be down in just a minute. I want to unpack a few things first."

"We're going for a walk on the beach in a few minutes, so come down soon. I'm going to put on some cologne and freshen up for Ms. Mary."

"Carson, for God's sake, leave the poor woman alone." Drew pleaded.

"Not a chance, movie man." Carson closed the door on his way out and had both of their eyes rolling.

"I can't wait to see that show. She's going to eat it up. Come here." She gave him one more kiss, "You ready to go down? I can unpack later. I don't want to miss the sunset."

"After you, love."

Everyone watched them come down the stairs, holding hands and smiling at each other. They had all agreed to give them some alone time since Drew had been out of town.

The girls picked on Millie for whining about missing him, but in reality, he had won their hearts. They had held her through the tears of heartbreak and the joys of being loved. Each of them agreed that they had never seen Millie this happy and content.

"Well, it's about time, you two. The rest of the crew arrived while you were up there." Rory leaned her head on Will's shoulder. She was always more relaxed when he was close. Millie stopped on the bottom step and kissed Will on the cheek. In a million years, she would never have guessed Rory to be the cuddly type. Love did incredible things.

"I'm going to say hi to everybody and get a drink." Millie squeezed Drew's hand. "Want anything?"

"Will you grab me a beer? Thanks, babe."

As Millie walked away, Drew gave Rory's shoulder a squeeze. "It's good to see you guys. Thanks for coming this weekend."

"Wouldn't miss it, man. Can't wait for tomorrow..." Rory pinched Will's ribs and shot him a "shut up" look. "Ouch! Damn, Rory. That hurt."

"I meant it to. Tomorrow is not on everyone's calendar."

"She's talking to Cate and John. No way can she hear us." Will pinched Rory back but knew better than to pinch hard. Instead, he nuzzled her neck and whispered something that made her grin ear to ear.

Drew went into the kitchen and found Mary and his parents sitting at the table, looking at their phones. "What are you guys up to? Everyone looks so serious."

"We're comparing calendars, just making sure everyone has any important dates." His mother was almost giddy beside him. "You know, in case anything comes up."

"Gretchen, here, has given me the skinny on the weekend plans." The two women beamed at each other. "With such a big family, I just wanted to make sure I have the basics."

Drew looked at his dad, "And you?"

"Just doing what I'm told."

"Always a good idea. Hey Audrey, great to see you." He gave her a hug and kept his arm over her shoulders. Of all the girls, he felt most protective of Audrey. She was such a kind soul, and after Millie told him what she had been through, he swore to himself that he would watch out for her like a big brother. "I heard through the grapevine that you're not on the market anymore. Are we going to meet him this weekend?"

Audrey stood with Drew's arm around her like a proud little sister. She wasn't afraid to admit that she adored him. "I didn't ask him. It's a little soon to feed him to the wolves. It's only been a few dates."

"What? We're nothing but nice." Millie walked into the kitchen and hugged Pete and Gretchen. "Except Cate, she'd play twenty questions with him and let everyone know when he got one wrong."

"I would not. I am the picture of Southern gentility. Isn't that right, John?"

"One hundred percent." John accepted one of the beers Millie was passing out. "Demure and delicate, and clever enough to grill someone without them even knowing they're being tested."

"You forgot ravishing."

"Well, that goes without saying, obviously." John smiled at his girl. He actually loved how scrappy she was.

"Let's get outside, people," Carson announced from the porch. "Sun's going down whether we're out there or not."

The herd moved quickly through the back door to the beach. Millie stood watching the crowd walk towards the water in awe. She had gone from her core group to nearly a dozen people she knew she could count on. She walked on the beach holding Drew's hand, laughing with everyone and knowing she was incredibly lucky to have all of this. As the sun set over the water, she felt a wave of gratefulness wash over her and held his hand a little tighter.

After dinner, the cards came out, and laughter continued to fill the house. When a few of the cousins went home a few hours later, Millie laid her head on Drew's shoulder. "Guys, I'm fading fast. I'm going to call it a night, but please keep up the party going without me." She patted Drew's leg. "I mean it. You're having fun. Stay and play."

He gave her a sweet kiss, "You sure? I can come up with you."

"Don't be silly. You've earned a night to relax and have fun. Besides, you're winning. You can't quit now." She gave him a wink and whispered, "I love you." She gave a wave to the room. "Night, y'all."

She walked up the stairs, hearing the laughter of her favorite people enjoying each other as friends, and smiled again that everyone got along so well. She got to Drew's room and saw her bag on the bed. She was too tired to dig through it for her pajamas, especially when she preferred Drew's shirts. Since their first weekend, she had been borrowing his shirts to sleep in and would only occasionally return them. Once or twice a month, he would steal them back, and so the cycle went.

She opened a drawer to find her latest borrow and saw something shiny underneath the stack. She pulled the shirts up a bit to find a framed picture of Drew. As she pushed the shirts further back, she saw the picture was of him holding a beautiful red-headed woman who was looking at him with pure love in her eyes on the beach they had just walked together.

Millie's heart was racing. She pulled the frame out of the drawer and sat on the bed, staring at it. Who was this woman? How had she never seen this in the drawer before? They had only been to the beach a handful of times over the year, but she felt like she would have noticed it before now. His smile in the picture was so genuine. He looked like he was on top of the world. It was the same smile he had given her countless times. That thought sent her from shock to rage. She would not have her heart broken again.

She stood up furious and slammed the frame on the dresser. It startled her how mad she was. She was surprised the glass hadn't shattered. She started packing the few things that had made it out of her bag, then went to the bathroom to make sure there was nothing else. Why was she this mad? She felt irrational and hurt, not a good combination. She felt her eyes starting to well but refused to cry. She looked at herself in the mirror and saw that it was too late to hold them back. Angry at the tears and the picture, she walked back to the bedroom to put her shoes back on when a very smug Drew walked through the door.

"Guess what, baby, I beat them all and won sixty-two cents. Where would you like to go on vacation? It's on me." He walked to the dresser to put his winnings down and saw the frame. His heart stopped for a moment before he looked up at Millie in the mirror and saw her tears.

"I'll only ask you once why that picture was hiding in your drawer. Whoever that is, she clearly loves you," her voice cracked, "and you clearly love her. So, I'll only ask you once why you're with me when there is someone out there who looks at you like that. And I'll only ask you once why you would tell me you love me when you love someone else." The tears were falling now. She hated that she was already crying.

Drew picked up the frame and looked at it with love and regret. Carson had told him so many times to talk to Millie about Laine, but he hadn't listened.

"We went to high school together. Her name is Laine, the love of my life," he looked up from the picture to find tears rolling down Millie's cheeks, "until I met you." He sat down on the bed, looking at the past. "This picture was taken almost five years ago, the day I proposed to her."

The wind was completely knocked out of her chest. "You're... married? I can't believe..."

"It was also the day before she was diagnosed with non-Hodgkin lymphoma." He took a deep breath and looked up at her, "I'm sorry I didn't tell you about her sooner. I can't even explain why I didn't. I don't have an excuse," he laid the frame on the bed and stood up, "other than stupidity."

He walked over to her and watched her step back in defense. He had done this. He had made her walls go up around her heart that he had spent the last year knocking down. Now, he had to tear them down again. Her presence in his life made him as happy as he had ever been. He knew he wanted to make her happy for the rest of their lives. He didn't want to lose her over this.

Millie watched him search for the words he wanted to say. She couldn't breathe. How could he not have told her about this? She was such a large part of his past, a large part of what made him *him*. Then it hit her, she was a hypocrite. He knew nothing of Taylor because she had never shared her heartbreak with him. She was so determined to block Taylor from her heart that she had never wanted to bring him up to Drew. It was different circumstances, but it was still heartbreak. "How long were you married?"

A tiny thread of relief wove through him. If she was asking questions, she was listening to his answers. "Two days."

Millie's eyes widened. "Please sit with me, Mil. I'll tell you anything you want to know." He held out his hand and laced his fingers with hers. They sat on the bed for a second before he continued.

"Laine was the life of the party. She never met a stranger. She was the opposite of me in high school. The beautiful girl who had a smile worth writing about. I wrote a story with her as the main character. That's how I asked her out. I nearly choked when she said yes. We were inseparable after that." He looked at Millie to gauge how she was doing. She hadn't let go of his hand, so he considered that a good sign.

"We got serious in college but agreed to wait until we graduated before we got engaged. This picture was taken the week after graduation. It was her last truly happy day." The swell of emotion was in his throat, but he needed Millie to know every detail. "I asked her to marry me in her parent's backyard. We had just graduated, so we had no money. We dined on Wendy's that night and celebrated with a bottle of champagne I got at a gas station. The ring had a chip of a stone, but she wore it like it was the Hope diamond. She made me feel like I could conquer the world. She believed in me more than anyone."

He looked at Millie and grinned, "You remind me of her in that way." He kissed her hand gently and held it with both hands. She could feel it in his grip, he was holding her hand out of necessity. She rubbed his hand with her thumb to encourage him to continue.

"She was feeling run down, just really tired. We all thought her body was finally relaxing after four years of hard work. Maybe if I had made her go to the doctor sooner…" He choked up before he could get the rest out. Millie scooted closer to him and put her head on his shoulder. "She was a biology major. She was going to be a pediatrician," Drew sniffed. "I married her in the hospital. She wore her mother's wedding dress but was too weak to walk, so I carried her down the aisle of the hospital chapel. She was a beautiful bride. It was an honor to be her husband, even if it was only a short time."

Millie could feel how tense he was. He was reliving this pain for her, and she felt her love for him grow. "Drew, you can stop. I'm sorry for making you go through this." She put her hands on his face so she could look him in the eye. "I'm so sorry for your loss, and I'm so sorry for throwing it at you like this. You could have told me about her. I love you so much. I'm so sorry."

The relief of her understanding and the memory of Laine in her wedding dress caused one lonely tear to roll down his cheek. She brushed it with her thumb and pulled him into a hug. Millie pulled him down on the bed with her and put his head on her chest, not knowing if there was more he wanted to share. Drew put his arms around her and held on for dear life, like a man who had lost a great love and never wanted to let go.

She didn't know what to do to make his pain go away. She kissed the top of his head. "Thank you."

Drew looked up at her, "Thank you?"

Millie brushed his hair back, "Thank you for trusting me with her memory."

"I'm sorry I didn't tell you. It's all I thought about for a few years, and then I just kind of stopped talking about it with anyone. I didn't know the picture was in the drawer, but I'm glad you found it."

"She is a part of you. She will always be a part of you. That makes her a part of us. Always love her, Drew. We can honor her together."

The love was too much for his heart to hold. He stretched up to give her a gentle kiss. "Thank you. Millie, I know you have the girls, but you're the best friend I've ever had. I can honestly say that I have never loved anyone the way I love you."

He kissed her again, moaning when Millie took it deeper. The passion he felt for this woman was more than he could contain any longer. He hadn't pushed her over their months together, but after bearing his soul and feeling her acceptance of him, he wanted to be as close to her as possible. He rolled towards her and trailed kisses down her neck with a whisper, "I need you."

Those three little words lit a fire within her like she hadn't felt with him before. "Drew, I want you…"

"Want me to what?" he was kissing her chest and sending flames through her with each touch.

"There's nothing else, I just want you." She took his head in her hands and brought his mouth to hers with all the hunger that had built up over the last year. He had been wonderful to her, never taking things further than she was ready for, but tonight, she felt closer to him than anyone else. She wanted to show him how much he had touched her heart. She wrapped her leg around him to pull him closer and saw his control break.

He rolled over, pulling her on top of him. "I want to touch you." He pulled her shirt over her head, slowly rubbing his fingers up her ribs. She found his mouth again and got lost in the heart-racing world they were creating. She had forgotten what pure lust felt like. His hands were creating an inferno inside of her. Overcome by need, she reached down to unfasten his buckle. It wasn't until that moment that she realized she was shaking.

"Are you alright? If you want to stop…"

"I don't want to stop. It's just been so long, and I… I just…"

"Honey, let's slow down. I want to make love to you. There's no reason to rush." He brought her hand to his lips and kissed each knuckle. "Have I told you today how beautiful you are to me?" He kissed her wrist and felt her pulse race. He wanted her to be comfortable, but he loved that he could make her heart pound like this. "From the very first time I saw you," he kissed up her arm, "I wanted to hold you."

She kissed his neck sweetly, "You knocked over the glass of water and said the party should include bibs and Band-Aids for the socially impaired who would be attending."

He chuckled, "I knocked the glass over because when you walked in the door, you took my breath away. Millie," he waited for her to look at him, "you changed my life that day. You made me look up again, to hope again. You brought me back to life. I have loved you from that day on."

She kissed him gently, "You humble me. I have never taken your love for granted. Knowing everything you have been through, it seems like a miracle." She kissed him again, this time with confidence and intention. "I want you to know how grateful I am for your patience, but Drew, mine has run out."

She pulled him to her and gave in to the need that had been building over the year. Their bodies fit perfectly together, and when they made love that night, she felt like it was exactly that: love. As the rhythm and heat increased, so did her need to be close to him in every way. And as they reached the peak together, she felt like time stood still just for them. They held each other all night with soft kisses and gentle touches, making all of Millie's dreams come to life. Finally, she knew what it meant to be cherished.

chapter fifteen

"Would you shut up! She'll hear you."

"She's outside with a dozen giggling girls. No way can she hear me from in here."

"I'm telling you, that woman has bat hearing. Shut up."

"You'd think on the happiest day of your life, you'd be in a better mood." Carson kicked his feet up on the chair with all the calm Drew wished he had.

"Don't give your brother a hard time," Pete said, popping the lid off a beer and handing it to Drew. "Tonight will be great. You've got a whole house full of people who support you."

"And a whole house full of people to get you drunk if she says no."

With that, Carson got a smack on the head. "Damn Ally, easy on the roids."

"Would you shut up! She might hear you!" Their sister had learned how to handle her brothers over the years, and she knew the only way to get through to Carson was a jolt.

He gave a dramatic eye roll, "Good Lord, y'all. I'm going outside with the women. They're nicer." He gave Ally a snarl, "Well, most of them."

"I can't wait to show his wife how to beat him up one day." She gave her dad a wink. "So, you ready, big man?" She patted Drew on the shoulder while she slipped his beer bottle from him to take a sip.

"Think so. Did you get the…"

"I got it all. You don't have to worry about the setup. Know what you're going to say?"

"Leave that boy alone," Pete stood up and smiled at his oldest son. "You'll know what to say when the time is right, the rest doesn't matter. I couldn't be prouder, Drew. You chose well."

His dad's approval had always been so important to him, and except for the time he took the car for a joy ride into the neighbor's yard when he was fourteen, he couldn't remember a time when he didn't have it. He hugged his dad, grateful for his blessing.

"What's going on in here?" Millie watched the two men curiously.

"Not a thing, chicken wing." Carson grinned from ear to ear. "What's going on out there?"

"Nuthin', muffin," she giggled.

Drew was always drawn to her, but after last night, he considered himself the luckiest man on Earth. He touched her cheek gently, "You're really something. You know that?"

She smiled at him but was very aware of their audience. Everyone seemed to be staring at her today, making her wonder if the whole house knew what happened between them last night.

"I'm something alright. Trouble with a capital T, according to Mom. I want to do something tonight, maybe a movie or something, but she says we have plans. Are we going somewhere?"

Pete spoke up first, "As far as I know, our only plan is to grill all that meat Gretchen has marinating in the fridge. You'll break her heart if you tell her you won't be here for dinner." He tried to be as casual as he could. "And I'm man enough to admit that I can't grill or eat all of it alone."

"Mom must have told Mary about all the new recipes she found in the cookbook I gave her." Ally said, determined to keep the plan on schedule, "It's a healthy twist on game food, basically."

Pete chuckled, "I'm pretty sure she's making every recipe in the book." He winked at Millie, "She knows how much you two like variety at the table."

"She knows the way to my heart, that's for sure." Millie hugged Drew's side, "This is the perfect weekend. We can see a movie some other time." She watched as the room took a collective sigh. "Alright, what is going on? You guys are up to something."

"Nah, just getting hungry. Let's go outside and figure out where we're going to put all this meat," Pete said a little too loudly. "We may have to buy another grill."

Millie looked around and smiled to herself. She watched as everyone walked through the living room and out the door, smiling to herself. The house was bustling with her favorite people, old and new friends, who meant so much to her.

She saw Drew across the room talking to his mom. He looked over at her and winked. He loved her. He was a good man, and he loved her.

"You look goofy," Cate bumped her with her shoulder. "What are you thinking about?"

"How beautiful you are, of course. How I want to be you when I grow up. Same old, same old." Millie laughed at the face of acceptance Cate made, like that was what most people would be thinking.

"You OK?"

"More than. This is great, don't you think?"

"What?"

"This. Us. All of us together. A big loud group to play with, laugh with, just be with."

"You always did want a big family." Cate bumped her friend on the shoulder again, "It's great. I mean, the house makes it awesome, but the people are alright too. Speaking of which, I love Drew's dad. Every time I see him, he has the perfect amount of sarcasm," she giggled, "but I can tell he's still a little scared of Gretchen. I want a marriage like that."

Millie stared at her for a second in shock. "Did you just admit that marriage is in the plan?"

"What? No! I just meant… shut up."

"That's coming up later, my friend. Probably at dinner in front of everyone."

"I'd hate to have to kill you tonight."

"You love me."

"I do." Then Cate did something rarely seen without cause. She hugged Millie with all of her might. "I really do." She walked away, leaving Millie standing in surprise.

"What was that about?" Drew handed her a fresh drink.

"I wish I knew."

"Up for a little walk before dinner? I haven't had you to myself all day."

"Sure, but shouldn't we help with dinner?"

"Just a quick one. We'll be back before they even know we're gone." He held out his hand for her and guided her out the front door.

"I don't think I've ever walked through the front door before."

Drew chuckled, "No one ever uses this door. That's why we can sneak out."

They walked hand in hand, enjoying the peace for a second. He squeezed her hand a little like a hug. "I didn't realize how loud the house was until right now."

"I know. I love it though, don't you?"

"Do you really?"

"Absolutely. Don't you?"

"Absolutely, but it can be overwhelming sometimes. I just want you to be comfortable."

Millie hugged his arm tightly. "Thank you for that. This is the best weekend. I love that everyone gets along so well and even enjoys each other. Cate says it's the house, but I can see it. They really like each other. Don't you think?"

"It's kind of eerie."

She stopped walking to look at him. "Why do you say that?"

"Eerie in a good way. I think it's wonderful, like they've known each other for years. Almost like it was fate."

She smiled at him, but it didn't reach her eyes. "Fate," she whispered. She couldn't say why that made her sad, but she started walking again in silence.

"Not a big fan of fate?"

"Where were you?"

This time, Drew stopped. "Where was I? When?"

"Never mind. Let's head back."

"Not a chance. What is going on up there?" He brushed a stray hair behind her ear. His heart was in his throat. "Is this about last night? I thought you wanted…"

She was making a mess of things again. What was wrong with her? Every time they got closer, she felt like she added a brick to the wall he had just knocked down. "Please, let's go back. I'm sorry."

"Millie, stop. Talk to me. Please. What's wrong?"

"I don't know!" She walked towards the ocean to feel the waves hit her ankles. "I need to tell you something." A year of holding back felt like lying, it always had, but after last night, it felt even more deceitful somehow.

"You know you can tell me anything." He wrapped his arms around her from behind. "No matter what it is, I love all of you. Do you hear me? I love you."

She felt the knot grow in her throat. "I love you too."

"Then we can make it through anything. What's on your heart, honey?"

"I was in love."

Drew's heart sank, and his arms fell to his sides. "Oh."

She spun around, "No, no, I mean before you. I was in love, or I thought I was."

Still hesitant, Drew put his hands in his pockets. "What happened?"

She looked down at the water over her feet. "He didn't love me. Or maybe didn't love me enough. He broke my heart."

"You've never said anything." He tried to put the pieces together, "That must have been awful."

"I was a fool. I look back now and hate myself for it. For falling so easily. For accepting so little."

"Sometimes there isn't a choice, it just happens without your permission."

"I should have known better."

Drew took a deep breath, "Do you still love him?"

She couldn't look at him. She knew she had a decision to make and that it had to happen now. "Sometimes I love the ghost of what might have been." She looked up at him, "but never as much as I love you. I didn't know it could be like this. I just wish…"

"What?" He wasn't comfortable yet and needed her to give him more. He wanted to hit pause on the world until he knew every ounce of her. She didn't open up often, so he knew he couldn't push too hard.

She hadn't felt this from him before and, for the first time, understood the frustration he must have felt with her. "I wish I met you first. I wish the hurt wasn't still there. I wish the damn memory of it all would go away! I wish it didn't keep me from trusting myself again! I wish I had told you sooner instead of blowing up at you right now! I wish I didn't frustrate you all the time. I wish…"

"Wait. Why am I frustrated?" He watched her kicking through the water and felt terrible that he was enjoying the fact that she was upset when it was clearly difficult for her, but it had taken a year to knock down this wall inside her and he knew another brick was falling.

"Are you kidding me! Look at me. I'm a hot mess!"

"And that's frustrating?"

She stopped and gave him a big eye roll, "You can't honestly tell me you're over the moon that I am the way I am right now."

He watched as she started pacing through the surf, splashing and releasing pent-up frustration from however long ago. "Never underestimate how beautiful you are to look at in the sunset, and didn't I just tell you that I love you?"

"Yes, but..."

"And didn't I just say no matter what?"

"Yes, but I..."

"And I believe I said I loved all of you, to include the hot mess."

"I know, but..."

"I don't think you do. I don't think you get it, Millie." He walked over to her and put her hands in his, "I also said we could make it through anything."

She felt a calm wash over her. "I'm terrified."

He kissed one hand and then the other. "Close your eyes. Close them. I want you to picture yourself happy."

"Drew, come on."

"Please, Mil. Do this for me."

She closed her eyes with a half-hearted huff.

"Thank you. Now, add details to that picture. Food, places, smells... people. What do you see?" Drew held his breath and hoped like hell her picture included him. "Tell me, honestly."

With a sigh, she looked into the darkness. "I see a front porch with rocking chairs. I see family everywhere, playing in the yard, grilling, talking, laughing."

"Anything else?"

She looked harder at her vision and thought what a shame it was that she had never really pictured what her happiness looked like. She wanted a home, family, and love. Nothing else mattered. She wanted peace. She opened her eyes and saw the love in Drew's. "I see you."

He pulled her to him and kissed her with passion and relief. "For the record, you only frustrate me when you squeeze the toothpaste tube from the middle."

Millie laughed out loud and hugged him tightly, "You're twisted. Thank you."

"For being twisted?"

"For being patient."

"I love you, honey. Patience comes with the package. I want you to be sure, though."

"Sure?"

"I don't want to push you. If you're…"

"I'm right where I want to be." She pulled away a little so she could look him in the eye, "It's what I saw. You are what I saw. You are the calm in the center of my chaos."

Another arrow shot right through his heart. "That's a terrific line. I'm stealing that one."

"It's all yours."

"Let's go back. I want to show you something." He kissed her gently and held her hand. "Have you noticed our best talks are on the beach?"

"There's magic in the air here." She said with her head on his arm.

"Agreed. Maybe I'll get a house here."

"You have a house."

"My family has a house. Maybe it's time I bought one. We could come down any time we want. You could decorate it any way you want."

"You really do know the way to a girl's heart, but I don't think you want me decorating."

"What do you think of that one?"

They stood on the beach, looking at a beautiful house that glowed from the inside. Millie pictured a family cooking dinner after a long day of playing in the water.

"It's amazing. I love all the windows."

"Let's go look inside."

"You're crazy. It's not for sale, and the owners are home."

"The owners are home, you're right." Drew grinned at her choice of words, "Let's go in." He pulled her hand to follow him through her objections.

"Drew, stop. You can't just walk up to someone's house to look through it. Drew, seriously, we can't just..."

Millie's breath filled her chest in a single gasp. At the top of the steps, she could see the glass doors of the house folded open to reveal the entire living space. Candles of every shape and height were glowing from the floor, giving the room the scent of clean ocean spray. Between the candles were crystal vases filled with dozens of magnolia blossoms. She tried to take in the awe of it all but couldn't believe what she was seeing. She was standing in the middle of a dream and was afraid to blink, fearing it would all disappear.

"I've been planning this for weeks. Well, if I'm being honest, since I held your hand while you were being stitched up after the Frisbee. I wanted our family here this weekend to witness a question I want to ask you. This house is for us to build memories in, and I wanted our first memory to be our beginning. This year has been the best of my life. Getting to know you, getting to love you, has given me breath again. You are a miracle to me, Millie. You will always be my angel, and I want to spend the rest of my life making you feel adored."

Millie's hands shook as she watched Drew bend down on one knee. "In all my life, I have never known anyone as incredible as you. I want to make you feel that way for the rest of our lives. Will you be my bride for the next eighty years and create a family with me in this house? Will you grow old with me and let me take care of you? Will you marry me and make me the happiest man in the world?"

The whole world had slipped into slow motion since walking into the light of the candles. Millie couldn't hear the ocean at all, only the emotion in Drew's voice. He was so confident that he loved her, so positive she was the person he wanted to be with forever. Having someone adore you for eternity was a dream come true.

The idea of him playing with their children brought a smile to her face. It gave Drew the first sign that this moment was headed in a direction that wouldn't lead to years of therapy and bourbon for breakfast. Her smile was also incomplete.

He rose to stand close to her. "Millie, this is a big step, but let me add one thing. When I took Mary out to dinner last month to ask for her permission to marry you, she told me a little about your past. I never brought it up because I wanted you to feel like you could trust me in your own time. I know you've been hurt, and I know that doesn't just go away. I also know that you are one of the most determined people I have ever known."

He looked around the room at the flowers. "I love magnolias because they symbolize perseverance and everlasting connections. You have the perseverance part already. When you put our ring on, I hope it will be your reminder that I will always love you and that our connection is genuine. I will always put you first and Millie," he put her hand on his heart, "I promise to always be the person you can trust not to hurt you."

She was breathless. She didn't notice her tears or that Drew was shaking as much as she was. She looked at his hand holding hers to his heart and felt the marching band beating in his chest.

She met his eyes with hers and really looked at this man who was offering her the world, and suddenly, she saw it—the house, the family, and years of beautiful chaos. She was humbled by his vision of her and hoped he wouldn't be disappointed in the reality.

She lifted up on her toes and kissed him sweetly. "Thank you for asking Mom. Thank you for creating this moment. Thank you for loving me." She kissed him again and heard an impatient voice from somewhere in the back of the house. "Is that a yes?"

Millie smiled at Carson's interruption but looked at Drew to whisper, "That's a yes."

Their kiss had the whole house erupting in cheers and clapping. As the lights came on, she saw everyone coming towards them in congratulations.

Mary hugged Millie with pride and nostalgia. Her baby was getting married. She kissed her cheek and felt the years rewind in her mind in a slideshow of images. How had life flown by this quickly?

The girls jumped in to hug the bride-to-be. Millie was so grateful to have them all there. She needed them just as much as Mary.

"So enough of the sappy, let's see the ring," Cate said, brushing a tear away.

"I haven't gotten it yet."

Pete shook Drew's hand. "She said yes without even offering the rock? You've got yourself a treasure, son." Pete pulled Millie into a big hug that made her feel like part of the family.

"We can get one later. The house sparkles more than any ring could tonight." Millie curled up to Drew, not realizing the ring had been sparkling from its box right next to her the whole time.

"Well, I guess I messed that part up," Drew pulled the ring from the box. "I'd ask for a redo, but I don't want to chance it."

Everyone laughed, but the breath left Millie once again when she saw the ring he was slipping on her finger.

"This was my grandmother's ring, but the sapphires on each side are Mary's.

She couldn't believe her eyes. It was the most beautiful ring she had ever seen, but those sapphires she knew immediately. She looked at Mary in tears. "The earrings?"

Mary nodded, "They are yours now. I hope they bless you like they did me."

Millie looked at the ring again in a blur of tears. It felt like the stars were aligned just for them. She felt the weight of it, but it was comforting in a way she didn't expect. Her life would be full of love.

chapter sixteen

THEY STAYED UP way too late, but the energy of the house wouldn't let anyone sleep. The dinner that had taken so many hands to plan and prepare, Millie now understood, was their engagement celebration. She was still stuffed from all her favorite foods laid out in a delicious smorgasbord of calories.

Maybe that's why she couldn't sleep. She laid still as Drew rolled over, and she envied his peace. She held up her hand to look at the ring for the thousandth time that night. It really was amazing. Drew had put so much thought into it. She loved that it held a part of both families.

The sapphires brought stinging tears to her eyes again. She had pleaded and begged to wear the earrings they came from when she was younger. Mary kept them locked tightly in her jewelry box, though. They were the only thing her great-grandmother brought from Spain when she came to America. They were priceless to Millie because they represented her family's hope for a better life and faith that they would have a family one day to pass them to. Now, four generations later, that was still coming true.

She heard a seagull call and looked at the clock. She huffed into the pillow at how little sleep she had gotten. The sun would be up soon and bring the beach to life. She got up quietly to take a walk in the quiet before sunrise.

Millie tiptoed down the stairs and pulled Drew's jacket from the closet. She walked into the breeze and felt the chill clearing her mind.

She walked towards the light, watching and waiting for every new color. How could there be a doubt that God exists when there were colors like this?

Millie stood in awe at the sight of the perfect painting. The breeze danced in her hair, but she only felt the warmth of the sun rising.

"It's magnificent, isn't it?"

The voice snapped her out of the trance she was in. She slowly turned to see Taylor watching her, equally surprised to find her on his beach.

His morning runs were his time to be free. Free from responsibility, free from worry, free from his past. Seeing Millie standing in the colors of dawn stopped his world from turning and brought the love he held for her to the surface with every beat of a racing heart.

Millie watched him in shock. She wasn't sure if she was happy to see him or afraid. She just stood there blinking at him until a "Hi" finally found its way out.

Good Lord, he was gorgeous...

Read on for an excerpt from the next book in the series,

Carolina Girls: Chesapeake Bay

chapter one

TODAY WAS ALL about her. It was a day to celebrate the start of her greatest adventure. She would look back years from now and remember with longing and love how the women she cherished most surrounded her with approval and support. They were showing their support by celebrating her fairytale love story.

There would be gifts and advice given. Stories would be told of their cute younger years, their embarrassingly awkward phases, and how she and Will had met and fallen in love. It was an afternoon based on the appreciation that she had found her soul mate.

It was a load of crap.

Her bridal shower was only two hours away, and she couldn't honestly say she was a bride anymore. The fight they had last night was epic. She couldn't even tell you how it started now. Will chalked it up to pre-wedding panic, but that turned into yelling and brutal truth-telling.

Some of the things they said to each other may have been true, but the way they said it was awful. All the frustrations of the last few weeks came to a head, and with two words, he shook her to her core, leaving her breathless.

"I'm done."

When he slammed the door behind him, she wondered if he meant the fight or their future. Rory stared in the mirror and was struck by the black circles under her eyes from tossing and turning all night. The girls would know something was wrong the minute they saw her. Her girls were her tribe, her people, her first loves, and her best friends. They were the people she was comfortable enough to be herself with, something she wished was easier for her.

She met Millie in the cafeteria, waiting in line for ice cream, their freshman year of college. They went to a small school and were bound to meet eventually, but they were both grateful to have met early on. Now, they had years of blackmail and inside jokes to keep them laughing and a genuine love for each other that anchored their friendship in the forever category. Millie was her sister from another mother, her partner in crime, and her free therapist when times got tough.

Rory looked in the mirror again. "Times are definitely tough now," she sighed.

She met Audrey in college, as well. Biology 101 had the potential to be torturous, but it came so easily to Audrey that being in her study group was a necessity. She still thanked Audrey for saving her life because if she had taken an F home, she was positive her dad would have whooped *her* biology. Audrey used that year as a stepping stone towards her dream of delivering "tiny humans" and was currently working on her residency at Rex Hospital. All the girls agreed that Dr. Audrey Jones, OB/GYN, would be their favorite epidural provider when the time came to start boarding the baby train.

Cate was the latest to join the group. In the five years since Millie introduced them, she had kept the group in shape from belly laughs. Her tales of the kindergarten classroom adventures she faced every day were hilarious. *She* made them hilarious, though. Cate had a sarcastic and sometimes blunt exterior, but anyone who really got to know her saw her optimistic heart of gold. It was that heart that would make her a great Principal as soon as her classes were complete.

Rory took a deep breath. They would see the circles under her eyes and know something was up. She added a little more concealer and blush. Estee Lauder was her hero today. She gave a pitiful attempt of a smile at the woman in the reflection.

She had just found her girly side a few years ago. She was nothing but a tomboy growing up – climbing trees, making fart noises from her armpit, and playing any kind of sport with skinned knees and ponytails all year long.

She had a great childhood, full of homemade adventures that seem so real to a kid. Nothing like kids today, she thought with pity. She was dirty more often than clean when she was young. Church was the only time she wore a dress, but she always put shorts on underneath so she could climb the old oak near the fellowship hall. She wondered if kids even knew how to make mud pies anymore. Or how refreshing it was to take a big gulp from the hose in the backyard on a hot summer day.

"You're stalling," she said to herself. She added one more layer of blush to brighten up her face and, hopefully, her mood, then turned off the lights. There was no sense in staring any longer. Being late would only make everyone more suspicious since she was never, ever late.

She got into her car and cranked the radio up to sing back up for Andy Grammar in the hopes that he could convince her that it was good to be alive. By the time she got to her aunt's house, she felt better and could at least smile enough to lighten her eyes.

When she walked into the house, the smells of her Aunt Patricia's baking had her moaning. She closed her eyes and breathed in the sweetness—her mother's pound cake.

"You're here! You look beautiful, sweetie!" Patricia hugged her tightly and whispered in her ear. "Your Aunt Ruby is in the kitchen. God bless her. She thinks you're joining the Army."

Rory pulled back to look at her. "What in the world? Where did she get that from?"

"Who knows! That woman was looney before the 'incident'," she rolled her eyes with finger quotes. "On the bright side, she's brought a great present you can use at basic training."

"Oh, Lord." They smiled at each other with understanding.

"How you holding up, darlin'?"

Rory looked down at their joined hands. Aunt Patricia had put her whole heart into this shower. She didn't want to take any of her happiness away today.

"I couldn't sleep last night, too excited about today. Thank you so much for all you've done."

"Oh please, you haven't seen anything yet, soldier. Come in!"

The room erupted in squeals when Rory walked in. She was hugged and kissed by one while another held her hand to get a look at the ring. She made her way through the throng until she got to Millie.

"Girl, thank God you're here," Millie hugged her. "Aunt Ruby was trying to sign me up with you so you have a wingman in the Army. I told her that I didn't look good in green. You know what she said? '*You're right. Maybe one of the other girls.*' As I am no longer being drafted, I'm going to get another mimosa. Want one?"

"A sweet tea, please."

Millie winked as she walked away but headed straight to Cate. "I'm getting drinks. Go check on our girl and tell me I'm crazy."

"Millie, please. Aunt Ruby has nothing on you."

"Listen, my life goal is to be like Aunt Ruby one day. I still say she's faking the crazy so she can say anything she wants and get away with it."

"She did that before the stroke, Mil. She doesn't need an excuse. Let's go back to your crazy. What's up?"

"I don't know. Something though. Talk to her, you'll see it. Something's wrong."

"You're drunk. She's having the time of her life." But as she said it, Cate saw the sadness. "Get the drinks. Make mine without orange juice."

"You want champagne?"

"Why yes, thank you for asking."

Millie rolled her eyes with love and headed towards the drink table.

Rory smiled her sweetest smile and did her best to appreciate the moment. There was so much love in the room. Most of it aimed directly at her.

Before she knew it, the gift-opening portion of the afternoon had begun. She was showered with china and towels, crystal and serving bowls, and an odd little gnome that her cousin Grace explained would create Feng Shui and good luck if put in the proper spot in the backyard.

"This is the last one," Patricia said excitedly. "It's from Aunt Ruby."

Rory smiled at both her aunts, who were eager for her to open the box. She didn't know how much longer she could fake smiles over cutlery and housewares. Her head was pounding. She just wanted to sleep away the headache and the dread of what was waiting for her when she got home. Or worse, what wasn't waiting for her.

All thought and breath left her when she pulled the tissue paper back. Rory just stared at the open box, like it held all the answers to life's mysteries. She wasn't blinking, wasn't breathing, wasn't moving. She felt Aunt Ruby's hand on her knee and forced herself to look up.

"I thought maybe you could wear it on your big day."

Rory looked at the box again. "How did you…"

"It's been in my closet all these years."

"But the fire. She was sure it burned in the fire."

Ruby squeezed her niece's hand, "You don't have to wear it. I just wanted you to have the option."

The tears came so quickly that there was no chance to stop them. "It's my mom's wedding dress. She's giving me my mother's wedding dress."

The whole room gasped, with tears all around and whispers of what a precious gift it was. Rory couldn't take her eyes off of it. She stroked the fabric as if it were sacred. It was sacred. It was a piece of her mother that she thought was gone forever. Planning the wedding had been a minefield of emotions without having her Mom there to help. Holding the gown made her such a big part of the day.

"Aunt Ruby, I don't know how to thank you..."

"Hush, child. Go try it on. You're about the size she was back then." Rory looked down at it again in awe. "She's going to try on the dress," Ruby announced to the room. "All you drunks, keep your cocktails under control until we get back. I'll introduce you to the sharp end of a switch if you spill anything on her."

Patricia stood up, "I'll help you get..."

"Sit down and host your party," Aunt Ruby said slowly, giving her knees a chance to adjust. "I'll take her. We're going to your room, Patricia. Let's hope we don't find anything with batteries."

"Aunt Ruby! Good glory!" Patricia sat down with a bright red face and took a good chug of her mimosa. "Crazy old woman."

When Rory and Aunt Ruby got to the bedroom, Rory laid the dress on the bed to take a good look at it.

"It's beautiful. She must have been so beautiful."

"She was, and you will be, too. Now get to changing."

Rory undressed while Ruby worked on the buttons on the gown. When she slipped it over her head, she smelled the faint scent of her mom's perfume and nearly fell apart. "It smells like her," she whispered.

"Chanel No. 5 Perfume. Never wore anything different. Let me take a look at you." Rory turned towards her to share the moment. She should have known better than to think her aunt would get mushy over her.

"There is something wrong with you."

Rory laughed, "You're one to talk. Why were you drafting people to join the Army with me down there?"

"Oh, that? I just like to mess with people. It's fun to watch their reactions. Especially that Millie, she falls for it every time. At my age, people just accept it." Ruby cocked an eyebrow, "Don't blow my cover, girl. I've worked years on those girls."

"I promise, but Millie is on to you."

"Is she? Huh." She was going to have to up her game, she thought. "So what's wrong?"

"Nothing. It's perfect."

"I'm not talking about the dress. What's wrong?"

"Just a lot going on."

"Hogwash."

"I'm fine, Aunt Ruby. It's all just a little overwhelming. It's a big change, you know."

"I do. What's wrong?"

"There's so much pressure to have the perfect…"

"The perfect what?"

"The perfect everything."

"Perfection is pointless if you ask me. What's perfect to one is imperfect to another. Who says you have to be perfect? If it's that boy, I'll get in my car right now and show him the perfect right hook."

"I'll store that offer for next time. Thank you."

"Then tell me about this time."

Rory sank on the bed with a long huff, billowing her dress to show off the miles of fabric in the skirt. "We had a fight last night."

"That explains the pancake makeup trying to hide the circles."

"I didn't sleep much."

Aunt Ruby sat on the bed beside her. "Rory. What's wrong?"

Rory put her face in her hands and began to cry. "Aunt Ruby, I don't even know how it happened." She lifted her head to plead for help. "Children. I'm... I'm not sure Will wants them. He's so good with them. He adores Hailey. When I told him Margaret had the baby, he was the first in line to visit her with a little pink bear. He's so good with kids. I'm just not sure he'll want one of our own."

Rory looked down at her hands. She hadn't noticed she was stroking the skirt of the dress for comfort until then. "What do I do?"

"Do you love him?"

"I do, very much."

"Will he be enough to make you happy?"

"I never planned my life around kids, but they were always in the picture somehow. I think I want a family... someday."

"Then you need to know if this is a reservation or a resolution of his. Which is it?"

Rory shrugged. She was embarrassed. "We never got that far into the conversation. The things we said to each other, Aunt Ruby, were awful."

"Oh please, I went after your Uncle Robert with a hatchet once. Would have used it too, but he came to his senses and apologized."

Ruby shook her head and smiled, "Lord, I miss that man. Kept me on my toes, he did. Never met anyone who could out-wit Einstein like he could. Smart ass."

Rory smiled. Theirs had been a great love. No matter what Ruby said, everyone in the family and the community knew how much they adored each other. "I want what you two had. How did you know Uncle Robert was the one?"

"Nobody knows that, honey. You just have to jump in and fight for it. Every day. Robert was no saint, but I knew I was a better person with him than without him. He made me feel sexy, confident, and smart. No one else came close." Ruby felt her voice begin to break with emotion and pulled back before she could show the loss she felt. "And he was a firecracker in the bedroom," she chucked. "Lord, I miss that man."

That made Rory laugh and gave Ruby a chance to collect herself. Now was the tough love. "No need to blush now, girlie. Men have been putting a pep in women's steps long before me. Let's get to my sage advice. Decide for yourself what your life will look like. Leave the details to fate, but know what will make you happy. Only you know what that is. Once you know, stand by it. If he doesn't board the train, tear up his ticket. This is your only life to live child, make it count."

Fate, Rory thought, then she jumped at the knock on the door. "Are you dressed yet? The natives are getting restless, and the mimosas are getting stronger. That's a bad combination."

Rory cleared her throat, "We'll be right out, Cate."

"I like that girl," Ruby got up, slower this time, Rory noticed. "She's a smart ass, too."

"High praise, indeed."

"Don't tell her I like her, though. I'm going to draft her next. Should be fun."

"On my honor." Rory crossed her heart and laughed.

"Let's look at you." Ruby turned Rory towards the mirror to give her a chance to swallow the knot that was forming in her throat. "It needs some alterations, but it's not too shabby. Not too shabby at all."

"Thank you, Aunt Ruby. For everything."

"You thank me when it's tax season. I've got shoe boxes of receipts for you to go through."

Rory cringed at that. "Haven't I told you to order carbon copy checks, woman? No one has time to go through all that."

"I've got a system."

"What you have is a hot mess. I'm going to drag you into the twenty-first century eventually. I'll swing by soon and pick up the box."

"There are a few this year, dear. Bring back up."

It relieved Ruby to see some spunk in Rory as she huffed out of the bedroom. Children were the one thing her Robert hadn't given her and it still broke her heart. She wouldn't have changed their love for the world, but in her soul, she knew even in Heaven, she would always regret not being a mother.

She watched Rory walk towards the tipsy women, oohing and aahing, and wondered if she would see her darling girl walk down the aisle this year or not. She may have to pay the groom-to-be a little visit now, though.

"Dumb ass."

www.ingramcontent.com/pod-product-compliance
Lightning Source LLC
Chambersburg PA
CBHW070926230725
29977CB00028B/354